GRACIE HART

A SIXPENCE
FOR CHRISTMAS

Complete and Unabridged

MAGNA
Leicester

First published in Great Britain in 2022 by
Simon & Schuster UK Ltd
London

First Ulverscroft Edition
published 2022
by arrangement with
Simon & Schuster UK Ltd
London

*A catalogue record for this book is available
from the British Library.*

ISBN 978–0–7505–4991–2

For Amelia and Oliver. With all my love.

1

Leeds 1895

Meg Fairfax threaded her way in and out of the busy Leeds market. She was on the scrounge for that night's supper and with little money in her purse, she needed to spend her sixpence wisely. Ever since Ted Lund had blackened her name, accusing her of stealing from the bakery that she had built up from nothing, she had been struggling to keep herself, her mother and her young sister, Sarah, fed. Now, even though the kind Joe Dinsdale had proved Ted Lund, the miserable baker, to be wrong, she could no longer work, looking after her dying mother. She was thankful that if things got too hard she had the love of her life Frankie to help her, but only if she truly was down to her last farthing. She had her pride.

Already, she'd bartered with the friendly butcher. He'd agreed to lower the price for pigs' trotters. Now, they sat in her basket, pink and pointing.

She made her way to her old friend Roger's stall. With a bit of luck, he might share vegetables that were past their best. The sounds and smells of the market filled the air, and for a short while she forgot her worries as she chatted to the local stallholders she had known all her life.

Every day was a battle to keep her pride and dignity, but better times were around the corner. She kept telling herself this as she stood in line. Then, she spotted Mick on the fruit stall.

He came over to talk to her in his soft Irish drawl. 'Now then, Meg — how are things? Mother still in a bad way?'

'Yes. Worse if anything,' Meg said quietly, as she shifted up the queue.

'I'm sorry, lass. You wouldn't let a dog suffer in the same way the authorities have let her. Come over to see me once you've dealt with Casanova, here. I'll give you something to take home.' Before Meg could answer, Mick glanced over at his stall, as a woman sorted through his fruit and looked around her to be served.

'Who's Casanova?' Meg asked, but Mick was already moving away, needing to serve his next customer.

Slowly, the row of women at Roger's stall shuffled along. Surely, she would be next to be served? It was only as she approached the front of the line that she realized who Mick was calling Casanova. A young woman was standing next to Roger, his arm around her as she heard him telling a customer that she was about to be his wife.

Meg knew in an instant that her days of free vegetables had disappeared. Not that Roger had ever been particularly generous with his offerings, ever since she had dismissed his request to walk out with him. Still, the odd free potato and onion would be missed.

'Meg, what can I do for you today?' Roger's long, greying hair was tucked behind his ears but his salt and pepper beard looked to be more trimmed than usual.

'Just an onion, thanks.' Meg knew that was all she had the money for in her purse. No freebies, today.

'Right you are.' Roger passed her an onion and held his hand out for payment.

Meg passed him a farthing and started to walk across to Mick when a hand touched her shoulder and she glimpsed two carrots being slipped into her basket next to the onion and trotters.

'They'll be better for a carrot with them,' Roger said, quietly. 'Have you heard that I'm to be wed? That's Ruth, from Wakefield.' Roger nodded across at the dark-haired woman who was serving his customers.

'No, I'd not heard.' Meg felt a blush coming to her cheeks. 'I'm glad for you,' she said sincerely. 'I hope that you'll both be happy. Thank you for the carrots — I can't pay you for them, though.'

'I know. I just want to make sure you're all right. I'll not be standing this market for much longer. I'm moving over to Wakefield. Ruth has two children there and she doesn't want to uproot them to Leeds.' Roger looked around at his stall's queue. 'Take care, Meg, I have to go.'

'You too, Roger. Thank you. I hope that you will be happy. You deserve it — you are a good man.' Meg put her head down and walked to see Mick at his fruit stall.

'That will not last, you know,' Mick said, nodding over at Roger and his lady friend. 'She's got him under her thumb already. She's after his money, that's all, ya can tell.' Mick shook his head and watched as his old friend started to serve his customers with Ruth giving orders.

'She might not be. She looks as if she loves him to me, she never takes her eyes off him. She didn't like me talking to him, I could tell.' Meg looked across at the woman who was staring back at her.

'No, because you may be after his brass! Anyway, there's no fool like an old fool; I can't do anything about it. Anyway, I hear that he's not the only one that has a new love in his life, Meg. You've got yourself a fella and a wealthy one at that.' Mick smiled and put some bruised apples from the back of the stall into her basket.

'I might have, but he's not that new. I've known him for a while now. But I don't expect anything from him. I have my pride. He's got his own problems and besides it isn't his brass I'm interested in.' Meg blushed. 'Although he is good to me and I like him.' She smiled and thanked Mick for her apples. He had always been good to her and knew that she liked to be independent and fend for herself and her mother. Their friendship was strong and she knew they would always be there for one another, no matter what.

'Like him, tha should love him before he puts that ring on your finger and make sure that he's not after nothing from you,' Mick grinned.

Meg grinned back. 'Well, it will certainly not be money or property because I've neither. It must be my charms Frankie's fallen for.'

'Aye, I can believe that. You have the charm of any leprechaun. You've charmed Roger and me out of many a piece of fruit and veg in your time. But I'm glad; it keeps your body and soul together. The world would be a sad place if we couldn't show one another a bit of charity, to be sure. With your mother being ill and you still not able to find work, it's the least I can do.'

'I'm always grateful; I'll bring you a piece of apple pie for your dinner if I get round to making it tonight,

4

but my mother isn't so good. In fact, I must be getting back to her, I shouldn't have left her, but needs must.'

Meg smiled at Mick. He was always kind to her, although he could ill afford to give anything away, with five children and a wife to feed.

'Well, take care. My prayers are with you and your ma. She's been ill for too long,' Mick said in farewell, before Meg made her way home.

★ ★ ★

Later in the afternoon, Frankie Pearson called in to see Meg to try to convince his fiancée to come and work for him. He looked around the sparse kitchen and listened to the heavy breathing of Meg's mother from upstairs. Meg had just come down from taking her mother a drink, and was now sat at the small table.

Frankie had loved Meg since the first time he had seen her with her nose pressed against his newly opened patisserie. The differences in class were of little consequence to him; they both shared the same love of baking and Meg was a kind, thoughtful lass who had just fallen on hard times through no fault of her own. It was love at first sight as far as Frankie was concerned.

'Meg, please come and work for me at my patisserie,' Frankie began. 'Only a few hours, just enough for me to pay you a small living. If your mother was too ill to leave, I'd understand and would manage without you. Please — give it some thought.' He sat down opposite Meg, wanting her to understand he was offering her assistance with no ties attached, but he knew her pride would not let her take a penny without earning it.

'Please change your mind, I wouldn't even have to train you, after the hours that we have shared together before your mother was this ill.'

She sighed. 'You know I can't leave my mother. Besides, I will never be accepted at the bakery upon the Headrow. I am more a backstreet baker . . . not even that, since Ted Lund and his spiteful words. I'd find it hard to work for you — I have my own ways — and I'd be tongue-tied every time a well-to-do customer entered the shop. And besides, my mother comes first. I can't leave her alone while she is so ill.' She felt her eyes suddenly spilling with tears.

Noticing immediately, Frankie reached out to squeeze Meg's hand. 'My love, I'm here for you, no matter what. I just thought that a few hours working alongside me would make a break in your day and help you financially. I'll support you and your sister, no matter what. You have no cause to worry.'

'I'm grateful, Frankie. Really, I don't expect you to, I don't need charity. I just need my mother to recover, which I know is asking the impossible. She's nearly at the end of her days, after all, which I'm finding hard enough to deal with. Give me time, and then I will happily be by your side and help out in the bakery . . . but not the shop.'

Meg tried to smile. After working for Ted Lund, she had come to realize that she would rather be the owner of her own business although the idea of that was like shooting for the moon.

'I'll look forward to that day. The tea room will soon be opening, too. I'll need some of your good wholesome baking to encourage my customers to partake of a cup of tea and a fancy of their choice.'

Frankie pushed back his chair and went to Meg,

putting his arms around her. 'I love you, you know that, I only mean to look after you,' he whispered. She stood in his arms for a minute quietly.

'You, your sister Sarah and your mother could come and live with me, you know,' Frankie said eventually. 'My house is large enough. We could get married and make it all legal, and then you wouldn't have to bear the worry all alone.'

Frankie held her tight and kissed her neck gently, holding her slim waist tight to him. Meg buried her head into his shoulder and smelt the French cologne on his clothes that she knew was his favourite and once again felt the comfort and love that Frankie had given her without question over the past few trying months.

'I know, my love. But this is where my mother loves, it is where her heart lies. I can't move her. Besides, Sarah will no doubt have something to say about our plans once she gets to find out what we are about?'

Frankie looked slightly irritated at the thought of Meg's unruly sister but tried to stay calm. 'Then if you are happy to stay here, I will help all that I can. If you need a doctor please tell me, I'll pay his fees. Hopefully, the laudanum that I brought with me will keep her free of pain for a while. She seems to be sleeping since you took it up upon my arrival.'

He held Meg close. With her mother being so ill, and her sister such a headstrong and abrupt personality, he sometimes wished that he could just whisk Meg away from her life of poverty living in Sykes Yard. He loved her but had not bargained for also having to love her family too.

'Yes, thank you. One day I hope I'll be able to pay you,' Meg said. 'And thank you also for the groceries that you had Dinsdale's deliver to me. There really was no need. I'd already visited the market this morning. It was very kind and too much . . . but most gratefully accepted.' Meg stood on her tiptoes and kissed him again. 'I do love you, Frankie.'

He left her arms and reached for his top hat from the kitchen table. 'And I you, my dear. I must go. I have an appointment to look around a property that is for sale in Headingley. Now that my patisserie on the Headrow is proving to be popular and the tea room is nearly up and running, I'm looking to expand. A good businessman doesn't stand still.' Frankie smiled at the surprise on Meg's face.

'Another property? A bakery?' Meg asked as she walked him to the doorway.

'Hopefully a patisserie, my dear — not just a bakery by the time that I have finished with it. It needs a lot of work . . . The building on the main street in Headingley is in a shocking condition, but that is how I like them. Then I can make a fresh start when I have new plans drawn up. One day, Pearson's name will be on every street corner in Leeds — and the whole of Yorkshire, if I have my way.'

Frankie kissed Meg on the cheek before saying goodbye to her on the step, leaving her to watch him as he made his way along the pavement.

Meg closed the door. Then she sat down in the chair that once had been occupied most days by her mother, back when she was well. She relished the silence, the peace of her mother sleeping upstairs, nursed and cared for, and the steady ticking of the clock on the mantelpiece. She could still smell the comforting scent of Frankie's cologne in the air.

Why did her husband-to-be want to be beholden

to her? She was not the same class as him; she was a penniless lass from the Leeds back streets. That's what she and her family had always been. Yet, he seemed to have given his heart to her and she had willingly given hers to him with every beat when she looked into his eyes with love.

Meg smiled as she thought of her handsome dark-haired beau with the slight French accent that made him all the more alluring. He did love her — she knew he loved her — but still, she couldn't understand why. She was not beautiful, nor eloquent or wealthy — none of the things that a man of his standing should look for in a woman.

He was an astute businessman from what he told her and the way he acted. His ambition to have a patisserie on every street corner would come to pass, if he had his way. However, she still felt uncomfortable to think that she would eventually have to get used to dealing with Leeds' upper classes if she was to support her husband-to-be. Those days were a long way off, though — surely?

She looked around the small walls of her home and listened for the pained sounds made by her mother as she battled the year's past cancer. This was a battle that would not be won. The weight had dropped from her bones and clearly the pain was becoming more intense as the days passed.

After her mother's death, Meg would have to decide what to do with her life — and that of her sister Sarah, who would soon be twelve.

Twelve. Only twelve.

The idea of going to live with Frankie, to marry him . . . That was uppermost in her mind. as she went to prepare supper for the three of them. At least, her trip to Dinsdale's Groceries had kept her informed of the local gossip. He was a good lad, George. He'd been the one who had cleared her name when Ted Lund had accused her of theft. She owed him a lot.

She began to peel the vegetables, placing them in a stockpot over the fire, along with pearl barley, onions and simmering pigs' trotters. A cheap but filling broth, accompanied by homemade bread, would be grand for Sarah to return to after a day at the mill. Warm her through; keep her strength up.

Once everything was settled above the fire, Meg quietly made her way up the stairs to the bedroom that all three women shared. It smelt of damp, mixed with the odour of the medicinal concoctions that helped to keep Agnes alive. There was very little furniture in the room apart from the two beds. Her mother lay in one, and the other she shared with her young sister.

Never had there been time for frivolities in Meg's life — but of late, things had worsened. Since her dismissal from Ted Lund's bakery, Meg had been searching for work, but her mother came first — always.

She looked down at her mother, asleep. Her lungs were silent for once, apart from the occasional rasping breath — a sign of the disease that had been eating the dear woman alive.

Meg straightened up and glanced at her reflection in the mottled glass of the mirror that hung on the bedroom wall. She tucked a loose strand of hair behind her ear and studied her features. She had a good figure but she found her looks plain. *Nothing for Frankie to be attracted to*, she thought as she heard the kitchen door opening. It would be her sister, returning from her shift at the weaving mill where she worked as an odd-job girl. Sarah never had been too caught up in school work.

'Meg, are you up there?' her sister yelled from the bottom of the stairs.

'Yes! Keep your voice down,' Meg hissed, stepping out onto the landing. 'Mam's asleep, for a change.' She made her way downstairs and into the kitchen, shutting the door quietly behind her.

Sarah was sat at the table, reaching down to unlace her boots. 'Your fella's been, I can smell him. That cologne he wears always lingers, even over the stink of those pig's trotters. He's never been away of late.' She massaged her toes and looked at the hole in her stocking that had become larger with the day's tread. She had been on her feet for twelve hours straight, running errands throughout the mill and ensuring the ongoing supply of cotton to all the weavers. 'I thought for a minute that you were perhaps rolling about in bed with him when you weren't down here,' she added, with a cheeky grin.

Meg felt her cheeks flare with heat. 'Sarah Fairfax, wash your mouth out! You shouldn't know about such things at your age. Those mill girls that you work with have a lot to answer for . . .'

'Well you can't say anything! Your best mate is Daisy Truelove and she's the talk where I work at Hunslet Mill — her and my boss, Tom. We all know what they get up to in the weaving sheds at dinner time and it isn't tiddlywinks.' Sarah sat back and looked at her sister. 'Shouldn't one of us wake Mother? She'll not sleep tonight if we don't, and you know what that means? Neither of us will sleep, either!' Sarah sighed.

Meg tried not to let her irritation seep through. Sarah thought only of herself and that was her way. 'No, let's leave her be. She's exhausted. Probably

11

from keeping us up all night reminiscing about the past. If she can't sleep and we don't get much sleep, it's not much to ask of us at the end of her days,' Meg said as she stirred the pot of broth and checked if the barley was softening. 'Frankie brought her some stronger laudanum tincture this afternoon. It seems to be giving her the comfort she needed.'

'I suppose that was good of him. Although you can buy anything if you have the money as he has. Has he asked you to marry him yet?' Sarah asked.

'I'm not for saying,' Meg retorted quickly.

'Or are we not good enough? I don't know why he's bothering with you. I've seen all the posh women coming and going out of his shop. Why doesn't he court one of them?'

Meg felt her sister's eyes looking at her up and down. Her words hurt but she was only saying what she herself had thought. Sarah disliked the man that had entered their lives. He was too educated and dressed too well, and she didn't trust him. Even at Sarah's young age, she knew toffs did not bother with the lower classes unless it was to their advantage.

'He's a good man, Sarah. I was going to wait to tell you but seeing that you have brought it up — yes, he has offered his hand in marriage to me.' She paused, and watched her sister's face cloud over, sending a shudder of guilt through Meg. 'I've said yes, but I'm in no rush,' she continued quickly. 'Mother's health comes first. You don't have to worry — he knows that if I do marry him, I'd expect you to live with us until you're old enough to set up a home on your own.'

Sarah's hands dropped from massaging her feet. 'What if I don't want to live with you both? Have you thought of that? Him and his posh ways, he's not right

12

for you,' she said.

Meg let out an exasperated sigh. 'I knew that you'd act like this. I was dreading telling you, but now you know. You'll have all you need if you come and live with us, it will be better all-round. This home of ours gets damper with every winter.' Even as she spoke, she could see the dark mould blossoming in a corner of the room. No matter how many times they washed it down, it always reappeared.

'This is my home, I'm not leaving it . . . and I'm not living with you and your fancy man!'

Anger contorting her face, Sarah went to the back door into the yard behind the house and stepped outside, even though she was barefoot, then slammed the door behind her.

Meg shook her head. Sarah was the bane of her life, but when or if she did marry Frankie, she would have no option but to take Sarah with her, whether her little sister wanted to live with them or not.

★   ★   ★

Agnes had lain awake for a good hour, fighting the pain. She tossed and turned and tried not to call out into the darkness. Her daughters were both asleep in the bed across from her. She managed to make out the shape of the bottle of laudanum that was now always kept by her bedside. She breathed in and fought a sudden bout of pain as she reached for the bottle. The laudanum that Frankie had bought her was strong — much stronger than the tinctures Meg usually brought home.

Shakily, she unscrewed the lid and drank direct from the bottle, then she lay back upon the pillow, turning her head to gaze at the bottle, only three-quarters full now. She shifted her glance beyond the stool that acted as a bedside table, to her two daughters, curled around each other. She thought about the lives that lay before them. She was a burden for them, a burden they could do without.

Another bout of pain wracked her body and she made her decision. Slowly and deliberately she drank the remaining laudanum, its bitter almond taste scalding her throat as it went down. If it was God's will, He'd welcome her into His kingdom.

She prayed for forgiveness and whispered her love for her girls. 'My darlings, forgive me. I have had enough of this life and you deserve your own without me as a burden. God protect you, my precious ones.'

Agnes breathed in deeply and closed her eyes for what she hoped was the last time, praying that death would come quickly.

2

'I hate him, I hate him! Don't let him into our home, Meg. He killed our mother!' Sarah yelled, as Meg went to open the door to Frankie. She knew he'd been told the news of their mother's death by the next-door neighbour, Betsy, who had rushed to tell him the news after hearing it from Meg.

'Hold your noise, Sarah!' Meg pushed her back. 'Mother was dying, anyway, and it was her decision to drink the bottle of laudanum. I'm as much to blame for leaving it at her bedside. Frankie had only been trying to help!' She took a breath. 'He couldn't have known that Mother was going to end her life that way.'

Meg stared at her young sister, who stood defiant and near to tears in the kitchen that had always been so much of a home to both of them. Now, with their mother dead in the bed, it was as if the heart had been torn out of the terraced slum and Meg saw it even more for what it was. The dirty unloved yard, the stinking necessary that was used by all the row, and the damp and dirt that covered each wall of her home.

'I'm not staying in the same room as him!' Sarah grabbed her shawl from the back of the chair and pushed her way past Frankie, as Meg opened the door to him. The young girl stomped out of Sykes Yard to make her way to the canal, no doubt to tell her friend Harry of the loss that was breaking her heart.

Frankie watched her go and then turned to Meg.

15

'I came to give you both my condolences. What did I do wrong? Your mother was alive when I left yesterday evening. Surely, it's the cancer that took her?'

If only it was, Meg thought.

'I'm sorry, Frankie. Sarah is angry, confused and heartbroken, if she would only admit to it. She blames you because my mother drank the full bottle of laudanum, whether by choice or accident we don't know. The doctor said nothing could have been done for her. Who are we to judge if she decided to end it all? She was in such pain.

'Sarah has to lash out at somebody, though, and I'm afraid you are the one that she's decided to blame.'

Frankie placed his hat on the table and then offered his open arms. He embraced her gently, and she felt comforted, even if it didn't remove the guilt she still felt over her own actions.

'I'm sorry, my love. The last thing I wanted was to cause you pain,' Frankie said quietly. 'Have you everything in hand? As soon as I heard the news, I had to come.' Frankie kissed Meg on her brow.

'I'm all right. I would never tell Sarah this, but I'm relieved in a way. Mother was in such pain, she couldn't go on like she was.' Meg wiped a tear away. 'The doctor has written his certificate. Mrs Bentham, from two streets down, has laid her out. I couldn't bear to touch her, even though I loved every bone of her body. The vicar has already been and the funeral will be next Thursday. So, yes, thank you — all is in hand. I'm afraid it will only be a pauper's funeral. I can't afford any more than that.'

'Then I will pay for a decent send-off. Your mother was good to me. She made me welcome and never questioned once why I loved you, only asking that I

16

would look after you and Sarah. Which I will.' Frankie spoke quietly, as Meg wiped away her tears.

'No! Please, no. I couldn't let you pay for the funeral. It is our responsibility to see that my mother gets a decent burial . . .'

'Shush, now. Tell the undertaker that a good, solid oak coffin is all that is needed. He can send the bill to me. Your mother needs a safe resting place. Please don't hesitate to ask if there is anything more you need from me.' Frankie hesitated before adding, 'Perhaps now that your mother is at peace, our lives can begin.'

'Thank you.' Meg felt a flush of relief, despite herself. She didn't want to take Frankie's money and yet . . . To see her mother buried with decorum would mean the world to all of the family.

And yet . . .

Had Frankie given her the extra-strong laudanum on purpose or had he simply meant well? She swept away her doubts. He could only have meant good . . . couldn't he?

★   ★   ★

Sarah strode out of Sykes Yard and into the street. Her thoughts made no sense at all, and in the meantime her heart was breaking.

She couldn't face the other workers at the mill. She knew Meg had arranged for a message to go to the foreman but she didn't care if she had been given the time off or not. She had to see Larry, whether he was busy at work or not. She needed to talk to him. He was still her closest friend, the only one who really knew her.

Sarah fought back the tears and anger and pushed

17

past the burly men who worked on the canal's wharf, to find Harry. Finally, she glimpsed him standing on a load of sacks being hauled from a barge. He was grinning as he sailed through the air, balanced on the crane's load as it lowered the cargo into the safety of the wharf. He waved his cap and shouted cheek at one of the young prostitutes who walked the canal sides touting for trade. 'I'm too young for you lot, I'd wear you out for the day.'

He can stop that immediately! she thought as she wiped her nose on her sleeve. She pushed her way past the busy dock workers to where Harry was just alighting from his brief flight in the air.

'What are you doing here again, Sarah? I've told ya, I'm busy at work when I'm down here. I haven't the time for you.' Harry leapt off a load of sacks and started to unload them with his fellow dock-side workers. 'Why aren't you at work?' He lifted a sack onto a waiting cart.

'You'd time of day to shout at that trollop over there!' Sarah said sharply as she looked at the young dark-haired lass who was not much older than herself, hanging around the docks up to no good. She folded her arms. 'My mam's dead. She drank a bottle of laudanum that our Meg's fancy man gave her and now she's gone.' She tried hard to hold back her tears in front of all the canal workers but without success.

Larry paused in his work. 'Sarah, I'm sorry. Come here, I'm sure I can spare a minute or two.' He turned to whisper something to his boss who shot a glance at Sarah.

After seeing the tears on her face, she heard the foreman speak. 'Go on, lad. Five minutes, then I'll expect you back at it.'

'Come and sit down in the building we use for our brews and bait.' Harry put his arm around the lass who he'd grown up with and guided her to where they could have a little privacy. 'Now, what's this about drinking laudanum and Meg's fella?' Harry sat down on an upturned crate and urged Sarah to do the same as they warmed their hands around a brazier's flames.

She couldn't hold it in any longer. 'He's bloody well killed her. He left a bottle of laudanum with my mam and she's drunk the lot last night when we were asleep. He did it on purpose, I know he did. He just wanted my mam out of the way and then he could get our Meg to marry him and bake every day for him. Well, I'm not going to live with them both in their little love nest. I hate him, and our Meg is a fool if she thinks he loves her. He's just going to use her! I hate him, I hate him! My mam would still be with me if he'd not turned up on the doorstep.'

When Sarah stopped, overtaken by sobs, Harry said, 'Shush now, Sarah. Your mam was riddled with cancer. You know that she wasn't long for this earth. He didn't kill her. She'd had enough, by the sound of it. If she is put out of her misery, you should be thankful. And if Frankie wants to rescue you from Sykes Yard, that is something to be thankful for, surely?' He paused to take a breath. 'I haven't said anything to my mam . . . but I'm saving as much money as I can. As soon as I've enough, I'm stirring my shanks and getting out of Leeds.'

'You can't . . . you can't leave me! I'll have *nobody* to talk to.' Sarah started to sob again but then suddenly realized just what Harry had said. She looked up at him with a beam on her face. 'I'll come with you. Go on, Harry! We can run away together. The two of us will be a lot safer than one of us on our own. We can look out for one another.' Sarah tried to control her excitement.

Harry didn't look convinced. 'I don't know, Sarah. I'd planned to go on my own. Besides, it's only a dream and if I do go it'll not be for another year. I've to save my brass up first.'

'Why can't I come? Is it because I'm a girl? I can do everything you can. I can look after myself. I could go with you, Harry — believe me! I can start saving, just like you. Especially if Meg and I move in with Frankie Pearson. I can put up with that for a few months if I knew I had a way out of there. Go on, it'll be grand for the two of us. Where are we to go? Liverpool, Manchester? We could even go to London, if we saved enough?'

'I don't know. Let me think about it. At least it's put a smile back on your face.' Harry sighed, recognizing that now wasn't the time to upset Sarah further. 'Perhaps it is a blessing that your ma passed,' he suggested. 'Your Meg can get her life back now. If she marries Frankie, don't you spoil it for her. She's her own life to live as well as looking after you.'

'If I know I'll be leaving with you, they can do what they want.' Sarah looked at Harry with purpose in her gaze. This would be their secret — and she knew she would have to keep it to herself when she got home.

'Aye, well . . . we will see about that. Now, if you've calmed down, I need to get back to my work. The boss will be looking for me. He might dock my pay, and then we'll never get to London.'

Sarah grinned and stood up. 'So, you are thinking about it?'

'We'll see. I'm not promising 'owt. I don't even

20

know what I'm doing myself from one day to the next. All I know, I need to get away from my father who drinks, my mother who has more men callers than the whores down here on the cut, and the constant wailing of one or the other young'uns in our house. Your life is a luxury compared to some. Even more so if Meg marries her fella. She'll want for nowt — and you won't neither.' Harry turned to leave.

'Aye, it'll be a good life for our Meg — but not for me. Please, Harry — let me come with you! I'll not be any bother.' Sarah followed him out of the hut and took him up in a sudden embrace, clearly embarrassing him in front of his workmates.

'We'll see. It's a long way off yet. I've hardly saved anything. Now, get yourself home and be right with Meg. She'll miss her mother just as much as you. She'll need you.' Harry unpeeled her arms from around him, making Sarah feel unwanted and vulnerable in her grief.

'She'll be too busy with her fella to notice me,' Sarah muttered to herself, as she watched Harry return to his work unloading the barges and Tom Puds. She'd go home, and she'd be right with Meg — but from now on, she'd put a penny or two away from the money she made at the mill. Enough for adventures with Harry.

⋆ ⋆ ⋆

'You're back!' Meg's hands were on her hips. 'Well, you need not come out with rubbish like Frankie poisoning our mother again! Else, I'll tell you exactly what I think of you. Frankie was really upset with your hard words. He'd only tried to help!'

21

Sarah slumped into the chair that her mother had used to sit next to the fire. 'She died, so it is his fault and I'm not going to apologize. I take it that he's buggered off?'

'Yes, he's gone. He's telling the undertaker to put our mother in an oak coffin and to send him the bill. So, don't you say another bad word about him, Sarah Fairfax! We could hardly afford to bury her. We owe him a lot.' Meg looked at her sister, feeling a pulse of guilt. 'Are you all right? I know that you're upset. We'll both miss her. She was always there for us, no matter what.' Meg bent down and took her sister's hand.

'But that's not true, is it? You have Frankie. You'll make me go to live with you both. Him and his French ways and his posh suits. What's he doing courting you? Why does he bother with us?' Sarah sobbed.

'I don't know, Sarah, but we love each other. Try and be happy for us. He wants you as a friend, not an enemy.' Meg hugged her sister. 'It'll be right, Sarah. Things will take a turn now, you'll see. I can go to work now Mam's passed and you're doing well at the mill. And if and when I walk down the aisle with Frankie then neither of us should have any worries.'

'Well, you won't but I will. He'll not put up with me forever, especially if you have children with him. I'll have no one.' Sarah pushed her sister away from her.

'You'll always have me. We're sisters and always will be,' Meg said and wiped away a tear, holding her arms out to be loved. 'I'll never turn my back on you, Sarah. When you think you are on your own, Frankie and I will do all we can for you. Don't you forget it.'

* * *

22

Both sisters watched as the procession of mourners threw a handful of soil onto their mother's coffin as the commendation was said over it by the vicar whom they hardly knew. Frankie stood by Meg's side for her support and looked lovingly in sympathy at her.

'I thought Harry would be here for you,' Meg whispered as she put her arm around Sarah's waist and squeezed her hand.

'He's too busy making money, although he said his boss wouldn't let him have the day off, seeing my mam's not family,' Sarah whispered back, wiping a tear away.

'Never mind, you've got us, and we will soon be on our way back home,' Meg said before shaking hands with the few friends who had paid their respects at the graveside and then were about to made their way home.

With the last mourner gone and the gravediggers waiting to do their job, the small family group walked together. 'Lord, I'm glad that's over,' Sarah exclaimed as they headed down the path through Saint Mary's churchyard. The grey stone church building stood proud and noble, surrounded by the hurriedly built rows of mill workers' houses.

'Don't say the Lord's name in vain, our Sarah. Show some respect.' Meg felt her body sink with exhaustion. 'It's been a long week. Perhaps now, we will be able to sleep more soundly. It has not been the best, sharing our bedroom with a corpse in a coffin.' Meg peeled away her black gloves and took her sister's hand.

'You should have let the undertakers take her to their parlour. I would not have minded paying for the extra service,' Frankie said as he watched Meg consoling Sarah as tears fell down both sisters' cheeks.

'No, we wanted her to stay at home as long as she could,' Meg replied. 'Neither of us could bear to think of her lying by herself. But thank you for your offer.' She tried to smile at Frankie as they walked through the wrought-iron gates and back into the busy city. 'She'd hardly ever moved more than a street or two away from Sykes Yard since she got married to my father. It was only right that she stayed there until her burial.'

'I don't know what I'm going to do without my mam,' Sarah sobbed. 'She's always been there for me, no matter what.' She suddenly realized that she was now independent of her mother and remembered all the times that she had rebelled just for the sake of it.

'It will be all right. I keep telling you, we'll always have each other. Dry your eyes. Mam wouldn't want to see you so upset now that she is at peace.' They walked towards the hackney carriage that Frankie had made provision for.

'Now, my dears . . . let's get you back.' They hadn't wanted a wake or any fuss at all, and Frankie had insisted on catering for the sisters at his home. 'I told my maid to make something appropriate for the day and she was only too willing. I wouldn't like to think of the two of you returning to an empty house.'

Sarah squeezed Meg's hand and looked pleadingly at her. The last thing she wanted was to have to stand on manners at the posh house of Frankie's in Headingley. All she wanted was to go home.

'That's kind of you,' Meg said. 'But I think both of us need some time to ourselves — to grieve and contemplate what to do next. Sarah is at work tomorrow at the mill and I aim to see what employment I can find now Mother has passed.'

Sarah stopped in her tracks ready to turn down the street that led to Sykes Yard.

'I understand,' Frankie said, after a pause. 'I'm not part of the family yet. However, surely an hour and just a sandwich won't hurt? My maid would be so disappointed if her work went to waste.' Frankie looked at Sarah and felt a pulse of pity for the young girl. 'I want you both to know that I'm here for you, no matter what. And I mean both of you!' Frankie bent to kiss Meg's cheek, wanting to hold her tight but knowing that it would not be proper in public, especially when the sisters were in mourning.

Meg hesitated, glancing at her sister. 'Perhaps a drink and sandwich . . .' Silently, she pleaded with Sarah not to protest. 'Then we'll return home.'

Frankie opened the carriage door, and the two sisters clambered into the darkness of the horse-drawn cab — but not before Sarah had chance to nip Meg's arm in protest. They sat down against the studded leather seats. Opposite them, Frankie took his own place. He was dressed in his finest black mourning suit, a diamond stud glistening against his cravat.

'It will give you chance to see my home, Sarah. I understand that Meg has told you that we are to be married. As part of that arrangement, I am all too happy to make our home your home too.' Frankie leaned on his swagger stick and looked across at his sister-in-law-to-be who looked to be hiding in the dark shadows of the carriage.

'She has — not that I've been allowed to have any say in it,' Sarah retorted.

Meg put her head down, hurt at the bitterness in Sarah's words. She felt her stomach churn as she

25

hoped that there would be no further confrontation between her sister and Frankie, today of all days.

'Sarah, be thankful. Frankie is offering you a home. He's under no obligation to do so.'

'Whatever I say or think, no one gives a damn, so I'll just shut my gob.' Sarah folded her arms, making the atmosphere in the cab unbearable as the horse and carriage made their way down the busy street and out to the leafy suburbs of Headingley and the well-to-do houses of the businessmen who lived there.

★   ★   ★

'Here we are: my home. My grandmother lived here and now I do, thankfully. My mother hates the place, says that it is depressing compared to her flamboyant apartment in Paris.'

Frankie opened the carriage door and alighted, holding his hand out for Sarah and then Meg as they stepped down onto the pavement.

Meg gasped. 'Do you own all of it?' She walked up the sandstone steps and looked up at all three floors of windows, with their net curtains and expensive velvet drapes. She noted the brass plaque beside the door: *Grosvenor House*. Even though they had known each other for months now, this was the first time she had visited Frankie's home. They had always met at his patisserie on the Headrow or at Meg's home, Frankie hesitant to show Meg how he lived in fear of making her feel inadequate.

'It's not as big as it looks once you are inside. There are much larger places in Leeds. This really is quite modest, and there's very little garden, except the piece that you can see that runs around all sides of the

26

house.' Frankie turned the brass door handle on the green painted door and removed his mourning hat as he entered the hallway.

'I'm sorry, sir, I never heard the coach arrive! Please let me take your coats.' Frankie's housemaid scurried up to the group and bobbed and curtsied to Meg and Sarah. 'Welcome, to you both. May I say how sorry I am to hear of the loss of your mother.' The girl took Frankie's coat, and Meg and Sarah's shawl and bonnets from them, then hung her master's coat on the coat stand that took pride of place in the richly decorated hallway.

'Thank you. Sorry, I don't know your name?' Meg said, doing her best to ignore her sister, who was pulling a face behind the maid's back.

'It's Ada, Miss. Ada Smith.' The maid smiled as Frankie watched Meg and Sarah look around them.

'Now, ladies. If you would like to follow me into the drawing-room? Ada, we will take tea in there. Miss Fairfax and her sister, Sarah, are intent on not staying long as they wish to return home before darkness falls . . . which is understandable after the day they have had.'

'Of course, sir. I'll bring the sandwiches and cakes through directly. The fire is lit and I hope everything will be to your liking.' Ada curtsied and disappeared down the hallway.

'Ladies, please follow me, we will take the second doorway down for the drawing room.' Meg recognized that Frankie was nervous and thus was burbling. 'The first doorway leads to my study and the one here is the morning room, it catches all the light and is a delight to sit in after breakfast but the drawing-room is more homely. I didn't want you to feel as if you were standing on ceremony eating in the dining room across the other side of the hallway, after all, it is just us three and I feel that you must want to withdraw from the world at the moment, which is just what the drawing-room is for.' Frankie stopped for a breath, turned around and smiled at the two of them. 'There's a bathroom upstairs if you two ladies wish to use it.'

'A bathroom, Frankie — how opulent. I've only heard about them, never dreamt that I would be in a house with one.' Meg blushed as she realized she was showing herself up.

'Please, both of you go and see it for yourselves. Ada will be a while with the tea. I'm sure there is enough time for you both to go up there and powder your noses or whatever young ladies do in such a place.' Frankie smiled as Meg and her sister walked up the broad carpeted stairs. The two of them gasped as they opened the bathroom door.

'Lordy, Meg!' Sarah cried. 'He has hot and cold water and — look! — a toilet that flushes. You'll never have to sit in that stinking earth closet in the yard ever again, once the two of you wed. He's bloody well got everything we haven't. What does he see in you?'

'Don't say that, Sarah. He loves me for what I am, he's not bothered that we are poor.' Meg ran her hand along the roll-topped bath and wondered whether she dare turn on one of the taps to watch the water fill the beautiful white enamel.

Sarah sat down on the toilet. 'It's too good to be true and you know it. He doesn't fool me for a minute. Why should he bother with us? We are right at the bottom of the pile and he's right at the top. Folk like him usually look as if we are a piece of dirt on their shoes, yet here he is asking to marry you. Something's wrong!'

'Will you stop looking on the dark side of everything? It's simple, he loves me and I him. Why can't you be happy for us? This will be your home, too — don't you forget.' Meg went over and took Sarah's hand. 'Now, come on. Enjoy your tea with Frankie and try not to look too sullen. Then, we'll go home. Although it will never be the same now Mam has gone and left us. I looked down into the grave and thought, *This is the end of an era*. For better or worse, I don't know. However, looking around here, I doubt it will be for the worse.'

'Happen not for you, but it will be for me. This will never be my true home, no matter how fine it is. And he certainly does not love me nor I him.'

Sarah walked towards the bathroom door with her sister after both had washed their hands and marvelled at the water coming out of the tap and the smell of the expensive soap that was placed on the sink in its own little richly embellished dish.

'Just try to show him some gratitude, Sarah, that's all I ask — for all our happiness. Mama's gone now, and there's no bringing her back.' Meg swallowed hard, trying to keep the tears from falling. She had everything, and yet she felt as if she had nothing. A whole new world was about to be hers, but a silent niggle kept rocking her confidence. Was Sarah right in what she'd said? Why was a wealthy businessman looking twice at her?

★   ★   ★

Meg and Sarah walked back into the poverty of Sykes Yard, their stomachs full but their hearts aching. By

29

Meg's side walked Frankie. He'd invited the two of them to stay the night, but a warning glance from Sarah to Meg said that his invitation was not to be accepted.

Now, Meg let her hand linger on his jacket sleeve as Sarah walked by herself down the yard, taking her plain black bonnet from her head and letting the ribbons trail in the yard's dirt as she walked up the steps to their silent, empty home.

'Sarah's feeling our mam's death; we are better returning home today,' Meg told Frankie. 'I'm sorry, my love, but I have to consider Sarah's feelings. She's still young. Your tea was very thoughtful, and both of us were astounded by your home. I thank you for your kindness.'

Frankie squeezed Meg's hand. 'No disrespect, my dear, but sometimes you should think of yourself first — you can't kowtow to Sarah all the time.'

'I know, but she's heartbroken. We both are. We will be there for one another today and then we will have to get on with our lives. There will be plenty of time for you and me to be together.' Meg stood on her toes and kissed Frankie lightly, her head dizzy with the love she felt for him. 'I'll see you tomorrow.' Meg walked down the yard, glancing over her shoulder at Frankie, who stood looking dejected.

She had to be here for Sarah, today of all days. Tomorrow, and the days after that . . . ? They would be different.

★ ★ ★

Meg walked into the kitchen to find her sister stoking the fire that was nearly out.

'He's gone, then?' Sarah said, angrily shoving a poker between the coals. 'I thought you were going to say yes to him and stay the night at his posh home. It wouldn't have been right. All I really want to do right now is to curl up and cry.'

'It wouldn't have been right, the two of us stopping in his house alone; besides, I knew that you didn't want to stay. Come here, give me a hug.' Meg lifted her sister to her feet. 'It's been a hard day for both of us. Mam would have been proud to have seen so many faces in the church. She was well liked.' Meg held her sister close and kissed the top of her head as she sobbed. 'Now, come on, enough tears. Mam would not want it. Let's have a drink, at least. We filled our boots at Frankie's and will not want much to eat for the rest of the day. I noticed you didn't hold back on the cream horns!' She laughed, and dried the tears from Sarah's young face.

'I don't care, they were fiddly and I enjoyed them,' Sarah smirked.

Meg shook her head. 'Now, Mam had some relations down South. I'd better put pen to paper and tell them that we've lost her. I should've told them earlier that she had passed but with everything going on I've never got around to it.'

'Where down South? I've never heard of them before.'

'Somewhere in London. Holborn, I think it's called. I've never met them. She used to say they were from the uppity side and that they'd be disappointed if they knew how low we had come in society.'

Sarah released herself from Meg's embrace and placed two chipped teacups onto the table. 'We might be poor, but we have our pride, Mam made sure of

31

that. Can't you remember her saying that even rich folk fart?' Sarah said.

Meg stood with her hands on her hips but couldn't help but grin. 'Sarah Fairfax, sometimes your mouth is like a gutter! Just think of what you are saying and doing. Especially when we move in with Frankie.'

'If we move in with Frankie, I won't be happy. Even though he has a swanky bath and an inside lavvy. He can't fool me, I don't like him!' Sarah said as she got on with making the tea.

Meg scowled at her sister. 'I give up! Never look a gift horse in the mouth!'

'Aye, he's probably saying that, and we all know what gift he's getting from you,' Sarah said and then went quietly about her business warming the pot and making the tea. Leaving Meg to worry about her words and whether she was making the right decision when it came to marrying Frankie.

3

Ted Lund looked around the bakery he'd run for forty years. It was beginning to need money spent on it. A bit of love and pride wouldn't go amiss.

He eased himself into his usual chair next to the ovens and pondered what to do. Since the incident with Meg Fairfax, trade had steadily gone downhill. Perhaps the young lass had been right. He could make more of his bakery. But at his age, all the life seemed to have gone out of him.

But it was more than that — much more.

His time in Ireland had shown him the life he could have if he left the grimy backstreets of Leeds. The emerald isle had appealed to him, with its clean air and green fields. He'd thought of nothing else since his return. Maybe he could put one foot in front of the other, over on the other side of the Irish Sea. People were more amicable over there. He could see himself settled in a small bothy now he was in his dotage, doing what he wanted when he wanted. Perhaps it was time to sell, move on and leave. He'd sleep on it, and in the morning probably make a decision. With money from the sale of the bakery and no four o'clock start in the mornings, it was looking more and more attractive.

★　★　★

'Morning, Ted. What can I do for you today?' Joe Dinsdale, the owner of one of the largest grocery suppliers in the area, stood behind his counter, a white apron tied around his waist, looking through his ledger.

'I'm in need of some currants, if your lad has time to serve me,' Ted said and looked across at George. The shop lad was leaning across the counter, chatting to a young lass.

Joe glared. 'George! Currants for Mr Lund! Do your courting in your own time.'

'Yes, sir!' The lad straightened up immediately. 'A pound, is it, Mr Lund?' He abandoned the young woman and hurried to weigh out a pound of currants from a jar.

'Aye, a pound will suffice. I might not be needing them for much longer.'

'Why are you saying that, then? Have you had enough of baking? You've never been yourself since Meg Fairfax worked for you and you came back from Ireland — not that your moaning is anything new,' Joe grinned. 'You should have kept her on, I could have told you that. She's a good baker and folk like her.'

'That bloody lass has a lot to answer for. Folk are forever asking for her coconut tarts and tea cakes. Her 'baked goods'. I'm not making what she made, it is my shop after all. What do I want with all that work? It was a bad day when I took her on. Anyway, it all backfired on her, thieving bitch,' Ted swore.

Joe wasn't putting up with Ted rewriting history. 'Now, Ted, you know, she didn't steal a penny. Truth is, she made more profit running your bakery while you were away than you had done in a long time. She worked long hours and from what I heard, her baking was good.'

'You know nowt!' Ted cried. 'Apart from the fact that she lined your pocket with her wantings of

34

cherries and coconut and things that cost me a small fortune — stuff that any sensible backstreet baker would never use. I wonder what she'll do, now her mother's died. I'd have gone to the funeral, but I didn't think my face would be welcomed there.'

'Meg will be all right. From what I hear, she's walking out with the fella that owns the posh bakery on the Headrow. He'll have everything she needs. She's fallen on her feet well and proper, if he decides he's to marry her. She'll not be bothered about your bakery. Meg's going up in the world!' Joe grinned. It was good to have heard that Meg had found a good man. She deserved a better life after looking after her mother.

'She will only be trying to see what she can get out of him. Why would a fella with all that brass look twice at a lass like Meg Fairfax?' Ted said. He watched as George placed his pound of currants in front of him.

'Perhaps it's the other way around,' Joe suggested. 'She's a bonny lass and she'd be an asset for any good baker. Perhaps Frankie Pearson knows just what he's doing.'

'Well, it will make no difference to me because I am thinking of selling my bakery. I've had enough and things have never been the same since I employed *her*! She can do what she likes because I don't give a damn,' Ted growled. 'Now, put these on my account. I'll be paying you off for good at the end of the month. You'll miss my trade when I've buggered off, and then you won't be singing that lass's praises so much. Her fella hardly ever buys owt from you, I've noticed. Toffee-nosed he is, from what I've seen of him.'

'Now, Ted, don't sound so bitter. I've always thought you and me were good friends. Isn't it time to admit that you were wrong about Meg? Perhaps you should

35

rent the bakery to her? You know where she lives. Or come to some agreement, seeing that she'll not have the brass to pay you until she weds her man? That way you'd have a good bit of money coming in. Just what you need in your old age.'

'Over my dead body! Think of what you are saying, man! The lass gave me nothing but worry!

'Good day to you. I'd thank you for keeping your nose out of my business,' Ted scowled, picking up his bag of currants and grunting as he left the store, slamming the door leaving the doorbell clanging after he had gone.

Joe shook his head and looked over at George. 'That is one bitter man. Young Meg Fairfax made his bakery work. She must have made him some brass when he was away, but he won't admit it. He's a fool to himself. Nobody will want his bakery if they look back through his books and see what he truly makes when Meg's not there helping him.'

'Meg would have loved his bakery — but she's in no need of it if she's to marry her fella,' George replied and looked wistfully at the vibrating doorbell.

'Well, she'll want for nowt now. If what I hear is right, she's off to better climes. Good luck to the lass. I wish her well.'

Joe smiled and went back to his ledger, but not before he'd reminded George to go about his work and to stop daydreaming about a lass who was out of his reach. He ran his finger down the column of what Ted owed. Silently, Joe made a promise to himself to make sure that he got paid, before the baker closed his doors forever.

★ ★ ★

36

Sarah stood in front of Tom Askew's desk and she waited for him to look up from his papers. The Hunslet Mill manager's office overlooked the factory floor of burlers and menders where his workers checked and mended each length of cloth before it left the mill.

He glanced up at the lass who had worked for him for a good six months and had so far not caused much trouble — until now. 'Yes, what do you want?' he asked eventually.

'Dora Metcalfe is leaving at the end of the month,' Sarah began. 'She's telling everyone she's going to live at Hull when she gets married to her beau next weekend. I wondered if I could have her job. I think I've proved myself these last few months. I'm never late! And I'm a good worker.'

Sarah knew it wasn't her place to ask for a leg-up, but if she and Harry were to run away to London, they'd need every penny. Although Harry had not made himself known to her of late, she only hoped that she was still part of his plans. Not that she would let her boss know that!

'Is she, indeed? That's the first I've heard.' Tom sat back in his chair and steepled his fingers. 'She's said nowt to me.'

'I only heard her talking to Sissy Banks and showing off her fancy ring that her fella has bought her. She can't be making it up because the ring looks worth a good bob or two.' Sarah tried to read her boss's thoughts.

Tom paused, looking her up and down. 'How long have you been with us?'

'A little over six months, sir. I really need that burler's job. It was what I came here for originally.' Sarah felt her jaw set with determination; she needed the

37

extra money.

Tom stood up from his desk. 'Leave it with me. If she is leaving, I'll need someone to do her job. I'm not promising owt but I'll bear you in mind.'

'Thank you, sir. I really need it, I need the money, and now my mam has died . . .' She allowed her sentence to peter out, playing on her mother's death. Well, why not? She needed the money.

'That's not what I hear. Apparently, your sister has caught one of the wealthiest men in Leeds and you are to live with them.' Tom walked around his desk and opened the office door. Sarah realized that Daisy, the young lass who was his lover and Sarah's sister's best friend, had told all the gossip.

'I'll not be going with her, it will be over my dead body if I do, and I don't know why she even looks at the smarmy devil!' Sarah blurted out.

'In that case, I'll see. No doubt Dora will tell me when she is thinking of leaving in her own good time. Now, back to work! There's plenty for you to be doing.'

Tom watched as Sarah left his office and ran down the stairs to collect and sweep the clippings from around the burlers' feet. She had cheek if nowt else, did young Sarah Fairfax. No wonder she and her sister did not see eye to eye. Perhaps he would offer her the position if Dora left. She'd shown plenty of interest in the past from what he had seen and she was beginning to look more clean and tidy of late.

★ ★ ★

'Now, look. The fellas bring you in the rolls of cloth from downstairs, they'll hang them up on the rollers for you. Then it's up to you to run your hands over the

38

cloth and feel for any imperfections and knots and wrong threads.' Sissy stood with Sarah by her side. 'You need scissors in one hand and tweezers in the other, you cut off the loose threads at the sides of the rolls. Then, if you find any knots, you pull the thread straight with the tweezers and straighten the material out if it puckers. If it's badly knotted and you can't mend it, you tell snotty drawers over there and she'll inspect it and mark it up with tailor's chalk.' Sissy nodded to the woman, Madge Evans, who everyone hated, who walked around all day checking their work.

'That seems easy enough,' Sarah commented.

The other woman's eyes opened in shock. 'You'll not be saying that after a day or two! You'll ache with concentration. We are the last point in checking the material before it goes on to be made up. So, don't make too many mistakes. Each roll you mend will be tagged to you, so don't you forget that, else you'll be out on your arse!' Sissy watched as Sarah carefully followed her instructions. 'Don't nick the cloth. Be careful!'

'I'll do it better when you're not watching me — you're putting me off,' Sarah said sharply and sighed with frustration as she ran her hands over the cloth.

'You'll feel Madge Evans' wrath, if you keep doing that. The old bag! She must have told Tom Askew that Dora was leaving. She made Dora's life hell before she left, finding fault with everything she did. She's always snitching, that nosy old bugger.'

Sarah concentrated on the job in hand. She had to prove she could do the work. She wasn't going to admit that it was her who had told Tom Askew of Dora's leaving, but it had held her in good stead for

the job she was now doing and that was all that mattered. With the extra money, it would not take her long
to save enough to run away with Harry. The wedded
bliss that her sister was talking about . . . She'd never
forgive. Not the man who had killed her mother.

She had a twinge of guilt as she thought about the
support her sister had given her and now she was
planning to abandon her. Then she consoled herself
by trying to tell herself it would be for the best, that
she would only be in the way if she stayed.

★   ★   ★

Meg watched Sarah bolt down the meagre supper of
potato and barley broth that she had made for her
after her sister's day working at Hunslet Mill.

'What have you been up to today then?' Meg asked
carefully.

Sarah didn't look up from her meal. 'Filled the wool
bobbins. Swept up. Did whatever anybody asked me
to.'

'I'll have to move my shanks and find myself a
job before the end of the week. We need the money.'
Meg sighed. 'I'd still like to keep my independence,
whether I'm to marry Frankie or not.'

'I thought you'd be going to work for *him* as well as
marrying him now that Mam doesn't rely on either of
us,' Sarah said, with a surly look on her face.

'Frankie has asked me to do both, but I don't know.
The shop on the Headrow is that posh. I don't feel as
though I belong there. I'd be frightened that I spoke
out of term to some of his clients. I've told him I'm
thinking about it for now,' Meg said and watched the
smugness come to Sarah's face.

'He's too posh for us and you know it. Mr Lah-di-da. Get yourself a fresh bloke, our Meg. There's fellas out there that are like us but have a bit of brass put to one side if that's what you are after.'

'Posh or not, Sarah, he's the man I love and hope to shortly marry,' Meg snapped, feeling annoyed at her sister. Why did she always have to be so negative? 'I might not want to work in his shop on the Headrow but that should not come between us. Don't waste your breath. I am marrying Frankie, whether you want me to or not.'

4

The house was strangely quiet. There were no more demands upon her for pills and potions. Meg felt lost and bereaved, and sat with her head in her hands.

In front of her sister, she had needed to be strong, but the death of her mother had shaken her to her core. Worse still, she knew that if she didn't find work soon she would have to bow to Frankie's wishes and become dependent on his goodwill at his patisserie as well as marrying him. She wasn't ready to lose her independence, although she was hesitant to tell Frankie that. She wanted to be her own woman for just a touch longer.

Meg sometimes felt a pang of envy as she watched Sarah come and go. She had never had that freedom, always needing to be there for her family.

She raised her head as she heard a knock on the back door. Immediately, it was flung open. It was Betsy, her nextdoor neighbour, with her baby on her hip. His cheeks were red and burning and dribbles were running down his chin. Meg could see that he had been crying.

'It's only me, duck. I thought I'd put my head in. I never got a chance to talk to you after the funeral and with this one teething and my Jim working all the hours God gave him, I've not had a chance until now.'

Betsy sat herself down next to Meg, placing the baby on the rug by the fire. She handed him a clothes peg from out of her pocket which the baby instantly started chewing upon to ease his teething. 'My youngest starts walking, and then I get lumbered with looking after my sister's two days a week. Silly bitch! You'd think she'd learn from me not to have bairns — but no, her fella got her up the duff and now he's nowhere to be seen.' Betsy glanced at Meg. 'You look as if you are missing your mam? Have you had some dinner? It's no good going hungry, no matter how you feel. I know you'll be taking her death hard and that you'll be suffering.'

'I'm all right. I've had a crust and a bit of cheese. I was about to put my shawl on and have a walk up town. I need to find myself a job and bring some money in if I'm going to look after myself and be independent. Sarah's wage only just covers the rent. We need some money to live on and now with Mam gone, I can work full time again.' Meg tried to look brighter. Compared to Betsy, she had no real problems. Betsy's life was filled with drunken men, crying babies and poverty. She couldn't complain in front of her.

'I thought you'd be getting wed as soon as you could? Get yourself out of this bloody square. Has he not put an engagement ring on your finger yet? Posh folk usually do that first. I suppose it tells other fellas that you are theirs and not to try owt on.'

'No, Frankie has said nothing about an engagement ring,' Meg told her. 'We are to wed, but I've asked him for a little time, to show my respects to my mother.' She paused. 'Sarah is still not keen on going to live with him. We have no need to rush into marriage. He will probably give me an engagement ring nearer the time, I hope.' Why did Betsy's questions make her feel so uncertain, suddenly?

Betsy must have sensed Meg's anxiety. 'That'll be

why he's not got you a ring — the time isn't right,' she said, hasty to reassure. 'After all, since he came into your life your mother's been so ill. He's good to even consider taking Sarah with you. Does he know what a handful she is? Even our Harry says she's a mind of her own. I think he's embarrassed when she comes to see him down at the wharf. Stupid lad! Folk are teasing him.'

Meg tried to smile. 'Yes, Frankie knows all about our Sarah. I'm afraid she lets him know exactly what she thinks of him. She's not keen on him at all — sure that he's too well-to-do for us.'

'Aye, well he is posh. You've done well to catch him. Just you make sure you hold onto him. I'd be moving in with him tomorrow if he was mine. Anything to get out of this yard and the poverty that goes with it.' Betsy sighed and looked at her nephew as he started to bawl yet again as his teeth gave him more grief.

'He's in a twined way with himself,' Meg said and looked at the baby, even worse dressed and muckier than any of Betsy's ever were.

'Aye, he knows he's not wanted, poor lil sod, but he'll get up and soon be a man, God willing. I don't suppose you have any clove oil I can borrow, just to numb his gums. His teeth are taking their time to come through and they're giving him some jip,' Betsy said as she stood up and put the baby back on her hip.

'I should have. We both take it for toothache; we can't afford the dentist, so we make do when we can.' Meg went and looked in the wooden cupboard next to the back door that held anything they needed for medical emergencies. Meg noticed there was still a bottle of laudanum unfinished by her mother. She

44

passed Betsy the small brown bottle of clove oil and smiled. 'Here, it's awful stuff but it'll stop the pain. I'll have it back if there's any left after you have used it; you never know when we might need it again.'

'That's grand, that should settle him while I make Jim's dinner. He's been working nights so he'll want some peace when he comes home, else there will be hell to pay, especially when he knows we have this'en with us today. It's not as if we haven't enough of our own.' Betsy placed the small bottle of tincture into her pocket and made for the back door. 'Get that man of yours wed. Don't keep him waiting; anything's better than living in this yard of hell. Don't you go and lose him, my girl, your mam would never forgive you.' Betsy looked keenly at Meg. 'Make a better life for yourself, don't waste it like I have done mine.'

Meg watched Betsy climb ungainly over the short red brick wall that separated their backyards and listened to the wails of the baby and demands of Betsy's own children as she made her way into the house. Her friend was trapped by her own doing, Meg knew, and she had no intention of doing the same thing and be left looking after her house and home with a baby every year.

Perhaps Betsy was right. Maybe she shouldn't wait too long to wed Frankie, engagement ring or not. However, she wanted just a year to herself to do what she wanted to do. She reached for her shawl and decided to go and look for work, then call in to see Frankie at his bakery. Perhaps she and Sarah were more alike than she had realized: both were selfish and set in their ways.

★ ★ ★

45

Meg had wandered the streets of Leeds all day asking for work, but to no avail. The only places she had not tried were the factories, but she knew she could not stand the noise and monotonous work. Now she stood on the Headrow, not far from Frankie's new patisserie where she had first met him when it was just newly opened with beautiful cakes in the window. Perhaps she could work for him, just until they got married.

'Now then, love,' came a voice. 'Are you up for a penny fumble? Where do you want to go?'

Meg was taken aback as a soldier, dressed in the scarlet uniform of the Hussars, leaned over her in a drunken stupor and propositioned her. He had clearly mistaken her for a prostitute loitering outside the inn, and was seeking to take her up a nearby alley.

'I am certainly not that sort of woman, sir!' Meg said sternly. 'I command you to take your hands from off my waist. Get off me, you lech!'

She snatched his hand away as he rocked unsteadily on his feet. Passers-by shook their heads at the state of the man who should be there to protect them, not assault them. How could a soldier of the Queen's regiment be so intoxicated at that time of day?

A passing gentleman stopped and prodded the soldier with his stick. 'Move on man, go back to your barracks. Can't you see this lady is not for you!' He watched the soldier rock on his heels then think better of taking on a gentleman.

'Suit yourself, then,' he slurred as he went on his way. 'There's plenty more I can choose from, you bitch.'

Meg made her escape from him, dodging between carriages and the horse-driven trams with people sitting on the open top decks, looking down on the throning crowds of Leeds shoppers, making for the safety of the patisserie. She might not have any money, but she would never sink to that level.

For a few moments, Meg watched as the upper-class ladies and gentlemen came and went at the patisserie. She noticed that upstairs in the tea room windows, luxurious palm plants had been placed in readiness for the tea room's opening. Trying to compose herself, she went into the shop.

Norah looked up after serving her latest customer and saw the distress on Meg's face. Meg welcomed a face she already knew.

'Are you all right, Miss Fairfax? You look perplexed.' Marie glanced up, too.

'I'm a little ruffled,' Meg admitted. 'A soldier mistook me for one that walks the streets and accosted me. I feel more embarrassed than anything.' Meg tried to compose herself and breathed in deeply.

'I bet he came out from the Horse and Trumpet,' Norah said. 'The Hussars have come back from campaign and they are making up for lost time, drinking and womanising. They're not a good advertisement for our brave troops.' Norah gave Marie a knowing glance then said to Meg, 'Mr Pearson is upstairs. He's taken delivery of a counter for the fancies he is to serve upstairs. I'm sure he will want to comfort you.'

Meg noticed Marie smirk and then thanked Norah before climbing the stairs to seek out Frankie.

'Meg, my love. I didn't expect to see you today.' Frankie kissed her tenderly on the cheek.

'I thought I'd stop feeling sorry for myself and start to look for some employment.' Meg sat down on a chair as she felt her legs giving way beneath her, as she suddenly realized that she could have come off a lot worse from her encounter with the soldier.

Frankie sat down beside her and took her hand. 'You look drained. Are you all right?'

'Some idiot of a soldier accosted me. It has shaken me up; it could have been a lot worse if it hadn't happened in broad daylight on the Headrow. I feel such a fool! I'm worried — is that what folk think of me? That I'm no better than someone who walks the streets?'

'By God, I'd have shown him what I thought of him if I'd caught him,' Frankie said furiously. 'Don't be silly, Meg. Stop thinking of yourself as so low in life! If you are good enough to marry me and work alongside me, like I keep asking you to, all would be resolved. It's probably because he saw how beautiful you are, just like I do.'

'I'm fine. A little shaken and annoyed at myself. I thought that I would be able to find work straight-away. But unless I'm willing to take work in a mill or factory, it won't be that easy.'

'I've told you, there is no need to work. Marry me! Or, if you are still adamant about waiting a while, to be respectful and mourn your mother's passing, come and work here for now. The tea room is finished now. Look! The counter is waiting to be filled with pastries and cakes, the crockery is all on the shelves and the tables are waiting for customers. I will need to adver-tise for a baker shortly. Along with my delicate pastries, I will need to sell the things that you used to bake. My customers will expect everyday fayre like scones and sandwich cake. I don't have the time to do that myself — especially now that I've managed to buy the new patisserie at Headingley. I'm going to have to spread myself thin for a while until the alterations

48

have been done to my satisfaction and I can leave it to run with good staff in it.'

For a moment, Meg could see Frankie's brow furrow with anxiety, before he smiled. 'You see, I do honestly need you. Else, I will have to advertise for someone to work for me.'

'You've bought the other bakery, then? I'd forgotten to ask about it with losing my mother. You must be proud of yourself, your name to be above two bakeries.' Meg linked her arm into his. 'Perhaps, I should work for you here? But as I keep telling you, I'm not used to dealing with posh folk.'

'Well, if you want to work here in the tea room instead of the bakery and shop, I'll get you the same uniform as the rest of the staff — a plain black skirt and white blouse . . . not that you dress badly anyway,' he added hastily. 'Or if you would like to work just in the bakery then you would be in the back and no need to associate with the customers. Of course, I'd pay you well, as I would any employee that I take on.'

Meg thought for a moment then said, 'You're not taking me on out of sympathy, are you? I couldn't bear that!'

'I'm employing you because I am to take you to be my wife and I would like you to be by my side. It's that simple, and to buy you some new clothes would be a delight. You deserve to be wearing the best! Your beauty outshines many of the rich and famous who shop within my walls. So, never feel belittled.'

'I don't know. Look at your tea room and the shop downstairs. I feel out of place. Perhaps I could work in the bakery. Nobody would see me there,' Meg said quietly.

'You are to be my wife, Meg. I want to show you off

to the world. If you think you will be happier in the bakery, at first, then that is what we will do. However, not before I take you shopping — or give you some money to go shopping with. Visit the new arcades. All the women come here with their arms full of purchases, discussing the stores' delights.' He grinned at the astonishment on Meg's face.

'Oh my goodness, me go shopping in those expensive places?' Meg exclaimed.

'Yes, and charge it all to me. Ask them to send me the bill. It cuts out the vulgarity of money.'

'Oh, Frankie, I couldn't do that. I wouldn't know what to spend the money on or how much.' Meg lowered her eyes.

Frankie squeezed her hand. 'I'm sure you could. Take Daisy with you. It is time you had money spent on yourself. Treat Sarah to something as well. It might be a way to get her back into my good books and prove to her that I'm no heartless murderer.

'Now, I'm at the new property quite a bit next week. How about you start work for me on Monday after you have been shopping on Saturday? You know most of my recipes now. The following weekend, we shall announce the grand opening of the tea room. You can stand by my side, in your new clothes. Then, we can announce to the world that we aim to be the perfect couple who will own the best bakeries in Yorkshire!'

'Oh, Frankie. What can I say? I don't deserve all this.' Meg smiled and kissed him gently. Despite her constant worry that she really wasn't good enough for him, she was thrilled at the prospect of her new life at the patisserie and being beside him.

'Don't worry, you'll earn your keep. With two bakeries, we will be busy, especially once the one in

Headingley gets up and running. I may love you, but don't forget I'm a businessman at heart. I don't do anything without weighing up the risk. Though when it comes to loving you, I know there is no risk involved at all. I've jumped in with both feet first, Miss Fairfax.'

'You are giving me so much, Frankie, and I have nothing to offer you,' Meg said quietly after he had kissed her.

'Nonsense. You have given me much more than you'll ever know, Meg. You have given me the love and support that I have always craved. Now go with Daisy on Saturday. I'm sure she will be able to guide you on how to spend a man's money.'

5

'Well, I think that you are foolish to keep him waiting. Get that ring on your finger, woman!'

Daisy Truelove linked her arm through Meg's as they walked down Briggate together.

'I do love him, but I think I'm too young yet, in honesty. I hardly know men. How do I know he's the right one for me? Besides, this affects Sarah as well and I need to show some respect after losing my mother.'

'Lordy, you do like to make life hard for yourself! There he is, a good man, with money to burn. Yet you insist on making him wait. No disrespect, but you don't know how lucky you are. I'll never have the man that I love by my side.' Her face fell slightly as she thought of her love for the already-married Tom Askew, the manager at Hunslet Mill.

'Oh Daisy, I'm sorry. It must be hard giving your heart to someone who is already married. Do you not think you should stop seeing him? It can't be good for you.'

'No, I could never do that. I love him too much. He keeps telling me that he'll leave his wife for me but then something happens and he has to stay. One day, we'll be together. Until then, I'll keep faithful to him and enjoy the money he spends on me.' Daisy forced a laugh, clearly trying to shake off her worries.

Meg thought a great deal of Daisy, but she didn't agree with her relationship with Tom Askew. Her thoughts were with his wife and four children, whom he obviously had no problem betraying. She wished that Daisy would see that her love was wasted.

'Right, enough of me, where are we going? Has your man told you how much to spend and where to go?' Daisy asked.

'He said to buy what I wanted, and he didn't care where we shopped. His name is good throughout Leeds. I've to tell the shop owners to bill him and ask for the goods to be delivered back home. Although I think I'll not do that; I'll take what I buy with me. Imagine the look on the delivery boy's face if he saw Sykes Yard! Besides, all the neighbours will only talk when they see parcels being delivered.' Meg grinned. 'It would start them all gossiping.'

'Oh, I can just see the look on old Mrs McEvoy's face!' Daisy giggled. 'She likes to think herself better than the rest of you down there. Her nose would be pushed out, right and proper. After all, she's the only one who has a full tea service, and don't you all know it. Snobby old cow! Her husband only worked at the tannery. He always stank.'

'Frankie told me to go down the new arcades but I don't want to do that,' Meg mused. 'There's nowhere I would feel happy about buying from. I thought we could go and spend the day browsing around The Grand Pygmalion — it's that glorious large shop on Boar Lane and Duncan Street. I want to see the new clothes that they've been advertising in their windows. They're made by John Barran in his factory and also Hepworth & Son; everybody says they're really well made.' If they were made in Leeds, they would be, Meg knew — she was proud of the cotton and wool products made locally. 'I've seen them and I can't believe that you can buy a ready-made dress in your own size, instead of taking the material home and making your own. I'd love to buy one.' For so long she had thought about the dress she had longed for in Pygmalion's window when she had occasionally passed that way and now she had the chance to buy it.

'Yes! They're called 'off the peg', don't you know.' Daisy squeezed Meg's arm. 'It won't be long before all the shops are stocking them. Apparently, the dresses can be made in a matter of hours now that the factories have the new Singer sewing machines. Although you wouldn't get me working for John Barran. He makes his money from the sweat of his workers. He might have got a knighthood so that we all have to call him sir, but I doubt the Queen will know what goes on inside his factory walls.'

'I had set my heart upon the dress in the window,' Meg admitted. 'It's my colour and not too fancy.'

They walked past the game and butchers' shop owned by R. Boston & Sons. Fresh fowl hung in the window and they could smell the fish that sat on wet slabs. Both young women held their noses until they had walked past.

'I'll treat you,' Meg announced. 'Or, should I say, my Frankie will treat you. After all, he did say that I had to bring you along and it would only be rude not to buy you something. He's opening the tea room next week and I'm to work for him for a while. That's why I need something smart.'

'You really have fallen on your feet, Meg Fairfax, just like your sister. You'll be proud that at long last she has got the burler's job at the mill. She'll be able to help you out a bit more with the extra pay for her rent and keep. Not that it's still a lot,' Daisy said as they came to stand outside the three-storey building, with the metal sign announcing: Hopkin's Stores.

Meg tried not to look too surprised. 'What's that you say?'

'Sarah! Didn't you know? She's a burler and mender now. Surely she has told you?'

'Yes, she's done well, hasn't she?' Meg said quickly. 'Sorry, I didn't quite hear you.' Meg would have words when she saw Sarah later in the evening. 'Now, where do we look first?' Meg smiled as she pushed the revolving doors of the first department store to be opened in Leeds and entered a world that she had never dared visit before in her life. She looked around at all the glass cabinets, crammed with perfumes, gloves and jewellery. The shop girls smiled in greeting.

'Heavens, just look at it all!' Daisy cried. 'Look at the shoppers! Look at her, with the fox stole around her neck and her hat. It has a bird perched upon it!'

Meg shook her head in awe. 'Just imagine what this place will be like at Christmas. I bet it's packed to the rafters with everything that your heart could desire. I couldn't ever have believed that a person could ever need so much! And this is only the ground floor!'

Daisy examined a pair of kid gloves before quickly placing them back down as she spotted the price label. 'Come on, ladieswear is upstairs — look! They're advertising the 'off the peg' dresses. Don't they look lovely?'

Meg made her way towards the grey marble steps and delicately walked up the stairs holding onto the shining brass handrail before suddenly pointing. 'I can see the dress I want! It's there, on that dummy — the green one with the small daisies. Isn't it beautiful?' She ran up the last few stairs and stood in awe at the

55

sight of the dress that she had wanted ever since it had first appeared in the window. 'Do you not think it is me?' Meg turned and grinned at Daisy.

'Yes, I could see you in that and I could see you in that red one over there. The one with the full red skirt and lace collar. They're all lovely and they are all different sizes, isn't that wonderful?' Daisy exclaimed. She picked up a tartan plaid dress and held it against her body. 'I wish I had the money, but I don't suppose Frankie would pay for something as expensive as this, would he?' she whispered before putting it back.

Meg grinned at her friend. 'Should I buy two? One for you and I'd better not forget Sarah, else she'll never forgive me, even though she does call Frankie fit to burn!'

'Oh, Meg, won't Frankie say something? Don't you think it is a bit extravagant? Tom would never buy me anything like this!' Daisy held the dress to herself again and admired her reflection.

'This will test him,' Meg said quietly. 'If he truly loves me and isn't just interested in my baking skills, then he won't mind paying. I've been worrying that he's never mentioned an engagement ring even though he says he can't wait to get married. And I keep worrying that all this just can't be for real. A girl like me does not get courted by someone so handsome and as wealthy as Frankie without a reason.' Meg felt her face colouring at this admission, and walked over to the assistant for help.

'Frankie loves you and well you know it,' Daisy said, following her. 'It is simply a coincidence that you both love baking. As for engagement rings, who put that notion into your head? Although they are getting more popular, it's still only the well-to-do that places them on their women's fingers. They with a lot to lose if they back out of their arrangement.'

'Betsy was talking about it,' Meg said.

'Oh, her with the brass washer for a wedding ring and a headful of dreams. Don't listen to her.' Daisy placed the tartan dress on the counter. 'I'd like to wear it the next time I see Tom outside of work. I can just imagine his face when I tell him another man has paid for my outfit. That will keep him on edge!' Daisy grinned mischievously.

Meg placed the two dresses that she had chosen next to Daisy's. 'I wonder if I dare buy one of those high-necked white blouses, they would look smart when I'm in the bakery and I could buy one for Sarah as well for her work,' she said, then walked over and felt the quality of the white brocade.

'Go on, they're not expensive, he won't mind paying for those,' Daisy replied encouragingly. 'Your green dress is the most expensive, I saw the price tag, but it'll make Frankie's tongue hang out every time he looks at you in it, the bodice is so low.'

'It's not too daring, is it? I don't want to look like a trollop!' Meg exclaimed as she placed two blouses over the sales assistant's arm. She had spent more money on herself in the last half hour than she had in the rest of her life.

'No, it's just right, it'll suit you down to the ground. A little bit of temptation does everybody good,' Daisy said loudly, making Meg blush and the sales assistant smile.

'Would madam like to take these today or would you like them delivering?' the woman asked.

'We will take them with us, thank you,' Meg replied. 'Could you send the bill to Mr Frankie Pearson at

Grosvenor House, Headingley, please? I don't think that he has an account with you, so will that be all right?' Suddenly, Meg felt sick at the thought of all the money that she and Daisy had spent.

The sales assistant wrote something down on her invoice pad. 'That will be no pro. We know Mr Pearson well, or should I say, we know his mother. She often shops with us when visiting.' After the necessary packaging had been carried out, the shop assistant smiled and passed the beautifully wrapped clothes to Daisy and Meg, who looked at one another like a pair of giddy school children.

'I hope I haven't spent too much. I've always had cast-offs and second-hand clothes from the stall in Briggate. These smell all new and pristine,' Meg said as they walked out of the store.

'You can shop here every day once you get your man married. That's even more reason to marry him quick. His mother shops here, after all — that's what the assistant said.' Daisy peeped into her bag.

'Yes, that's strange. I didn't think that Frankie had much to do with his mother. Her ways are a little too bohemian from what I can gather. However, she must come and see him some time. But I'm not marrying for money, I'm marrying him for love. I don't want to be a rich man's plaything and be a bored wife who has no say in her life. I'd rather remain poor than lose my identity,' Meg said defiantly.

'Then I think you are quite mad. All I want to do is set up home with Tom and not sneak about all the time. I'd do anything to stop having to work in that mill and be a kept woman with him by my side.' Daisy sighed. 'I suppose we will have to agree to disagree. We both know what we want. Whether we will ever be lucky enough to get it is another matter.'

'Yes, let's not fall out. We're both strong women. Let's hope that we will get what we want in the end and have happy lives. At least we are loved . . . I think we are.'

Meg squeezed her best friend's hand and thought to herself that she was in better shoes than Daisy when it came to having a man who loved her. Tom Askew would never marry Daisy. He was too much of a family man, from what she had heard. He was just having his cake and eating it.

★ ★ ★

'I don't like it! You'll not get me wearing that.' Sarah looked at the blouse that Meg had given her and decided instantly that even though she thought it the most beautiful thing she had ever been given, she'd not like it on principle.

'Don't be so silly,' Meg said sharply. 'How can you not like it? It's brand, spanking new and the height of fashion. Plus, it will fit you so well. It's not the blouse that you don't like, it is who has paid for it.' She glared at her sister.

'He might be able to buy you but he'll not be buying me so easily,' Sarah spat. 'A few frills and ruffles don't mean to say that I'll decide to like him.'

'You, madam, need to be thankful that he has even bought you anything. Don't you spoil our chance of happiness because of your petty ways. Besides, you need to look a little smarter, now I hear that you have become a burler and mender. No wonder your hair has been looking neater and your apron kept clean of late. When exactly were you going to tell me? I felt such a fool when Daisy mentioned your news and I knew nothing about it.'

Immediately, anger clouded Sarah's face. 'Bloody Daisy Truelove! She cannot keep her gob shut! I've only been a burler for the past two weeks. I'm still being watched by old hawk eyes Madge Evans and she would get rid of me tomorrow if she had her way.' Sarah scowled. 'And before you ask, no! I haven't had a pay rise yet. That tight arse, Tom Askew, says I've to prove myself first.' Sarah avoided her sister's gaze.

'I just don't know why you didn't tell me. I'm so proud that you've got the job that you really wanted. I'm sure they will pay you the rate when they know you can do the tasks at hand.' Meg hugged her sister but got little response in return.

'I didn't tell you because it makes no difference what I do. Besides, we are no better off; the only difference is that I'm working harder while you keep house and entertain Frankie,' Sarah said curtly.

'I told you, I've decided to go and work at the patisserie and Frankie says he'll pay me a wage,' Meg said, trying to be patient. 'At least that way I can repay him for the kindness that he's shown to both of us over the last few months. He's virtually kept us fed and now clothed, although your contribution has paid to keep the roof over our heads, and for that, I appreciate every minute that you work at that mill. Once I do decide to marry Frankie, you may have no need to work. Perhaps you could re-attend school or something similar?' Meg smiled, remembering her time at school and the enjoyment that lessons had given her. 'I would have dearly loved to have had a better education.'

'I'm definitely not going back to school, so you can

forget that.' Sarah crossed her arms. 'Having to live with you and Frankie would be bad enough, but going back to school will be the last thing I want to do.'

'Ah, well, we will see. Now stop screwing that blouse up in your hands. You know it is lovely and that you will be the envy of the mill. Don't cut your nose off to spite your face.' Meg watched as Sarah held up the blouse to her body again. Sarah did like it, Meg knew she liked it, but clearly, her sister didn't want to lose face. *One day, Sarah will grow up*, Meg thought. And she would welcome that day with open arms.

6

Meg threaded her hand through Frankie's arm and smiled. It was the perfect Sunday afternoon. The sun was shining, she had the man she loved on her arm and the flower beds of Roundhay Park were in full bloom. Although it was quite a stretch from where they both lived, Roundhay was the place to promenade with the one you loved and admire the many beautiful flowers and plants within its walls.

To make things even better, Sissy Banks had called for Sarah to go and walk around the Arcades with her. When Sarah was with Sissy, Meg didn't have to worry, as she knew Sissy had been brought up correctly and would never do anything wrong. She'd trusted them so much, she had given Sarah a silver threepence out of their meagre savings to spend on what she liked. She watched Sarah, dressed in her new blouse, link arms with Sissy, and the two of them left the yard, heads close together as they laughed at something. Maybe Sarah *was* growing up at last.

Now, Meg strolled happily around the park's gravel paths and watched as Frankie greeted fellow visitors with a tap of his straw hat and a few words. She knew how lucky she was to be with such a handsome man, dressed in his blazer and matching trousers, his hair and moustache immaculately groomed. Likewise, she was wearing her new printed dress and felt like royalty as they stopped next to the main fountain and admired the rainbow of colours that cascaded from it as the water caught the sun's rays.

'I love you, Meg,' Frankie whispered, as they sat on a bench to watch the world together.

'And I you, my dear,' Meg replied. 'This is such a perfect day. I don't want it to end.'

'This is just the beginning. We will have many days like this in the future. I aim to take you wherever I go. We will visit Paris and perhaps even Rome, if you wish. United, there is nothing we can't do. I am so glad that you have agreed to join me in the patisserie. I have even brought the opening of the tea room forward to tomorrow, because I have faith in you running the bakery while I charm and greet the new customers in the morning.'

This was news to Meg. 'You are opening the tea room in the morning? It is the first that you have spoken of it to me. I hope that you don't want me to serve in there?' she exclaimed.

'No, my dear, I'd not ask that of you. I know that you are happier helping me bake. I'm sorry that I have not told you until now, but the time seemed right for the tea room to be at last opening. I've employed two more young girls to attend to the tea room's needs, Martha and Hattie.' Frankie sighed and looked at the ground. 'I would have suggested that we employ Sarah, but she is still reserved towards me. It is best that she keeps her job at the mill, for now.'

'She will come around to liking you,' Meg replied confidently. 'Every day, she grows a little more mature. She did appreciate the blouse that you bought her, just as Daisy and me appreciated the money spent on us.' She squeezed her lover's hand tightly.

'Ah, that Daisy! She's a flirty madam. She will make the most of her new dress, I am sure — but she will never look as beautiful as you, my love.' Frankie held Meg's hand tightly and kissed it gently. 'One day, Sarah will realize just how much I love her older sister and that I am to be trusted.'

Meg smiled. Frankie knew Daisy all too well, and as for Sarah, it was good to know that Frankie saw the best in her sister. 'I'm sure she will. Hopefully, she will grow to love you as much as I do.' Meg sighed. If only she had as much faith as she was trying to portray.

★ ★ ★

The following day, Meg was in a rush as she spoke sharply to her young sister. 'You'll get yourself to work on time? Promise me, our Sarah, just because I'm not there to get you up and going.' Meg pulled her slip on and watched Sarah rub her eyes in the half-light of the late summer's morning.

'I'm not a baby. I can get myself to work. Now, leave me be. I still have time for another hour of sleep.' Sarah growled and turned her back on her sister.

Meg pulled her skirts on and hurried downstairs. It was five in the morning. She was back to working early mornings, but now it was with a happy heart, working next to Frankie. She took a sip of water and buttered herself a slice of bread. There was no need to relight the fire if both she and Sarah were to be out most of the day.

She closed the back door behind her, walking out into Sykes Yard. Neighbours were already up and astir. She looked up at next door's window as she heard a baby crying and Betsy shouting at her son as he disturbed her sleep. The street cleaner was out in the main street with his dustcart and brush, sweeping up after the horses that had deposited their waste, for use in people's gardens.

Meg's heart beat a little faster as she reached the broad street of the Headrow. She might be working next to Frankie, but she thought herself not in the same league as his baking and hoped that she would be able to manage. She also worried about the customers that visited; she hoped that she would not be thrown into the deep end by Frankie as he knew she could already bake almost anything. Would the customers realize that she was just a common lass from Sykes Yard? Would they accept her into their upper-class bakery, even though she was dressed finely in her new blouse? Most of the staff knew where she came from and was now accepted by them, but the customers were a different matter.

'Good morning, my darling.' Frankie turned from the bread that he was making for his baguettes to welcome Meg into his bakery at the back of the empty shop. 'You nearly made it here earlier than me, I've only just started making the dough. I'm running late this morning. I've been up half the night worrying if my new purchase in Headingley will prove to be a foolish one along with the tea room. I sometimes think my passions run away with me.' Frankie smiled and kissed Meg on her cheek.

'I'm sure they won't be. You know what you are doing,' Meg smiled and returned his kiss. 'I hardly slept as well, worrying that I would perhaps not fit into your bakery. It is a lot different to Ted Lund's.'

'*Patisserie*, my dear — and you will fit in perfectly. You are not the only new one here this morning. Martha and Hattie are also new to us. It will be all fresh for everyone.' Frankie wiped his hands on a cloth rather than sully his spotless white apron and passed Meg a similar apron. 'Here, put this on and I will give you your first task of the day. Are you up to making some puff pastry? We will need plenty, as *Slippers a la Crème* and vanilla slices both have puff pastry as their main ingredient.' Frankie pointed at various cupboards. 'All dry ingredients are stored in those, all fats like lard and butter are stored in the cold store along with milk and cream just at the back door. Everything else you will find as you go along.'

Meg put the crisp white apron around her and tied the strings at the front of her stomach. It was a little too large and obviously made for a man. She smoothed it down and went to investigate where everything was kept.

'Don't forget to wash your hands! Cleanliness is my one main rule and both of us must show it to the rest of the staff. I expect it from whoever works for me.' Meg watched in awe as Frankie moulded and shaped his baguettes, twisting the dough and tucking the ends of each stick under before placing them to rise next to his state-of-the-art gas ovens. The ovens that Meg dare not say again that she was wary of.

'Yes, of course, sorry. My head's full this morning. I'll be fine once I've got my bearings.' Meg walked over to the white-tiled sink. Frankie came over, and put the tap on for her. She reached to wash her hands and was surprised to find that there was hot water, provided by a wall-mounted gas boiler whose flame smelt pungent.

'Nail brush above the sink, if you need it,' Frankie prompted. She used it quickly before she started to make, roll and shape the puff pastry that she knew would take a good hour to make from previously making it with him.

Priorities were certainly different to working with Ted Lund. She had expected a bit more chat from Frankie but instead, he was going about the business of baking. She watched him weighing out some ground almonds into a large bowl and looked at his strong arms that had kneaded the bread with such love and now were turning to making a delicate pastry. He had a passion for his work and his stunning good looks were just a bonus.

Frankie sensed her watching him and looked over. 'I'm making little bites of love — macaroons. My ladies love them.' Frankie grinned. 'Pink and white loveliness. Sugar, finely chopped almonds, a little flour and egg whites . . . and a drop of orange water. I colour half and leave half white, pipe onto wafer paper in small rounds, then bake. Once they're cool, I put two together filled with whipped cream.'

'They look beautiful. I've never seen them before,' Meg said as she watched Frankie place the mixture into a parchment paper cone and pipe them into small circles. Then she returned her attention to her own work, folding and rolling her pastry.

'You just wait until they are made,' Frankie said when he had finished. 'They are just like small bites of love. I thought they would be apt for today, my wife-to-be in the kitchen and the tea room opening. Next, I'm going to make *Tourte aux pommes* and *Tartlettes de Cassis* before I start on a Genoese sponge. All these should sell well and impress our tea room diners.'

Frankie placed the small macaroons in the gas oven and then walked over to inspect Meg's work. 'You see, I do need your help. An extra pair of hands before the shop and tea rooms open for the day makes all the difference, especially when I have new staff to train. That pastry looks fine, rest it for a while in a cool place. You can make the crème filling,' he said gently, kissing her on the cheek.

'When you've renovated the bakery at Headingley, it will be nearer your home. Will you be the main baker there?' Meg asked with interest, thinking that the good people in Headingley were perhaps not quite ready for French baked goods.

'No, I was hoping that you might step into the shoes there once we are wed. Or, if not, I'll employ and train somebody. Don't you worry, that's all a long way off. Just settle into working here and we will see how things go.' Frankie started making what looked like a shortcrust pastry, ready for his tarts.

Meg looked at the gas stove and dreaded lighting it to warm her milk for the slices' custards that Frankie had shown her how to make when they had first met. She poured the required milk into the pan and reached for the cornflour and eggs. Gas was a new commodity and she had heard so many tales of people blowing themselves up or gassing themselves with the fumes.

'Would you like me to light it? You look nervous.' Frankie came over. 'Look, you light your match and then just slowly turn this knob until you hear a slight hiss and then put your match to the gas. It will go pop, but then the flame will start to burn.' Frankie struck the match and held it to the hissing gas, then blew the match out once the blue and green flames started to burn. 'See, simple! You'll soon get used to it.'

'I don't know if I'll ever get used to it, or the smell,' Meg replied, but smiled as she gingerly put her pan of milk on to nearly come to the boil before adding her cornflour and egg yolks. Stirring gently, she watched as the mixture thickened. She put it to one side and began to mix a thin icing to cover the slices of pastry. Once the custard was cool, she sandwiched the pastry and custard together and drizzled a covering of icing on top. She looked at her vanilla slices and compared them to the trays of delicate desserts that Frankie had prepared. Hers looked as if no care had been put into them at all. They were rough and ready next to Frankie's perfect bakes. She felt inadequate, a dropping sensation hit her stomach and her face flushed as a bitter taste of disappointment passed over her.

A similar thought had clearly crossed Frankie's mind. 'Meg,' he said gently but firmly, 'I'm in no doubt that your pastries will taste absolutely marvellous, but . . .' He shook his head. 'Presentation is not your strong point. You, bless you, are used to filling an empty stomach, but the ladies who come here will be more refined in their tastes. I thought that you would have realized that. Tomorrow, smaller portions. As it is, I will try and tidy these up a little. I can't afford to waste all this.' He noticed the tears that welled in her eyes. 'Don't cry, my love. I should have kept an eye on you. After all, it is your first day with me.'

Meg nodded morosely. 'Yes, perhaps you should have, I'd forgotten that part of what you had previously shown me.' Frankie put his arm around Meg as she wiped her cheeks. 'They will taste wonderful and with a little care, no one will ever know that I've touched them,' he reassured her. 'Remember, half the size tomorrow. The ladies that come here are always thinking of their waists, not their stomachs.'

Meg smiled and tried to look happy as she heard the shop door open. She guessed that it must be Marie and Norah, arriving for the start of their working day. The last thing she wanted was for them to see her tears.

'Yes, smaller and neater,' she repeated. 'Forgive me. Tomorrow they will be perfect.' She watched Frankie cut the slices down to size and make the *Slippers de la Crème* more presentable before taking them out to place under the shelves in the shop.

'No harm done. Now, come and say hello to Norah and Marie. They are here to help us both in the shop and keep the customers happy. As my future wife, you must stamp your authority with them.'

'I'll try to. But it's not Norah and Marie I worry about, it's the customers. They're of a different class to me. I don't want them to think badly of me.'

Frankie paused in carrying the trays out front. 'Meg Fairfax, you are as good as any of my customers. Now, stop belittling yourself. You are not the only new employee today, but you are the one that has my love and commitment. I'm proud of you, so have faith in yourself.' Carefully balancing the tray, Frankie bent and kissed her on the cheek. Then he walked through the bakery door and instantly transformed into another person: Mr Pearson, owner of the Headrow's finest — and only — patisserie.

'Good morning, Mr Pearson!' Marie and Norah said together, as they each bobbed into a small curtsey.

'Good morning, girls. It's all change, this morning. Miss Fairfax has been helping me in the bakery since the early hours of the morning.' He indicated Meg as she followed him out into the shop front. 'And I am expecting another two new employees to be waitresses upstairs in the tea room to arrive shortly — Martha Robinson and

70

Hattie Parker. Both have previous experience in service, as they have both worked in The Royal's tea rooms.'

Meg watched Norah and Marie glance at one another and wonder where they stood with three new employees working in the shop.

'I know Hattie Parker. She's worked at The Royal since she left school, and she'll know what to do,' Norah said quickly.

'It's nice to see you here as well, Miss Fairfax. Mr Pearson will need your help now the tea rooms are open,' Marie added and smiled at Meg and then glanced at the slices and slippers that Frankie had set out under the counter. Meg noticed a sly look at Norah as Marie realized that the pastries were not up to the usual standard and instantly felt another wave of shame flood over her as her presentation skills were put on show for all to see.

Gathering herself, Meg tried not to think about the shared glance between the two women. 'I'm looking forward to working with you all,' she said, pasting on her bravest smile. 'It might take me a while to understand how everything works, but I aim to learn quickly.'

'I'm sure we will all work well together. Look!' Frankie indicated the shop window. 'Here come our other two employees, looking very smart in the patisserie black and white uniform. Let us all hope for a busy day, with the tea room packed and the pastries selling well.'

Frankie opened the patisserie door and welcomed his two new employees. He introduced them to everyone. 'My new team.' Frankie's smile took them all in. 'Now, Norah, turn that notice board to Open and put out the large boards proclaiming our tea rooms are up

71

and running. Not only have we a first-class patisserie but also a first-class tea room. Let's hope for a good day of trading. Everybody to their posts, please, you should all know what to do and if you don't, please ask. Meg, if you could make a second batch of eclairs, the ones that I made will soon go and I know that more will be wanted.'

Frankie stood at the bottom of the stairs and watched as his two new waitresses climbed up them, then turned to Meg. 'Remember, *petite*, and you will be fine. I'll have to give instructions to these two and then I'll be with you.'

'Yes, I'll remember. I'll do better this time,' Meg said quietly.

Frankie followed the two upstairs to the tea room where they would work most of the day supplying customers with coffee and tea from the huge urns or tripping up and down the stairs for freshly made sandwiches and sweet delights.

It wasn't long before the first customer of the day arrived, but as Meg walked back into the bakery she heard Marie whisper to Norah, 'She'll not last long.'

Meg felt a spurt of anger course through her body. Of course, her baking wasn't sophisticated enough. She had made the vital mistake of thinking she was feeding the backstreet people whose bellies needed to be filled cheaply and substantially. She'd not make the same mistake again. Her eclairs would be perfect. They would be so gorgeous that Queen Victoria her-self could have them presented in front of her, she thought as she mixed the choux pastry and listened to the posh voices coming from inside the shop and the noise of busy feet along the floorboards of the upstairs tea room.

This was a different world from what she was used to, but she was going to have to get used to it if she was to marry Frankie. She was more than the second baker here. She was Mrs Pearson-to-be and she would show she could bake just as well as her husband.

A thought crossed her mind. Perhaps Norah and Marie were just jealous of her. After all, they knew she was to marry Frankie. Perhaps they had hoped to catch his eye, especially Norah with her sickly smile.

★ ★ ★

Later — much later — Meg unlaced her boots, kicking them off to sit back in her mother's old chair. Her head was swimming with the noise and heat of the bakery, and the amount of talking done by ladies of leisure in the newly opened tea rooms. They held themselves upright in their tightly laced corsets, sipping their tea delicately while comparing each other's fine hats and listening to the day's gossip. She had watched them when she had run upstairs with some wanted eclairs when the shop girls had been busy. They were oblivious to any woman or girl who served them, but had swooned and smiled at Frankie as he checked their requirements. No wonder he had said that her eclairs and slippers were too large; each customer only ate a mouthful or two.

Food is for eating, Meg thought and shook her head. She had loved her first day in the patisserie, but at the same time hated it! It was filled with people shopping and having tea that she would never usually share the time of day with. Yet, Frankie was in his element, swarming his way around the tea room and knowing each of his customers by name. She was going to

73

have to get used to that, and get used to Frankie flirting with his customers. After all, when the patisserie's doors closed it was her that he walked back home. It was her that he kissed goodnight to. The patisserie was just a front to the good and great of Leeds.

Frankie's head would never be turned. Or, at least, she hoped not.

7

It was late Friday afternoon and Frankie grasped the deeds to his new shop in Headingley. He knew it would cost him dearly. Too much, by the time he brought it up to the standards of his new patisserie.

Headingley was one of Leeds' more affluent areas. Many a rich mill owner lived there. The air was clear and the houses spoke of wealth. Their occupants demanded the best service, and that was what Frankie was determined to give them.

His spending was beginning to attract his mother's attention. Her letters of late had been terse and to the point, declaring that his standards were far too high and that if he wanted to live a Parisian lifestyle he should have stayed in France. If only his twenty-fifth birthday was closer. Sadly, he had another eighteen months to wait until he could take full rein of his father's inheritance. Everybody thought of him as rich, but the truth was that he was still tied to his mother's apron strings. The sooner they were un-tied, the better.

Frankie gazed out of the old bakery's window and thought about Meg. She wasn't enjoying working in his patisserie, he could tell. She felt herself inferior. Another fly in the ointment was that he had not broken the news of Meg to his mother yet. He knew exactly what her reaction would be. His mother might lead a decadent bohemian lifestyle, but she was never short of a man with money in her life and he knew that Meg would not meet his mother's standards, no matter how much he loved her. Thank the Lord, she was happy in France at the moment. Otherwise, she would have been picking holes in everything.

'So, you don't think you are wasting your brass here, do you?' Jed Hurst joined the man who was asking for miracles when it came to his work in the new premises. 'The whole place needs gutting and you'll struggle to get a gas pipe for your fancy ovens into this hole.'

'You'll do it, I know you will. You did me proud with the patisserie on the Headrow. If you do the same here again, it will suit me. Only quicker this time, if you can. I need some return on my investment.' Frankie patted the builder on the back and hoped that he wouldn't decline the work. He paid well and on time the last time, which was more than some folk did.

'Let me put something together. We'll see what we can do. My men can start knocking it about at the end of the month. The weather will soon be changing and at least it's an inside job. But you are asking a lot. The joists aren't strong.' Jed looked up to an opening in the downstairs ceiling and peered. 'Are you sure you don't want the building re-roofing? You'll be spoiling the ship for a ha'porth of tar, if you don't.'

'If you think the roof will not take the strain, I suppose you will have to.' Frankie swore under his breath.

'Your roof is the main thing,' Jed pointed out. 'It's no good you having a flash bakery, only to find that you have rain pissing in every day. I'll add that to my quote and then you can make your mind up.' Jed patted Frankie's back and laughed. 'You can't take your brass with you when you are six feet under, but it can take you a bit earlier to your grave if costs worry you.

I'll do as good a job as I'm able, and I'll be kind with my quote. But like you, I've to make ends meet.'

Frankie felt a sickness come into the pit of his stomach and he wiped his brow with a handkerchief. 'Thank you, Jed. It will work out, I'm sure.' Frankie led the way to the door and locked it as both men walked out onto the busy street.

'You'd have been better buying the one on York Street. Didn't Meg once work there?' Jed checked that his horse and cart were still securely tied to the railings. 'It only went up for sale last week. Ted Lund the owner is selling it himself, and he's put a notice in the window. 'No time wasters!' it says. Nobody will want it on that back street and with his bad books. He'll not have made much over the years.'

'What? Ted Lund's bakery is up for sale? I didn't know!' Frankie exclaimed. 'I wonder what's made him sell up. Meg made good money when she ran it.' Frankie wondered if Meg knew.

'He's a lazy old sod. His stuff is worth nowt. From what I hear, he's off to Ireland. It's about the right place for him. He can do what he wants over there. Perhaps that's the next one to be snapped up by the Pearson Empire, especially if your lass already knows the customers. Although I'd have thought you were a bit too posh for those backstreets.' Jed climbed onto his cart. 'I'll be back with my quote. I'll do my best for you, don't worry my friend. You'll hopefully soon make your money back.'

Jed flicked his reins over his horse's back and left Frankie looking up at his new bakery, with its bowing roof. Another expense that he would have to explain to his mother and hope that she would understand. If only Jed was right and that he would soon be making his money back . . . But, so far, this place had simply drained him of his money.

Meg would prefer me to buy Ted Lund's place, he mused as he walked home. But a patisserie was not the right place on those backstreets. He only hoped that she had not heard that it was for sale. But he knew that, sooner or later, the news would reach her. And what would he do then?

★ ★ ★

Sarah sat across from Meg and stirred her bowl of porridge.

'You're not hungry? That's not like you.' Meg went over to feel her sister's brow. 'Well, you've no temperature, at least.'

'I never said I was ill, but I hate that bloody mill and I hate Old Cow Evans even more. If she picks on me once more today, I'm sure I'll hit her.' Sarah rattled her spoon against her dish. She really was hating working at the mill and her dreams of running away with Harry seemed to have vanished just like her friend, who was always now too busy to see her. 'Do I have to keep working there? I didn't realize how hard the work is and how boring. Can't we manage without my money? I'll even go back to school if you want me to. Anywhere but standing on my feet all day, staring at a piece of cloth and getting bad-mouthed by the she-devil.'

'No. We can't do without your money. Things are tight enough and I'm not asking Frankie for any more. I'm not pulling my weight at his bakery, as it is,' Meg said. She too was not enjoying her lot in life, not that Sarah was ever bothered about her.

78

'*Patisserie!* Don't you let him hear you call it a bakery, posh snob!' Sarah said sarcastically.

'Sarah, you're not the only one who isn't happy in your work. I don't think anybody is if they were to tell the truth, but we have no option if we are to survive. I'm struggling . . . ' Meg broke off and put her empty bowl to one side. 'I'm sure Mrs Evans will leave you be, once you've got it right.'

'Oh! Are things not that happy between you and *him*? Has Cupid stopped firing his arrows and sense come into that head of yours?' Sarah smirked.

'No, we are perfectly happy,' Meg snapped. 'Simply, I'm saying that I'm learning like you were when you started in your job. Now, eat up, else you'll be hungry.' She found herself blushing. She didn't want to let Sarah see that she too didn't want to go back to work, either. That she had heard the girls giggling about her and that she couldn't get her hands to manage the pastries' decorations.

'Don't worry, I'm going! I'll be on time — and even if I am not, it won't matter. Sissy will say I'm at the toilet or something.' Sarah wiped porridge from her chin before scraping back her chair, making for the kitchen door.

'You'll be sacked, or your wages deducted, if you aren't careful. We can't afford either!' Meg called after her sister as Sarah's clogs clattered out into the yard, her apron half tied behind her back, hair brushed hastily.

Sarah doesn't care about anything, Meg thought, as she sat back down for a quick respite. She, on the other hand, did care! She'd not slept for thinking of the many ways to decorate fancies, how to thinly roll pastry, how to correctly serve the pastries from behind the counter — and most of all — not to speak in her broad west Yorkshire accent. It was an entirely different lesson in baking. She was learning to be a lady. No matter how posh she pretended to be, the more refined customers still looked down their noses at her. Frankie had told her that there were always those customers, that it was part of society. But the girls in the patisserie seemed to take great delight in seeing her fail.

She knew why. They all secretly imagined themselves on the arm of Frankie, after all. He was handsome and wealthy and showed a kindness to everyone, whether rich or poor. Perhaps she should marry him as soon as possible? It would make the staff more respectful of her if she became Mrs Frankie Pearson.

She wanted a little longer to respect her mother's death and to still be single. Independence. That was not too much to ask . . . was it?

★ ★ ★

'Good morning. my dear.' Frankie was weighing out the flour and already had the gas ovens alight, the smell still disgusting to Meg's senses. The first batch of croissants and baguettes were rising as he turned to greet his fiancée.

He had told her the night before to come in a little later than usual, saying that she looked tired. Still, the hour or two before the shop girls and the tea room staff arrived was special to Meg.

'Good morning, my love.' Meg stepped into his open arms as he took a minute away from his task in hand. Snuggling in, smelling the newly baked bread on his apron mixed slightly with his smell of cologne . . . she felt at ease.

'How are you, my love?' she asked.

'A lot better for seeing you; I count every minute while we are apart. When are you going to let me set a date for our marriage?' Frankie kissed her gently on her brow.

Meg looked up at Frankie. She did love him, but she knew she was young and she didn't want to be smothered in his world. Her emotions told her to marry him quickly but her head said wait. 'Soon, I promise, soon. I do love you so much. Give me a little more time.'

She pulled out of his arms, and put on her apron over the blouse and skirt that she tried to look smart in. 'What would you like me to start on this morning?'

'The usual, *Slippers a la crème*, *Parissiene* creams and . . . could you make the macaroons this morning? They seem to sell so well.' Frankie looked at Meg. 'I'm toying with the idea of perhaps letting you bake more everyday fayre for the tea room. Rock buns, Victoria Sandwich, perhaps. Scones are always asked for. Would you be happier to make those?'

'It isn't necessarily the baking, Frankie. It's that I don't feel that I belong in this world, it is alien to me. I don't speak posh enough. I don't dress right. Sometimes, I have to hold my tongue so much that I need to come downstairs to the backyard and swear out loud. Looks and words hurt. I know I am just as good as your customers, but I'm not used to the posh ways of higher society.

'I sometimes think I'd better look for employment elsewhere. I don't want to drag your business down.' Meg looked across at the love of her life and the clouding of his face. She quickly regretted her words and tried to make things better. 'Once we are married, I hope we can start a family of our own. A daughter or son to carry on your business, so my time would be spent raising them.'

Frankie paused in his work. 'Why do you think so little of yourself? It makes no difference to me who you are and where you come from. Why does it bother you so? As for children? All in good time, my love. My work comes first, and I have a lot invested. When we do become parents? I don't want my children to go without anything, although I know nature will take its course and there is nothing either of us can do about it. However, I'm not prepared for them yet.'

He watched Meg start to make the puff pastry, her head bowed low. 'I love you and I want you happy.'

'I love you,' she said, after a pause. 'But I'm not a fool, so please don't treat me like one. Perhaps I'm doing right giving us time before we are to wed. After all, we hardly know each other, I'm starting to think; we have both been wrapped up in our own worlds and have not discussed what is dear to us. I thought that you would welcome children into our lives once we were married, so I'm glad that I know how you feel.'

Her heart beat fast in her chest at the speech she'd just made. She looked over at Frankie. He looked concerned and worried and she suddenly realized that she was seeing him with fresh eyes. Frankie had slowly been taking her world over and she had been infatuated with her love of him. Now she was beginning to understand that perhaps they did not know each other that well.

'I shall welcome children into our marriage . . . eventually. My business comes first and I thought that you would understand that.' Frankie walked around the table to Meg's side. He wrapped his arms around her and kissed her neck. 'Let's not fall out. I want us to be happy. I love you and never want you to be unhappy.'

'And I love you. It's just that we are so different.'

Gently, Meg stepped out of his embrace and went to carry on with her baking. She'd show him what she could do, given a chance. She was starting to create pastries almost as good as his; she knew she was improving.

Still, she could not dismiss the conversation they'd just had. The two of them hadn't discussed babies before. What else had they failed to discuss? Their differences were emerging now that they worked together all the time.

If she went ahead with this marriage, it was to be a union not just of two people, but in business, too. And there would be a family, if she was to have her way.

She was definitely right in making Frankie wait for a little before their marriage. After all, she had to get to know him in more depth and she felt she needed to show him that she was his equal when it came to both baking and business. Despite being in real need of his support, she knew it would be wrong just to marry him for the security he would provide.

8

'I can't understand you, Meg Fairfax. Why are you so bloody stubborn?' Daisy said as she sat at Meg's kitchen table.

'I'm not stubborn! I just want to be sure I'm marrying the right man. It's been such a fast-moving romance. It started when my mother was ill and I was just so glad of his care and attention. I was impressed by him and his budding business empire and my head was turned by his knowledge of the things that I love. Now I'm working with him every day, I realize that perhaps he's not the man I thought he was. He does think something of himself even though he pretends to be there for the likes of us.' Meg sank deeper into her chair despondently.

'He is something! That's why I can't understand why you don't get on with marrying him. You've the perfect life on a plate but from what you're saying now, it sounds as though you're pushing your whole future to one side for the sake of a few petty details,' Daisy exclaimed.

'I want to prove myself, to be as successful as him when it comes to baking. I want to be my own woman, which I know is not something you hear of in this day and age. He doesn't want to rush into having a family around him so why shouldn't I see what I can achieve? Once married, it is inevitable that children will come along, or I'd expect them to, and then he will be weighed down with the responsibility of raising a family. I also think that he has enough worries trying to run two bakeries. He is already worried about the new bakery in Headingley and how much it is going to cost.' Meg looked into her tea cup and thought she might have said too much about Frankie's affairs. Daisy was not exactly discreet when it came to secrets but she was her closest friend and confidante, and she just needed an ear to listen to her concerns.

'That's what all these swanky folk do. They worry about every penny when it's us that don't have a penny to our names. They don't become wealthy by spending recklessly.' Daisy snorted with laughter. 'The man's got brass, believe me! Think about those dresses he bought us — never said a word about what they cost, did he?' Daisy's laughter faded away as she took in Meg's furrowed brow. She reached across the table and patted her friend's hand. 'It'll be right, lass. You carry on working with him and getting to know him. You know that he loves you. All will be well.'

Meg shook her head. 'I don't know, Daisy. I do love him, but perhaps our Sarah is right. Perhaps he's not the man for me.'

'When was your Sarah ever right about anything? She needs to keep her mouth shut and concentrate on her own job. She's got a good one, if she did but know it and listened to Madge Evans. She might be an old dragon but she is always right when it comes to her work.'

'She doesn't like anybody with authority. Lord knows where she's going to end up in life.' Meg gave a small smile. There was a small secret part of her that wished she was more like Sarah, not caring about anybody or whose feelings she hurt. *Life would be so much easier*, she thought, then changed the subject. 'How are you anyway? I've told you all my troubles — what about you?'

'Oh, I'm all right, the 'other woman', you know how it is. Tom comes and sees me when he can and keeps telling me he will leave his wife for me.' Daisy smiled and held her head up. 'I don't think he ever will. He loves his children too much but I'm a fool and lie to myself every day thinking that I will win him from his family. I wish I hadn't lost my heart to a married man.'

'Oh, Daisy, don't you think you would be better without him? Move on, you are good-looking — you turn many a man's head,' Meg said, feeling sorry for her friend.

'But I love him, Meg, despite everything I love him. My mother has lectured me about him, my father hardly talks to me nowadays but I can't stop my heart from loving him, despite me knowing that it will eventually end in tears.' Daisy bowed her head. 'We are both idiots and both of us should know better.'

'I'm sorry, Daisy, but he might be yours one day,' Meg said and thought about Tom's wife and children who she doubted he would leave for Daisy. 'We are a right pair! Wouldn't it be nice if life and love was not complicated.'

Daisy suddenly let go of Meg's hand and shifted back in her chair, looking nervous.

'What is it?' Meg asked.

'There's . . . There's something I need to tell you. There's a For Sale sign up in Ted Lund's bakery window. He must have decided to call it a day. I wonder where he's going, because his house is up for sale and all.'

'It's up for sale?' Meg felt her eyes widen. 'Lord,

86

I'd love to own that bakery! I could make money running it. Frankie would have been better buying that than the one in Headingley. All the folk knows me; he would have had ready-made customers.' Meg felt her pulse quicken. If she only had the means to take over the run-down bakery.

Daisy grinned. 'Then ask him to buy it for you. Forget a ring — it would be an engagement present that would pay for itself within six months. Surely he would like that idea? You could bake what you are happy with, serving the folk you know, and make just as much money as he does every day. Our part of the world has missed you. All the mill girls complain that you have gone. They'd soon come back if you were to take it over.'

'I couldn't. Frankie has done so much for me already. Besides, he already has the new patisserie in Headingley. I would love it, though.' Meg saw images dance behind her eyes, of a future that seemed just out of reach. 'I could do so much with it, if it was mine.'

'If he loves you, he would buy it for you. Money should be no problem to him. Like I said, he didn't bat an eyelid when we went on our shopping spree.' Daisy egged her friend on.

'Buying a couple of dresses and buying a shop are two completely different things! Besides, he wouldn't be happy at the state that it's in. He'd have to rearrange and put in those infernal gas ovens that he loves. I still don't trust them — give me a cast-iron range like in Ted Lund's any day. I often wonder if the gas makes the baking taste odd. It's such a strong smell!'

But, despite her protests, Meg felt her heart beating fast. Could she ask Frankie if he'd buy it for her?

He had been so good to her in the past but this would definitely seal their union. She could create the things she loved in her own bakery and supply the patisseries with more traditional goods — the odd currant bun or the lightest loaves of bread for their cucumber sandwiches. From what she could see, it would be an answer to both their needs. Meg thought for a minute and then said out loud to Daisy

'I will ask him. After all, he can only say no!'

* * *

Meg had thought of nothing else but Ted Lund's shop all weekend. She had even walked to York Street to gaze at its closed up windows and doors looking unloved as she stood across the street from it, and imagine what she could do with a place like that. Walking out on Frankie's arm the following Sunday, she had resisted saying anything to him. He had seemed to be lost in his own world of worries, anyway. Making her way to the patisserie on the Headrow now, she decided that she would see how Frankie felt about Daisy's suggestion. Her heart felt a little lighter as she walked into the warmth of the bakery from the nip of the coming autumn frost that had started to appear on her early morning walk to work.

'Good morning, my love. Monday morning comes all too soon, I think.' Frankie looked up from the table where freshly made baguettes were waiting to be taken into the patisserie's shop front. The aroma of freshly baked bread made Meg's mouth water and wish that she had eaten more of her breakfast of stale crust of bread and jam.

'Yes, Sunday went all too fast. I suppose it is the

same for anybody. But, at least, we are doing a job that we love.' Meg went and gave Frankie a light kiss on his cheek. 'How are you, today? You look tired?'

Frankie reached for a baking tray to place the raspberry tarts on. 'I didn't sleep very well. My mind was racing with the plans for the new bakery. It appears that it is in a worse state than I first thought. And my mother is on my mind. She can be so demanding. She will expect me to be with her every moment, if and when she visits. I hope that she decides against her trip.'

'So, she has written to say that she is coming? I'm looking forward to meeting her. I'm sure she can't be that bad.' Meg smiled as she tied the oversized apron around her waist and started about her work.

'You don't know her. She drains every inch out of you with her demands and wants and nothing I ever do is right.' Frankie sighed. 'Lord, I can't help hoping that she won't make it.'

'Is the new patisserie giving you problems? I suppose you could always sell it on again if you decided it was too much worry,' Meg said, testing the water.

'I'll not be doing that. It is set so nicely on the high street at Headingley. It's only that the costs are high. Once I've had the main work done, and open its door, I'll soon make the money back. I seem to have spent so much of late.' Frankie looked over at Meg as she cut the pastry she had just made into strips. 'Remember, small and delicate. That's what my customers like.'

'I know, they're just as you showed me the other day. You're too much the perfectionist and like to be in control of everything. I'd not let you down on purpose, you know?' Meg said and looked straight at him.

89

'Forgive me, I sometimes ask too much, the pastry is perfect,' Frankie told her.

'Frankie,' Meg held her breath and wondered whether she dare ask the question that she could not stop thinking about. 'I know that you've already done so much for me and my sister but I have something that means a great deal to me that I need to ask you.' Meg felt her stomach churn. Was now the best time to ask such a big favour from her beau? However, she had thought everything over and over in her head, and for him to buy Ted's bakery made perfect sense to her.

Frankie paused in his work and looked at Meg. 'What is it, my dear? You look so serious. Is everything all right?'

'I think that you know that Ted Lund is to sell his bakery. Well . . . I've been pondering over it and I just wondered if you might be interested in buying it, after all. I know the clientele and I'd be happier baking there.' Meg rushed the words out and watched as Frankie's face darkened and he shook his head, clearly not at all happy with her suggestion.

'Why would I want to buy a run-down bakery?' he asked. 'To take over a place there . . . It would not be in keeping with the Pearson name.'

'I see . . . Of course not. I should've known better.'

Meg couldn't help but think Frankie was showing his snobby side and had said what he had been think-ing all along. She had been a fool to think he would buy it, a backstreet bakery was not for a man of his standing.

'I'm sorry,' he said. 'If circumstances were differ-ent, then I would have gladly bought you Ted Lund's shop. I'm just a little stretched at the moment.'

'I understand. I'll get on with the tasks in hand. I should never have asked. You've already been kinder to me than anyone else in my life,' Meg said quietly.

'I'm sorry, Meg.' Frankie looked crestfallen. 'If I could, I would. I don't mean to offend. If the bakery is still up for sale in another twelve months, then I will be in a better position to speculate. It can be my wedding present to you. I know you would feel more at home with baking there, although you fit perfectly well into this patisserie and always will do. Please don't let my refusal come between us.'

'Of course, it won't. I'd love you whether you were a pauper or a prince. As you say, our love is not about money or class . . . I hope. Now, forget I even asked you.'

Meg turned back to her work and tried to bury her hurt. She had hoped above hope that he would say yes to her idea. She wished that she had been born into a rich family or even one that just didn't have to struggle like she did or live on the street that she did.

It wasn't that he'd said no to buying the bakery that hurt. It was his comment about her neighbourhood. No matter what he said, did he secretly think of her in that light? She was always more than aware that she was from the poorer classes but she had her pride and manners. From what she had seen, she had more of both than some who came into the shop.

A determination filled her soul. She had given her heart to Frankie Pearson but she had also set her heart on Ted Lund's bakery. She prayed that it might still be up for sale in twelve months and that their love would still be as strong and that Frankie would see the sense in buying it. But one way or another she had to make it hers.

9

Madge Evans stood in front of the mill's manager. She had been pushed to her limits by Sarah Fairfax and she had to say something.

'I'm sorry, Mr Askew, but that girl is impossible. She doesn't listen! She's cheeky, ignorant and I know very well that she pulls faces at me behind my back. I can hear the other girls titter at her pranks.' Mrs Evans sighed. 'She'll lead the other girls astray, you mark my words. She and Sissy Banks are a bad combination. Sissy has the brains and Sarah has the gall. They think I was born yesterday with their caper of covering for one another in the mornings. I know what they are up to covering for each other when they clock in of a morning and they do one another's work and show no respect at all for me.

'I didn't want to bother you, you are busy enough without wasting time on two stupid pig-headed girls who I thought I could straighten up myself. But I feel I'm just wasting my breath when it comes to that Sarah Fairfax.'

'They are young, Mrs Evans,' Tom Askew replied when it was clear she had finished. 'In fact, Sarah is one of the youngest girls we have had as a burler. Do you have a problem with her work? Is she making a lot of mistakes? If so, I'll have to pull her up myself — but that will mean you lose face if I have to override your authority.'

Tom knew all too well what the problem was. Sarah

92

Fairfax had a mind of her own and the more Madge Evans reprimanded her, the more she would fight. Sarah had spirit, admittedly, but her work was without fault. He had no intention of losing her.

'Her work is good enough. It's simply her attitude to folk! She cares not what she says, or if the world can hear her say it. I've never had such an outspoken lass.' Madge shook her head. 'I'm at my wits' end with her.'

'Persevere with her, Mrs Evans. She is young and has only recently lost her mother.'

Tom looked at his faithful employee as she left his office. Things must be bad, else Madge would not be complaining. He'd have to keep an eye on Sarah Fairfax.

★　★　★

'You've a long face. What's up, have you seen your bum?' Sarah asked her older sister as they sat next to the fire that Meg had lit on their return from work.

'Stop being so rude. I'm exhausted,' Meg said and tried not to look at Sarah, else she would only lose her temper when she saw her surly face. Her sister had no worries compared to her.

'That's my day every day! I hate work! I hate Madge Evans and I hate most of the workers in the mill,' Sarah complained.

'I know, you tell me every day. But you forget that it keeps us fed.' Meg slumped down in her chair.

'What's up with you, then? Fallen out with the man himself, or are you like me? Fed up of working for folk who don't give a damn about you?'

'I did a stupid thing,' Meg admitted. 'I learned

93

that Ted Lund has put the bakery up for sale on York Street. I asked Frankie if he would buy it for me. I shouldn't have — he's done more than enough for us.'

'Did he say no? It can't be because he's no brass! Everyone knows that he's rolling in it!' Sarah's eyes lit up. 'Perhaps he doesn't love you that much, after all!'

'Stop it! You love to hurt me, and you'd love for me to stop seeing Frankie. Well, it's not going to happen. He's just bought another bakery in Headingley and he's concentrating on that. He's promised me if the bakery is still for sale in a year he will buy it for me!' Meg spat out.

'A year's a long time. Things change,' Sarah said.

Just occasionally, Sarah had wisdom beyond her age, Meg realized. 'I know, but I was the one who said we should wait to marry. I'm beginning to have my doubts now. Perhaps I should marry him as soon as I can? I'd get more respect from the staff in the shop, then. I can't help but think the same as you — I'm just a passing fancy from off the backstreets and that he's waiting for someone better. Even though he has asked me for my hand in marriage, I still think he should be doing better for himself.'

Frankie's words were still ringing in her ears and they hurt. She had always thought that class would never come between them, but today he had shown a different side to his personality.

'I could have told you that!' Sarah said, unable to keep a note of triumph from her voice. 'He's a snob. He wants you to help him in his posh bakery, that's all. He and his slimy ways! But you are as good as any of those lasses behind the counter. I'll come in and tell them that, if you want?'

'No, don't bother yourself,' Meg said quickly, surprised and pleased her sister was still willing to stand up for her. 'It's all right, it's just me. I've had a bad day and my head can't make its mind up about anything or anybody. I can look after myself.

'We're a right pair, aren't we? I miss Mam so much, she was so ill and I can't help but wonder if I did enough for her. Besides, there's some folk dying on the streets, and we are moaning about nothing. We've always get each other.' Meg smiled at her sister.

'Aye, I suppose . . . But I want a better life. One day, I'm going to have it,' Sarah said, with a look of determination. 'As for Mam, you couldn't have done any better than you did so stop worrying over that score.'

'I know but I can't help but think of her sometimes. And when it comes to wanting a better life, I do too. So, stop making trouble for Frankie and me and at work, just behave yourself. It'll all work out right in the end,' Meg said quietly.

'I hope so, for your sake, our Meg. We both deserve a bit more cheer in our lives.'

Sarah went up to her room, where she could count what money she had saved and dream of the day that she could run away with Harry. He was not being as friendly as he used to be. Harry had changed, acting like an arrogant fool and hardly talking to her now. He thought he was a big man on the wharf side of the canal. To her, he was still Harry, the gobshite of a lad who had always been her friend and she hoped that he thought the same of her, no matter how he tried to avoid her.

Meg wasn't the only one with worries. Sarah's plans were falling apart too.

★ ★ ★

95

Frankie Pearson took out his pocket watch and shook his head.

'Where are those two girls? It is way past eight, we will be having customers queuing for the tea room in another hour. They have the tea urn to fill and tables to polish. I'd expect at least one of them to show their faces.'

Frankie stood on the patisserie's doorstep, looking onto the Headrow. People were going about their early morning business, but at the corner of Park Row, there seemed to be a commotion of sorts. People were standing in groups looking at something happening further down the row. A horse-drawn ambulance rushed past from the local infirmary. The crowd parted to let it through.

Frankie felt sick and worried as he strode out and looked at the carnage that had befallen one of the morning horse-drawn trams. The two-tier tram lay on its side and bodies were strewn along the road, attended to by passers-by and now the ambulance staff, who quickly got to bandaging wounds and cuts and accessing the injuries. People were crying and wailing and sitting at the side of the pavement, looking on at the accident that had happened at one of the busiest times of the morning.

The tram's horses were snorting and neighing in agony, still attached in their harness. Both thrashed and foamed at the mouth until the least hurt one was unharnessed and was able to get free from its workmate that lay in pain, its broken legs beneath it. There was blood running down the road and women covered their eyes crying, seeing the road littered with injured people and their belongings as well as the dying animal.

A voice rang out above the crowd. Frankie gasped, sickened as he heard the words he knew had to come. 'Stand back, everyone! This has to be done. The horse will never be fit to work again.' It was a stocky man with a bowler hat. He pulled a gun from his leather bag and aimed it at the horse's head.

A shot rang out.

The ladies in the crowd screamed and their husbands comforted them as the horse was put out of its misery. The remaining horse reared and the man holding its reins struggled to control it.

Frankie returned inside, but moments later everyone turned to look at the doors as they were flung open, hitting the back wall with a clatter. 'Mr Pearson, Mr Pearson! I'm sorry I'm late for work, but I was on the tram and it overturned! It turned the corner too fast and lost its balance. It was terrible, terrible! I don't know what to do.'

Hattie ran to the side of Frankie and looked up at him, scratches on her face and arms. She was visibly shaken, blood running down her face with a look of panic in her eyes. Frankie's initial relief that she was alive disappeared when she relayed what had become of Martha.

'She was up top! She fell right out onto the road! The ambulance folk are seeing to her now. Look, she's just being loaded onto a stretcher.' Hattie started to cry. 'She doesn't look so good, Mr Pearson.'

Frankie felt the blood rush from his face. 'Hattie, are you injured?' He put his arm around her and could feel her body shaking.

'Yes, I was at the right side of the tram. I didn't take the full force. But Martha . . .' Hattie's voice trailed off.

97

'Stay here. I'll go and see how she is. Then I'll get you a carriage to take you home,' Frankie assured Hattie as he pushed his way through the crowd to the ambulance and nurses. 'Excuse me, that girl that you have just put in the ambulance — she works for me. How badly is she injured?'

'She'll not be working for you today,' one of the nurses told him. 'She's the worst of all our casualties. Unconscious, numerous breaks. It doesn't look good. Can you tell us her name and address?'

'Yes, yes — of course. Martha Robinson. She lives with her parents at 29 Chadwick Street. Please do all that you can for her. She's a good person.'

Frankie felt shaken as he watched the ambulance driver flick the reins over his horse's back and the co-driver ring the brass bell to clear the way to get to the infirmary.

'Thank you,' he managed to say. 'I hope she will be all right.'

'It doesn't look good.' The nurse moved on to the next injury.

Frankie put his head down and walked back to Hattie, not wanting to tell her the news.

'Is she going to be all right, Mr Pearson? She usually sits downstairs with me, but there wasn't room this morning. I do hope that she'll be all right,' Hattie sobbed.

'She's in the best place now. They'll do all they can for her at the infirmary. But she's badly injured.' Frankie said. 'Now, come take my arm and we'll see to your own wounds in the patisserie. Then I'll get a carriage and take you home.'

'I'm all right, Mr Pearson. I can work if you want me to.'

'You certainly will not. You have had a terrible shock. You must go home for today, at least. Don't worry, I'll still pay you for the hours that you would have worked. I'm just glad that you are not in the same state as poor Martha.'

'Thank you, Mr Pearson, you are a true gent. I'm so grateful that I'm still on this earth and not like that poor horse or Martha.' Hattie turned and looked behind her and watched as a knacker-man put ropes around the dead horse's hooves and started to hoist it onto his cart.

'Yes, let's hope that Martha pulls through,' Frankie sighed. He hoped he did not sound shallow and uncaring but Martha's accident would be just another worry for him, a worry he could do without because of his mother's announcement of a forthcoming visit in a fortnight's time.

'Oh, Hattie, you look so white! Here, sip your tea and sit down,' Meg said and looked at the shaken girl. 'Thank heavens you've got away with only scratches! I never have liked those trams at this time of the morning. They're always packed and the horses are never looked after properly.'

'I just hope Martha's all right. She works to keep her father. Her mother died of consumption a few years ago and her father's breathing isn't good after working in the glass kiln. If anything happens to her, it'll mean the workhouse for her father for certain.' Hattie raised her head as Frankie came to tell her that her hansom cab was waiting outside for her

'Don't you worry about Martha. The hospital will do their best to look after her. Go home and get yourself better. It really does shake you up, a thing like this.'

'I'm sorry. I'm leaving you with nobody to look

after the tea room and folk will be coming. Folk will want to know the gory details of the accident. They all stood about like vultures. They'll want to discuss it in detail over a slice and tea.'

'You've not to worry your head about that. We will manage. Meg will fill in for you and Martha. Norah and Marie will help when they can. We will be fine. Go home and rest.' Frankie helped her into the carriage and then returned to the bakery.

'Meg, if I help you set up the tea room, could you serve in there today? The shop is going to be busy and we will have half of Leeds in this morning, discussing the accident.'

Frankie could see the disappointment on Meg's face at him asking for her help in the tea rooms. He knew it was not her favourite place in his business but he needed her in there instead of the bakery.

'Yes, I suppose I must,' Meg said reluctantly. 'However, if Martha is that ill, you'll need to look for someone to replace her. I hope that I'll not be permanently placed to work in there — you know it isn't the sort of work I enjoy. However, today is an exception and I'll help out.'

'It's all hands on deck today, I'm afraid,' Frankie replied gratefully.

'Right. I'll put a smile on my face and serve the great and the good.' Meg looked for support from Marie and Norah but customers had started to come in and they were busy serving behind the counter. Frankie was heading for the bakery. She'd have to manage, whether she enjoyed the job or not; after all, poor Martha might be lying on her death bed and Hattie had looked so badly shaken and battered as she got into the coach home.

10

'Yes, madam, of course. Whatever you wish.'

Meg took a deep breath and walked back to the counter, where Hattie patted her on the back. She'd seen in the last few days that Meg was to be trusted and was as good at her work as she was.

'Mrs Braithwaite is an old minx,' she whispered. 'She thinks herself something special. You should tell her who you are — that you're about to marry Mr Pearson and that you're only serving on in the tea room because of Martha's accident.'

'That shouldn't have anything to do with how she treats people. She should be right with everyone, no matter who they are.' Meg turned the tap on the steaming silver tea urn to fill the teapot for four that Mrs Braithwaite had ordered, along with a selection of fancies. *Special fancies, ones that only I have.* Those had been her exact words.

'Do you want me to finish serving her? She is awkward.' Hattie started to make up the tea tray. 'You could serve the lady who's come in on her own over in the corner. I've never seen her before.'

Discreetly, Meg looked over at the woman on her own and was thankful to Hattie for giving her an alternative. 'Would you mind? I might not be able to hold my tongue if I hear another word from her and her friends.' Meg placed a silver teapot and warm water pot onto a tray for Hattie to take away. Then, she plucked up her notepad, grateful for escape.

Mrs Braithwaite was sat overlooking the Headrow with three friends, all of them bedecked in their finest clothes. Hattie served the group with the two-tier cake stand stacked with fancies, before she poured the tea. A shocked expression came over Mrs Braithwaite's face before she looked Meg's way. Then she said something to Hattie, turned her attention back to Meg and smiled. Whatever Hattie had said had made a difference because Mrs Braithwaite put her arm out to gain her attention as she went to serve a lady sat partially hidden by a parlour palm in the corner of the tea room.

'My dear, I had no idea that you were the intended of Mr Pearson.' Mrs Braithwaite looked Meg up and down as her friends politely sipped their tea. 'Congratulations, he is such a handsome young man.'

'Thank you,' Meg said curtly but smiled to herself as she went to her customer in the corner. It was true; it wasn't what you did or what you looked like that Mrs Braithwaite judged people upon, it was connections and who you were that counted in her world. How false was that, she thought as she went to serve the next customer.

Meg glanced at the woman, who was tidy but nowhere as decadent in dress as Mrs Braithwaite and her friends. 'Good morning. What can I get you?'

'A cup of tea, if you don't mind please.' The woman took in the prices on the menu. 'I'd have liked to try one of those macaroons, but they are a tad expensive. Maybe, a plain scone?'

'I'll get your tea, then,' Meg smiled, but as she passed Mrs Braithwaite's table she heard one of her friends whisper, 'He could do so much better.'

The words hurt like an arrow through her heart.

Meg knew they were talking about her. She went back to the counter and placed a free macaroon on the delicate china with a cup of tea. She'd look after her own if nobody else.

'I'm sorry, I didn't ask for this,' her customer said as Meg placed the plate in front of her.

'It's a gift from me. My husband-to-be showed me the same kindness, so I thought that I would do the same. He owns this patisserie and he believes in treating people, so you enjoy.' Meg took in the delight on the woman's face as she picked up the delicate almond macaroon.

'Eh, I've never had owt as fancy. Wait until I tell my Bert. Bless you, lass.'

Honestly, Meg didn't know how much longer she could keep working in this tea room. Frankie was expecting her to help in the bakery early in the morning and then in the tea room later. She was here, there and everywhere filling in wherever she was wanted the most. Working with Frankie was not going as planned.

★ ★ ★

Meg pushed off her boots and sighed, glad that she was home, out of the gaze of the upper classes. Looking over at her mother's empty chair, she realized just how much she missed her ma. Now she understood the struggles that her mother had endured to bring her family up and wished she had shown more care towards her. She hated every minute of serving in the busy tea room and only wished Frankie would uphold his promise of employing somebody to replace poor Martha.

11

Sarah looked at her mistake — the great big knot in the material that she should have seen straightaway if she had been concentrating.

'Are you listening, miss? You're a disgrace! If it was up to me, I'd send you home right now. Nobody in the whole of Leeds would want to employ you with your attitude and slovenly ways.' Madge Evans grabbed Sarah by the shoulder and shook her.

'Get your hands off me. Don't you touch me!' Sarah shouted. 'There's nothing wrong with my work, you old bitch!'

'That's it! I'm not having any more cheek from you. Get yourself to the office and explain yourself to Mr Askew. You'll be lucky if you leave with your job.'

Madge stood with her hands on her hips as the rest of the room watched the confrontation that had been simmering for weeks.

'Make me, you old bitch!'

Madge Evans' face turned bright red.

Sarah grinned nastily. 'You know there's nothing wrong with my work, you just have it in for me, since the day I started.'

Every girl went silent.

Madge reached to grab Sarah's shoulder to push her up the stairs to Tom Askew. However, Sarah was wiry and tough and a lot stronger than her manager. She lifted her fist as Madge shoved her.

Sarah's temper got the better of her and she punched

Madge Evans straight and hard on the nose. The whole room gasped and watched as blood spurted, and Madge's spectacles lay broken on the floor.

Madge paused, then wiped her nose and stared at Sarah. 'Get out, *get out of this mill*! I never want to see your face again!' She shrieked so loud that Tom Askew came out of his office to look down at the commotion.

'Sarah Fairfax, my office now!' Tom's voice boomed.

'No! I'm off! You can keep your job and you can shout all you like. I hate this place but most of all I hate her!' Sarah stomped past Madge to the stairs that led down to the mill's exit.

'You come back here, madam! I've not done with you. I'll not have you assaulting one of my staff!' Tom Askew threw himself against the railing as he watched Sarah flounce out. 'Damn that lass!' He glared down at the staff below. 'Get back to work! And, you?' He crooked a finger. 'Here!'

Doing as she was told, Madge Evans dragged her feet up the stairs to his office after picking up her damaged glasses.

★ ★ ★

Sarah ran like the wind, tears streaming down her face as she headed towards the canal. She shouldn't have hit Madge Evans, she should have kept her calm.

She didn't really hate her job, it was just her that she hated, and besides she needed the money. Meg needed the money; what she would say to her she didn't know. She bent double, leaning against the red-bricked wall to catch her breath as she watched the barges and Tom Puds sail up and down the murky canal.

If one of them would stop, I'd run away here and now! she thought. But then, the peelers might come a-knocking on her door. Had she broken Madge Evans's nose? It had certainly looked like it, with the blood. There would be hell to pay if she had.

Her sobbing started again and she curled up in a heap by the side of the canal. A few weeks ago, she would have run down to the wharf to find solace with Harry but of late he had been even more dismissive of her. He'd changed since he'd started work down at the cut; he never waited around to see her or hardly spoke when he did. He was no longer carefree. He worked every hour in order to put aside the money to get away. He no longer had time for her.

In fact, Sarah realized, nobody had time for her — except Meg, and she would be mortified to hear that she had lamped Madge Evans one. She ignored the passers-by who looked at her but showed no concern. No concern at all.

★ ★ ★

'She's done what!'

Meg stood in her kitchen. It was evening time and Sarah was nowhere to be seen.

'She's hit Madge Evans! Her overseer! A whopping punch. She's lucky that she didn't break her nose, else it would be serious for her.' Daisy sat down at the table, placing her bonnet down by her side.

'Oh, Lord. I knew she was struggling to get on with her new boss, but I didn't think she'd go that far.' Meg glanced out of the window, her eyes searching up the yard for her young sister. 'Have they called in the peelers?'

106

'No, thank goodness. Madge didn't want to make a fuss, but Sarah lost her job. Tom says he'll not have her back. He can't have a young lass like that getting the better of the staff.' Daisy sat back in her chair. 'Is she not here, then?'

'No. I thought she was dallying outside the music hall as she does most days. But she could be anywhere. I'd better check if Harry next door has seen her. She usually goes to him when she's in trouble and I heard him arrive home not too far back.' Meg went out the back door and shouted over the brick wall. 'Harry!' she yelled. 'Have you seen our Sarah today?'

Harry came and leaned against the door, still chewing his slice of bread and dripping. 'No, I've seen nowt of her today. She doesn't come down to the wharf as much as she did. Has she not come home?' Harry looked worried; Leeds was no place for a young lass to be roaming.

'No, she's got herself into bother at work. I hope that she's all right. I'll put my shawl on and go and look for her. If she's dallying at that stage door of the music hall it won't be the only bother that she's in.'

'Has he seen her?' Daisy asked, as Meg stepped back in through the back door.

'No. I'm going to have to go and search for her. Please God, don't let her have done anything stupid. I might curse her some days, but I do love her.' Meg grabbed her shawl. 'I'll go and look down East Gate and Vicar Lane and around the music hall's stage doors. If she's anywhere, she'll be there. It's where she always goes when she wants to escape the world's troubles. With her fanciful ideas of being a singer or dancer, she's often drawn there.'

'I'll help. I'll go down The Calls and up Briggate.

She doesn't want to be wandering there on her own.' Daisy put on her hat and wrapped her shawl around her.

'God, I wish I had a sensible sister,' Meg said as she closed the door behind her.

Harry was already emerging from his house.

'Are you going out to look for her?' he asked. 'I'll help. I'll look up York Street and George Street. She could be looking in the shop windows.'

'I'll give her looking in shop windows. I've been too soft with her, and my mam was too. Lord, I hope that we find her.' Meg felt tears bubbling up in her eyes.

'We'll find her, don't worry,' Daisy said, striding out next to Harry and Meg. 'She'll be all right. She has to be.'

* * *

Meg was exhausted. She had covered half of Leeds, calling out Sarah's name and asking everyone she met if they had seen her — even the whores and the drunks that crowded outside the hostelries. There had been no sign of her, and eventually she'd dragged herself home.

She met Daisy at the top of East Gate. She had not seen hide nor hair of Sarah, either. Now, both young women walked back to the yard.

'I hope she hasn't done anything foolish. What if she has run away or thrown herself into the cut? Or somebody might have taken her to work in a brothel.'

Meg had barely finished sharing her worst fears, when the two of them froze and shared a glance. The door to the sisters' home stood wide open, a glow from the oil lamp spilling out.

'She's back!' Meg ran down the lane and into her home.

Sarah looked up from where she sat at the table. Tears ran down her filthy face and she began sobbing as soon as she saw Meg. 'I'm sorry!' she cried. 'I couldn't take her bullying ways anymore, and I didn't mean to break her nose.'

'I found her in the yard's shed. You could hear her blubbing a mile away,' came a voice. It was Harry, stood over his heartbroken friend.

'Oh, Sarah! I could bloody murder you! I was worried sick!' Meg went over to her sister and hugged her.

'You haven't broken Madge Evans's nose,' Daisy cheerily informed Sarah, following Meg inside. 'You've just bloodied it and made her lose the respect of the girls under her. It will happen to teach her a lesson not to pick on the ones she takes a dislike to!'

'And my job?' Sarah said, as she tried to stop crying.

'No, you've lost that. Tom will not have you back and word will get about that you're trouble,' Daisy said quietly. 'Mill owners don't want workers who think for themselves. That's why they have the likes of Madge Evans.'

'Never mind, you'll find something else,' Harry said, placing his hands on Sarah's shoulders as she slumped at the table. 'But you are going to have to learn that you just can't do what you want. It's hard, but if you want to be fed and kept under a roof, folk like us have to work. That's why I can't talk when you come down to the wharf — else I'd lose my job. You needed that job if you had set your head on your dreams.' Harry glanced at Meg and Daisy for confirmation.

'Harry is right,' Meg said. 'It's time you grew up and acted like the young lady I know you can be. Just as our mother, God rest her soul, wanted you to be. Time to put your childhood behind you, like Harry says, and knuckle down.'

'I'm sorry. I'll try,' Sarah said quietly. She hid her head in her arms as Harry and Daisy made to leave. Meg thanked them for their help and closed the door behind them.

'Now, Lady Jane,' Meg said, turning back to her sister. 'You behave from now on, because my patience is wearing thin. Tomorrow afternoon we'll go to Hunslet Mill and see Tom Askew — I know Harry says that you'll not get your job back but I'll see if we can persuade them otherwise. You will apologize in front of everyone to Madge Evans. Do you hear?'

'Yes, I hear, but I don't want to,' Sarah choked out.

Meg was annoyed with her selfish sister but was thankful Harry had added his four-pennorth, whatever his reasons. Sarah and Harry were and always had been too close for her liking. 'Doesn't matter. You will do as I say,' Meg said firmly. 'Now, we'll have some supper and get to our beds.' She looked sternly at her sister. 'I've searched half of Leeds looking for you, even after a full day's work. That's how much you mean to me. So stop your blubbering. All will be well — as long as you do as you are told.'

12

'The answer is no! I don't care how much you beg — your sister will not be working at this mill or any other!' Tom Askew glared at Meg as she pleaded her sister's case.

'I know she's headstrong, but she is still young. Please give her another chance! We need the money,' Meg pleaded. With Sarah's money gone, there was even more pressure on Meg to marry Frankie as soon as she could just to relieve the poverty that they were both living in. But Meg was hesitant, knowing a marriage should have firmer foundations.

'She should have thought of that before she lifted her fist to Mrs Evans. There are plenty of girls at this mill who are ready to step into her shoes and not give me any trouble. I'm sorry, but we do not want her back and she should be grateful that Mrs Evans is not charging her with assault.'

Tom Askew looked at Sarah as she hung her head. He had heard too many reports of the young rebellious Sarah and had decided enough was enough.

'Now, good day. See the pay clerk on your way out.' He opened the door for the two of them to leave.

'Please, Mr Askew. Please give me my job back. I promise I'll behave. I'll even apologize to Mrs Evans in front of all the girls. I need my job!' Sarah sobbed as she followed Meg out of the office.

'I'm sorry. You've had more chances than most. I know Mrs Evans has reprimanded you several times,

111

but you chose to disobey. I don't need workers like you. However, I do wish you and your sister the best of luck.'

Meg put her arm through Sarah's as they left his office. 'I knew he'd not keep you on, but it was worth a try. I don't know who he thinks he is anyway; he knows that I know about him and Daisy. I've a good mind to go and tell his wife, but that would hurt Daisy,' Meg muttered, prepared to do pretty much anything to protect her young sister and get her job back — but not that.

'It doesn't matter. I'll find something else, I hated the bloody job anyway,' Sarah snivelled and then shouted at the top of her voice. 'Stick your job where the sun don't shine.'

★ ★ ★

'You'll never learn, will you?' Meg glared at her sister as they reached home. The pay clerk had heard Sarah's shout and had waited for Tom Askew to give his permission before he paid Sarah the little she was owed.

'I wasn't going to have him say anything bad about me. I did my job well and he knows it.' Sarah slumped down in a chair and kicked her boots off.

'You needn't take those off! You can go and find yourself a new job. The pay you got won't even cover this week's milk. You need to find something else to do — and quickly! — before word gets out.'

Meg wrapped her shawl back around her shoulders. 'I need to leave. Frankie will wonder where I've got to! I hope that he has coped with baking this morning. Lord knows what he'll think when I tell him what you've been up to.' Meg glared at her sister who she knew would sulk all day if left.

'He can think what he likes. He's nowt to do with me, so I ain't bothered!' Sarah said and folded her arms.

'He's everything to do with you. He's going to be your brother-in-law shortly,' Meg snapped.

'Only if you get on with marrying him. If he's any sense he'll run a mile,' Sarah retorted.

'Shut up! Get your boots back on and go and look for a job, even if it's just helping on the market. Surely someone will take you on.'

Meg knew that her words were falling on deaf ears as she rushed out of the door and made her way quickly to the already busy Headrow. The patisserie would have been open for over an hour. She should have sent him word that she was going to be late but she couldn't afford to pay the local lad that usually delivered letters. She could only hope that Frankie would understand.

★ ★ ★

She said a quick good morning to Norah and Marie behind the counter, but they were both too busy serving customers to reply.

'Ah, so I see that you have decided to show your face this morning,' Frankie said, as he placed a tray of tarts on the counter. The bakes were decorated with cream and raspberries, which must have taken him an age to prepare.

Meg reached for her apron and saw the stress and worry on Frankie's face. 'I'm sorry, I couldn't get a message to you. I'm late because I've had to go and plead with Tom Askew for Sarah to get her job back.'

'And what has our precious Sarah gone and done now?' Frankie said sharply. Clearly, he was tired.

'She's gone and lost her job at the mill, through being stubborn and awkward as always. I will always have her to worry about, it seems. However, you will always be my main love. You should know that,' Meg said softly and went to his side and kissed him on the cheek to try to calm him.

Frankie indicated the row of well-to-do customers queuing up to be served. 'We have been so busy this morning. Hattie is run off her feet upstairs.'

A bit later, out of earshot of customers and staff in the kitchen, Meg busied herself clearing Frankie's used baking bowls and confessed to what Sarah had done, feeling embarrassed by her sister's rash behaviour. 'Sarah hit her supervisor. She'll never get employment with any of the mill owners around here, not once they hear what she did.'

'It is a wonder that she's not been placed in Armley gaol,' Frankie said bluntly. 'She's lucky to have got away with that, *cherie*, and has only lost her job. Assault is a serious business, I hope that you have told her so?' Frankie looked at Meg as she made her way to the stairs and the tea room, knowing he was sending her back to the place that she hated but was most needed.

'I have. I've made it clear to her that she has to change her ways. Lord knows if it has sunk in. I can only hope that she'll find another job soon. You pay me well, but Sarah's little bit of income gives us both a little leeway.' Meg hesitated, turned back to him and asked, 'You couldn't find work for her, could you? We are one person down. Even if she just did the wash-

114

ing up, she would be a help.' Meg looked at Frankie's face and immediately saw her answer. 'I'd keep her in check. She wouldn't dare step out of line if I was keeping an eye on her.'

'No! Not in my wildest dreams would I have your sister working in here. She has little or no respect for me. Indeed she has little or no respect for anyone from what I've seen and heard. I love you, *ma cherie*, but your sister is another matter.' Frankie shook his head. 'In fact, I've been thinking about this for some time and perhaps it would be better if she did not come and live with us when we are married.'

Meg's voice showed her dismay. 'But I can't leave her behind! She's my sister and she's too young to have the responsibility of looking and paying for herself.' Meg felt her heart beating fast. Was Frankie asking her to choose between him and her sister?

'Then we will have to find a compromise because I want as little to do with the girl as I can. I'm sorry. I know that blood is thicker than water, but you are complete opposites and I thank the Lord that I love you, not her.' Ignoring the stricken look on Meg's face, Frankie went into the shop with his tray full of tarts.

Meg made her way up the stairs to the tea room. She'd have to put her cares behind her as she served and tidied the tables for the good and the grand of Leeds. Yet, all the time, her mind was on Sarah and Frankie's obvious dislike of her.

Her worries grew as the day progressed. She purposely kept out of Frankie's way, making herself busy and trying not to remember the expression on his face when she had asked for Sarah to work for him. She was more than thankful when Hattie informed her that Mr Pearson had gone to his new establishment in Headingley. 'He asked me to say that he'll call by at yours this evening.'

'Thank you, Hattie,' Meg said as she went to serve at the next table. She was grateful not to have to speak to Frankie until later, and then in the privacy of her own home. Things were not going as she had expected since she had started work with Frankie. She had a feeling that something was going on in Frankie's life. Something linked with his mother?

★ ★ ★

'Frankie, you've brought nowt but work with this place, which is grand for me but not so good for you. I hope that you are prepared to spend some money,' Jed Hurst said as he looked up at the new roof he was tiling. 'My men have had to replace all the joists. They were rotten to the core.'

'This place is costing me a small fortune,' Frankie said. He sank back against a wall and gazed around the rubble and destruction. He'd have to manage the rest of his finances with care and hope that he could convince his mother to back him. Maybe even, she might let him loose with his inheritance. But even as that desperate thought crossed his mind, he knew that he was fooling himself.

'Aye, it is not the best of places. But once finished, it will be worth a small fortune. You'll not lose out, don't worry.' Jed glanced down from his work and spotted Frankie's furrowed brow. He was glad that they had both come to a gentleman's agreement upon the work that had to be carried out. 'There's not going to be a problem, is there? You will see me and my men right,

116

once it's finished?'

Frankie shook his head clear. 'You need not worry on that score, my friend. Of course, I will.' Frankie patted Jed on the back and sincerely hoped that his words rang true. For now, he had to go and make things right with Meg. She'd not spoken to him all day and he had regretted his way with words over her sister Sarah — but the girl was a liability, and he really did not want her to work in any of his establishments, ever.

★   ★   ★

'What's up with you, then? You look even more down than I am,' Sarah said, as her sister poked about at her supper, even though Sarah had gone to all the effort to make sure that a meal was waiting for Meg's arrival home.

'I'm just tired. I've had a hard day and it didn't start off well with having to walk all the way to Hunslet on your behalf and for nothing in the end.' Meg sighed. 'I don't suppose you've been out of these four walls, and if you have, it won't be because you've been looking for work. Not if I know you.' Meg pushed aside her plate of scrag end stew.

'I did!' Sarah protested, immediately. 'I've asked all around the market if anybody needed help, but nobody wants me. I wasn't that bothered anyway because it's starting to turn colder now. You only freeze in your boots working outside at this time of year.'

'You'll be freezing in this house if we can't afford to keep the fire going. You need work, Sarah. Come to that, I could do with looking for something else. Working with Frankie is not going to plan, especially at the moment,' Meg sighed.

Sarah's eyes widened as she looked at her sister. Any other time, she'd have revelled in Meg's announcement but after this week's drama, it was another shock that she didn't need. Before she could say anything, there was a knock at the door. Without waiting for an answer, Frankie stepped inside. The cheek of it! She saw Meg's face light up to see him and felt herself scowl.

'Frankie! I didn't expect you this early. I've not even changed out of my work clothes.' Meg felt self-conscious as she looked at Frankie dressed in one of his best suits. Frankie glanced at Sarah as though he wanted her to disappear into thin air. Instead, she sat back in her chair and looked him up and down.

'Perhaps we could go for a walk,' he suggested, smoothly. 'In the churchyard perhaps, while there is still light? Have a talk.'

'Yes, that sounds like a good idea. Let me grab my shawl.' Meg pushed her chair back and looked guiltily at Sarah as she put her shawl around her shoulders.

'We'll not be long,' Meg said and took Frankie's arm as he led her out of the house.

'You can suit yourself!' Sarah called after them. 'I'm going to talk to Harry if he's about.' Sarah shook her head as she watched the couple walk out of Sykes Yard in the direction of the churchyard. Just as she'd thought her sister was seeing sense, he'd turned up — typical! However, things did not sound as rosy between them both. Perhaps if she was lucky, Meg had seen through her pompous baker and the love affair was at an end.

★ ★ ★

118

Frankie and Meg sat on a bench in the late evening's sunshine and watched as the reds and oranges of the falling chestnut leaves littered the churchyard. Frankie reached for Meg's hand and kissed it gently.

'I'm sorry, *ma cherie*. Lately, I have spoken to you without care. My worries have taken over and I can't make sense of anything at the moment. Forgive me?'

'Perhaps it would be better if you were to share your worries with me? Especially if we are to be married,' Meg said. 'And, Frankie, I know you like to call me *cherie*, but now I know you better, there is no need.'

'I thought you liked my French accent! Very well, I'll desist,' Frankie said, looking wounded. 'However, it is better that I don't share my worries. All will become more bearable once my mother has left after her visit. I always loathe seeing her. I can never do anything right in her eyes. But I'll tell her of our plans to marry, so no doubt she will ask to meet you.' Frankie kissed Meg's hand again. 'I hope that it is acceptable?'

Meg nodded and wiped away a tear. 'Yes, of course. I'm sorry I asked about Sarah. I should have known better.'

'I know I'm not the best person to work with. I am a perfectionist and my words about Sarah were inexcusable. However, I do believe to be right over her not being suitable to work in my patisserie.' Frankie squeezed Meg's hand tightly. 'If she is to be my sister-in-law, she and I will both have to grow to like one another. I'll try and win her over one way or another.'

'That would truly be a miracle when it comes to Sarah! She likes nobody, not even herself,' Meg laughed and put her head on Frankie's shoulder. 'I'm sorry. We both have our worries and sometimes they get in the way of our love. Once I've met your mother, it will be one less worry for you, I'm sure. I'll charm her, so you don't have to worry.'

13

Joe Dinsdale leaned upon his shop counter and stared at the shop door that was left swinging after Ted Lund's departure.

Ted had been moaning as usual about how bad his life was. The latest disaster was the sale of his bakery, which at least was now closed. Joe sighed and shook his head. What had Ted expected? If it had been Joe in his place, he'd never have got rid of the young Fairfax lass. She must have been making him money! Ted should have buried his pride, apologized, and kept her on to run the place. He could have sat back and watched the money roll in. But, of course, Ted would never lower himself to an apology. He glanced to one side as George served a regular customer.

'Three pounds of flour, an ounce of baking powder and half a pound of currants,' the woman read out from her list.

'Anything else, Mrs Brown?' George asked as he totted her total up and passed her the goods, all packaged and sealed.

'No, I think that's it, lad. That is unless you fancy doing my baking for me! Now, how grand would that be to be able to come in here and buy my old man his tea cakes and bread with no effort at all?' Mrs Brown smiled and passed George her money. 'I never thought I'd say this, but I miss that miserable old Lund's bakery — not that his bread was up to much.'

Joe's ears pricked up.

'Then that will be threepence ha'penny, please, Mrs Brown.' George smiled and rang up the till, wishing her good day as she left.

'Do many folk ask for bread and the like, lad?' Joe looked around his shop, turning over an idea.

'Aye, quite regularly, especially now that Mr Lund has closed his bakery.' George tidied the counter.

'Happen it's something we should think about. We sell just about everything else. Perhaps a place for baked goods would work a treat, just as you come in next to the door. Catch the customers with the aroma of freshly baked bread and fancy cakes. Folk are partial to a treat, especially on a Friday when they've just got paid.' Joe laughed to himself.

'But we have no bakery, Mr Dinsdale — and neither of us can bake,' George said.

'No, but I know somebody who can. We might be missing a trick here, lad. Just think what we could sell at Christmas. Puddings, cakes, them new fruity mince-pies . . . Everybody's wanting them.' Joe thought about his shop, full of seasonal baking. Aye, he reckoned he could make a tidy profit if his prices were right and the baking good.

★ ★ ★

Sarah put her chin in her hands and looked around her as she sat on the wall overlooking the canal. She had walked around the market and asked in various shops if there was any work going, but there was nothing. She dare not even look on the employment boards outside the many mills and didn't want to return to work within them anyway. But she had to find a job of some sort. Meg still expected her to work, even if

122

she was about to be wed to Frankie Pearson. That is, if she went through with it.

Sarah sighed. She had really hoped that the love affair between her sister and the posh Frankie had been on the wane. However, after her return from her walk out with him the previous evening, Meg had been humming to herself and looked to be still in love with the man Sarah hated.

'Now, then — what are you doing sulking here?' Harry said as he passed her with a hot mutton sandwich in his hand. He looked to be on his way back to work at the wharf.

Sarah lifted her head. 'Well, I'm not on my way to see you, if that's what you're worried about.'

'There's no need to be like that! You know why I can't talk to you. I need to keep my nose clean. So do you, although the way you act you wouldn't think it.' Harry sat down beside her. 'Here, have you had any dinner? Have a bite, they make a good sandwich at Murgatroyds and they don't charge a lot.' Harry passed Sarah the sandwich, then watched her eat greedily as he wiped the dripping fat from off his chin. 'A penny, that's all they charge — and it nearly does me all day. It's no fun, having a rumbling belly all day.'

Sarah took another mouthful and then passed his lunch back to him.

'I'm not hungry really. It just looked good.' Sarah wiped her mouth with the back of her sleeve and looked at Harry. 'Are you still saving to go to London? You've not mentioned it lately but I've been saving all I can so that I can come with you.'

'No, it was just a dream. I've spoken to a lot of folks that come and go on the tubs. They say life is just as hard, if not harder, down south.' He shrugged. 'If you're poor, you don't stand a chance anywhere. Anyway, it's winter coming and I don't want to be trailing on my own, especially at Christmas.'

'But you said you were going as soon as you had saved up. I was going to go with you! I've been putting money away and not telling Meg.' Sarah suddenly felt like crying.

'I never promised you that, you shouldn't take folk for granted, Sarah,' Harry said with a look of shock on his face. 'Give Meg your money, for now. She'll be struggling as it is without your wage coming in. Or if your head is set, then you'll have to go on your own, but you don't really want to be doing that, not now. It's time to grow up, Sarah, I've had to. Working on the docks soon makes you a man, else you don't survive.' Harry reached for Sarah's hand. 'You'll find a job, Meg will marry her fella and everything will be all right. You'll see.'

Sarah snatched her hand back. 'You're like all the rest! Everybody always lets me down. I hate you, Harry Truelove! You are no friend of mine.' Sarah spat and leapt down from the wall. Her promise of a different life was shattered.

'Nay, I don't think you do, you are just angry with the world. A world that's not going to change just for you. Now, I'm off to work and you need to get your arse moving and stop feeling sorry for yourself. Nobody likes a selfish brat and that's what you've turned into of late.' Harry leapt down from the wall, too. He'd had enough of the spoilt lass that lived next door. 'Sarah, I live in a house full of folk that sleep head to toe and work hard every day just to keep body and soul together. All you do is moan about your sis-

124

ter who bends backwards for you and tries to keep you safe. For Lord's sake, grow up!'

'I do hate you, Harry Truelove!' Sarah shouted yet again as she stomped off down the road and into Leeds. She headed towards the only place she could forget about the worthless life she was in, and how Harry had shattered her dreams. She'd go to the music hall.

★ ★ ★

Len Pickering shook his head as he posted up the advertisement.

Odd job person wanted, must be good at turning their hand to owt asked of them, most of all able to communicate well with the acting profession. Hours many, but pay could be good for the right person.

This was not the first time that he had put up the notice; needing new staff was a regular occurrence. The acting profession was . . . a challenge to work with. Actors were full of their self-importance and if anything at all was out of place in their shoddy rooms, shoes were thrown and colourful language flowed. Which was why his dad, manager at the music hall, was advertising the position yet again. The latest lad had left after being kicked out of the music hall by an inebriated so-called comedian. Some comedian. He'd nearly broken the young lad's leg! That was the trouble with their sort. What you saw on the stage was not what you got in real life.

'What are you doing, Len? What's your notice say?' Sarah appeared behind Len and read the advert. She had often had a conversation with Len and had on a

125

few occasions persuaded him to let her have a sneak into the mysterious backstage of the music hall.

'We need another bloody stagehand. These actors are a law unto themselves. They think themselves so grand that they can treat folk like muck.' Len gave a heavy sigh

'Oh, I'd love that job! But I suppose it's no job for a girl. Your father will be wanting a lad or even a man?'

'He'd welcome anybody at the moment, but . . .' He looked Sarah up and down, assessing. 'You are a bit puny to be lifting things, like the ropes between scenes.' Len looked at the excitement on Sarah's face. 'But it's more running after the various acts than any heavy work and making sure everyone is on time on the stage. You'd be able to do that, I'm sure. I can ask Dad, if you want? Besides, he's desperate at this time of year, with Christmas just around the corner. Some of the biggest names coming to play here. Come on! Come with me and we'll ask.'

'I don't know. He'll only laugh. He'll not want me. But I know I'm damn good no matter what he thinks,' Sarah said. 'I'd like a go at showing him just what I can do. '

'You might just be the right one for the job, one to dodge and dive for the acts and run errands for my father and anyone else. I can manage the sets along with Henry, who sees to the sets and lighting. He'll never know if you're right for the job if you don't have a go.' Len smiled as she followed him into the other world of the theatre. 'Besides, I hear that you're in need of a job,' Len grinned, always happy to tease a friend. 'Punching your boss was not the best move you ever made.'

126

'I hope that you've been out and about looking for a job, Sarah Fairfax! I came home to an empty house, the door wasn't locked and the dirty dishes hadn't been touched since this morning. It's not good enough.' Meg's lecture had begun the moment Sarah opened the door.

'Well, you can hold your noise and stop pestering me, because I've done just that!' Sarah smiled, feeling cocky in the knowledge that she had just secured the job of her dreams, working in the music hall.

'You have? Where . . . and is it suitable for you?' It was a treat to see how shocked Meg looked.

'I saw Len, my friend at the music hall. He was placing an advertisement outside for a stagehand and so I went in to see his father, the manager, and guess what? He's given me the job! I start on Monday evening, looking after Larry Hopkirk. I can't believe my own luck! Fancy me, looking after Larry Hopkirk — I just can't get over it.' Sarah felt herself smile like the cat that had got the cream as she swaggered into the room and threw her shawl down onto the back of a chair.

'But you're too young for a job like that!' Meg cried. 'You'll be working until midnight. It won't be fit for someone your age.' Meg sighed. 'What on earth did you ask to work there for? I'll worry about you every minute.'

'Nothing I do will ever be right for you. I will love every minute I work there and Len is going to walk me home each evening, so that is not your problem. Len's father has offered me the job and decent money, so you had better not stop me from doing this, our

Meg.' Sarah felt her eyes flash in anger. 'You are following your dreams, now let me follow mine. You've always known I love the music hall. I will work there, whether you want me to or not.'

'Bloody hell.' Meg swore out of desperation, 'Sarah! On your own head be it, but I'll expect no moans, and no chasing you to go to work . . . and you'll pay your way until things change and I get married. It is time to grow up, Sarah, just like Harry next door,' Meg said sternly.

'Him? I never want to be like him! He'll always be content with his lot. I know you can do whatever you want if you long for it enough. I have to take this job — it was made for me.' Sarah smiled, thinking of the day she had had behind the scenes at the music hall. She had found her place in life and nobody was going to talk her out of it, no matter who they were or what they said.

14

Florence Pearson looked at the porter with disdain.

'Take care with that, you fool! That is crocodile skin. If you scratch it, I will expect compensation.' Florence sighed and turned to her latest lover. 'You can tell we are back in England. No style, not like the French, my darling.' She cast another icy glance at the porter. 'Follow me. My son will relieve you of the luggage as soon as he meets me at the station entrance. At least he will take care.'

'Really, Flo! The man is doing his best.' Richard Fleming shook his head and followed her through the smoke-filled Leeds Station.

'Well, it's not good enough! Now, where is that son of mine? He promised me that he would be waiting for us with a horse and cab. I need to refresh myself, I must look terrible after the journey that we have had.' Florence adjusted her hat and wrap while she peered through the crowds of people.

'You always look magnificent, my dear,' Richard said and linked his arm into hers. He had learned that flattery worked best on Florence at every opportunity. As long as she continued to keep him in the manner to which he'd grown accustomed, and helped to orchestrate gallery viewings of his artwork, he would say whatever she wanted to hear.

Florence frantically looked through the crowds for her son. 'There he is, there he is! Over there, by the main entrance. Can you see him — the man with the top hat and the silver-topped cane?' Florence waved and quickly stepped out in her full skirts, nearly knocking the porter and her cases over in her rush.

'Mamma, how lovely to see you. Did you have a good journey?' Frankie kissed his mother on both cheeks and urged the porter to place her cases in the carriage.

'No! The crossing was stormy and the people tiresome. Just anybody seems to travel nowadays — and as for the trains! Well, don't ask.' Florence stood back and looked at her son from arm's length. 'You look peaky. Too much work and not enough play, perhaps? Or could it be the other way? I never know with you, you tell me nothing.'

'Don't start already, Mother. Are you not going to introduce me to your . . . friend? I don't believe we have ever met.' Frankie took in the debonair man dressed in a cream linen suit, completely unsuitable for the cold northern climate.

'This is my darling Richard. Richard Fleming. His work is absolutely exquisite. Paris and the world will be in awe of him — they just don't know it yet.' Florence smiled at Richard, who held his hand out to be shaken.

'An artist, I see.' Frankie shook hands. 'I'm pleased to meet you, Richard. I'm sure my mother will be making you welcome in her world.'

'I'm eternally grateful to your mother for her encouragement and it is good to meet you. She speaks very highly of you, and I thank you for letting me stay with you on this brief visit.'

'My mother never mentioned bringing a guest with her. I'll ask my maid to make a room up for you, once we arrive home.'

'There's no need, Frankie. We act as if we are married. A second room will not be needed.' Florence looked at the disdain on her son's face as he held her hand to climb into the carriage. 'Really Frankie, don't be so prudish. Your mother has to have a life, too. It is not regarded as scandalous in Paris. You should know I am used to Paris ways now, no matter what Yorkshire folk think.'

Frankie closed the carriage door behind them and took his place, looking at the couple. Florence did not like the expression on her son's face.

★   ★   ★

'I never did like this house, but your father insisted,' Florence said as she sipped her tea after supervising the maid unpack her many cases and inspecting her and Richard's bedroom.

'It's a good house, well built in an affluent part of Leeds, what is not to like about it?' Frankie said. He sat back in his chair, trying his best to temper his hostility towards the couple who had invaded his home.

'It does not let the light in enough. Our apartment in Paris is so airy, perfect for Richard and me to paint. Leeds is so dull and drab at this time of year. Thank the Lord that I visited you now and not mid-winter. I can't stand the biting winds that blow along these streets,' Florence said, looking down her nose. 'Now, Richard. My son and I have some business to talk about. Perhaps after you have finished your tea, you could go for a stroll?'

'Yes, of course. I will go straightaway and come back to my tea. I should not be privy to your conversation.' Richard gave a sickly grin. 'Nobody should come between mothers and sons.' He rose from his seat.

Florence held her hand out for him to kiss. 'Thank you, my love. I knew you'd understand.'

Frankie started as soon as Richard had left the room. 'Where has he come from, then? He's young enough to be your son!'

His mother looked appalled, as though she had no idea what he was talking about. 'He's very dear to me! You could say that he's the son that I really craved, only . . . slightly more intimate.' Frankie felt his stomach churn. 'He entertains me. In turn, I help promote his work. One day he will be rich and celebrated, and then I hope that he does not forget who helped him get there.' Florence sat back in her chair. 'Goodness, you are so much like your father, lecturing me when it is you that needs help.'

Frankie quickly remembered the arguments that his parents used to have and felt sympathy for his late father, who had always been honest and hard-working. 'I don't need help. I just need my inheritance. All I ask is that you release the funds nine months early. Then, I can progress comfortably with my life. Every penny I have is tied up in property or in renovating.' He took a deep breath and forced himself to continue with the truth. 'I'm . . . I'm facing a huge bill.'

His mother gave a sly smile. 'Now, whose fault is that? It's certainly not mine. Why you ever left Paris I do not know. A French patisserie in a northern mill town will never work even though you are telling me different! I sometimes think that I gave birth to a child with no brains, especially when he insists on buying a property that he can ill afford.'

'Please, Mother. The new patisserie is making good

money. Another twelve months and I'll have no worries. I'll have two patisseries and one will be making a good profit. You know I'm a good businessman and you know that I will spend my father's money wisely.' Frankie leaned forward in his chair. 'I also want to tell you that I have met the woman I wish to marry. Her name is Meg Fairfax. She is a baker, too. She means the world to me.'

'A baker! You mean that she's a common worker? Oh, Frankie — you could do so much better than that. I expected you to marry into a respectable family.' Florence shook her head. 'I should have known. You are so much like your father, never happy until you are living amongst the lower classes.'

'It is better than being a snob and pretending to be something you are not. You sometimes forget that you were a cobbler's daughter from Bradford. We are nothing special, Mother. Father made the money.' Frankie knew that his words would not sit comfortably, and from the look on Florence's face he was not wrong.

'That was different! My father had seen to me being well educated. Does this girl come from a decent family? Is she educated?'

'She's recently lost her mother and her father died some years ago. She lives with her younger sister, Sarah. She's far from dim.' Frankie tried to keep his voice under control.

'No, I'm sure she's anything but dim. She probably sees you, thinks money and has set her sights on marrying you. Really, Frankie, she's interested in you for your money.' Florence sat back in her chair and took a deep breath.

'What money? I haven't any!' Frankie snapped.

His efforts at control had disappeared. 'Well, not yet. Don't judge me — look to yourself and your lap dog, Richard.'

'How dare you comment on your mother's life? It is yours we have come to discuss. That, and your reckless spending.' Florence sipped her tea.

'Nothing that you say will make me change my mind about Meg. We are to be married.'

'She's not with child, is she?' Florence sighed, placing her tea cup down.

'No! And, as it happens, she is in no hurry to marry, out of respect for her late mother,' Frankie said and looked out of the window.

'Well, that's a blessing. Perhaps I should meet her although I don't know why,' Florence said sharply.

'Good, because she is coming to tea tomorrow. And my money . . .Will you even think about instructing the solicitor to release funds?' Frankie held his breath.

'I'll give it some thought after I've seen your new patisserie. I already know the shop that you have bought in Headingley. I could have told you not to touch it. I remember when you were a child, the Hodgsons nearly burnt the place down with an over-hot oven, the roof was badly damaged and then they made a hash repairing it,' Florence said and shook her head. 'It is no good following good money with bad.'

'Please Mother, it is only a matter of months before it is all mine, with your say or not,' Frankie pleaded.

'We will see. I'll tell you once I've met . . . Meg? Is that what you call her? Surely her name should be Margaret? Meg is so common,' Florence sighed.

'Mother, she's called Meg. And I like it that way.'

★ ★ ★

'Do I look all right? I'm trying to breathe in and keep my figure. I know she'll expect me to be wearing a corset, but I haven't any.' Meg looked at herself in the mirror and wished that she owned a set of corsets to make her figure look waspish, like all the ladies of fashion.

'Lord's sake, Meg! She's not the Queen. What does it matter what you look like?' Then Sarah saw the panic on her sister's face. 'You look perfect,' she said, more gently. 'You always do — apart from when you are black-leading the oven and fireplace.'

'I haven't any of that on me, have I?' Meg looked down at her long black skirt and white cuffed blouse and sighed with relief when she couldn't find any smudges.

'I'll never get this upset at ever seeing anyone, of that I'm sure,' Sarah laughed.

There was a knock at the back door. It was the coach driver that Frankie had sent.

'Go on, then — your carriage awaits. All the row will be watching you from behind their windows, wondering where you are off to now. Mrs McEvoy will be breaking her neck peering from behind her net curtains. Having a carriage pick you up is one up on owning a tea service.'

Sarah grinned and watched as her sister reached for her small posy bag. 'Just be you and stand up to the old bag if she tries to pull you down. We are as good as anybody.'

'I'm dreading this. If Frankie doesn't get on with her, then I'm not about to. I know now that she'll not think me good enough for him.' Meg put her bag on her wrist and opened the door to the driver of the hansom cab.

'Don't be daft. Enjoy your afternoon!'

'Thank you, I'll try.' Meg followed the driver out to the carriage that was about to take her to meet the woman who would decide her future.

★ ★ ★

'So, you are the . . . Meg that I have heard so much about. The one who wishes to marry my son.' Florence didn't deign to rise from her seat as Meg entered the parlour.

Meg instantly recognized the hostility of Florence's words. 'I am, and Frankie wishes to marry me,' Meg said quietly. She sat down next to him and he took her hand.

'The trouble with arty types — of which my son is one — is that we are drawn by good looks.' Florence looked at Meg. 'And I can see that is the case here. However, from what he has told me, you are without the desirable family background that I had wished for my son's intended. Perhaps you are attracted to him by his money or do I presume too much?'

Meg felt herself shrinking inside. Her future mother-in-law was as fierce as she'd dreaded. She reminded herself what Sarah had said. She decided to take courage and stand her ground.

'Money has nothing to do with it. We love one another.' Meg looked at Frankie and smiled. 'We have so much in common. Our love of baking and one another. I never think of his wealth.'

'You see, Mother? Not everyone thinks of money when they marry. Meg and I are in love and no matter what you say, you cannot put a stop to our marriage.'

Florence stared at Meg. 'She is after your money!

It is as plain as the nose upon my face. Why you are throwing yourself on a backstreet girl, I do not know. You could have the choice of many a wealthy woman either here or in Paris.'

Meg stood up suddenly and looked down at the other woman, who spoke to her with no thought or care. 'I am not after his money. I care not if Frankie is a pauper or a prince. I will marry your son, with or without your permission, because we love one another.'

Frankie stood up and took his place beside her. 'Yes, Mother, we will be married. I don't know why I even broached the subject with you. After all, you can hardly dictate my life to me, not with the morals that you have in yours,' Frankie spat. Meg felt him squeeze her hand tightly.

'How dare you speak to your mother like that, in front of this trollop?' Florence retorted. 'If you want me to sign over your late father's money early, then you had better reconsider because you will not be receiving it or my blessing. This is exactly why the money was put in trust until you had sense and had grown out of womanizing. But I can see that this hussy has made you lose all your senses.' With a quivering hand, Florence placed a handkerchief to her mouth.

Meg gasped at the insults. 'I'll leave, Frankie, before I say something I regret.' She did her best to control her feelings. 'You should make peace with your mother. There is obviously more going on between you both than I know about.' Meg looked at Frankie's mother. 'However, you are wrong, Mrs Pearson. We do love one another. I know nothing about this inheritance that you are talking about and it is none of my business. If it is any consolation, I have been asking Frankie to wait to marry me. I wanted time to grieve over the loss of my mother. Perhaps if we are to marry, a longer length of time might make you happier, to prove to you that I do love him.'

Florence hid her head in her hands. 'No amount of time will make me want you as part of my family. My son deserves so much better than an alley-cat for a wife.'

'Mother, you have said enough. You do not need to lecture and to be so petty that you will hold me to ransom over my inheritance. An inheritance that Meg had no prior knowledge of.'

Meg reached for Frankie's arm. 'My love, I think that I am best going home. This is for you and your mother to settle between you. Please, don't argue over me. I do love you but not at the cost of coming between mother and son.'

With tears rolling down her cheeks, she stepped out of his arms and made her way into the hallway, nearly knocking the man lurking behind the door as she made for the horse and carriage that was waiting for her.

'Going home so soon?' the carriage driver asked, seeing tears rolling down her face. 'Is everything all right?' But before Meg could answer, Frankie burst from Grosvenor House as the carriage door shut behind Meg.

'Meg! Please come back in. My mother is a vindictive old woman. She cannot judge anyone, not the way she lives her life.' Frankie leaned through the open window of the carriage. 'Please, my love, come back.' He tried to reach for Meg's hand.

Meg sat firm. 'I'm going home, Frankie. You can tell your mother that she hasn't won. I still aim to marry you. However, it's better that you clear this talk of me wanting you for your money. I don't want to know any part of that side of your affairs. Please make that clear to her.' Meg struggled to speak from between her tears. 'I'll see you at the patisserie tomorrow. I'll come in a little earlier than usual so that we can discuss what is to be done.'

'Are we going home, miss?' the driver enquired as Frankie held onto the carriage door.

'Yes, please.' Meg kept her gaze fixed ahead as Frankie pleaded with her to stay.

'I love you, Meg. She'll not win!' Frankie yelled at the carriage as it drove away. As she swayed with the vehicle's movement over the cobbles, she wondered whether her love would win. Or would a love of money win Frankie's heart over?

15

'I will leave for home in the morning. I have sent Richard upstairs to see to the packing. There's no point staying in a house where I am not wanted.' Florence sniffed. 'She's not good enough for you, despite what she says. She is only marrying you for your money. Surely, you can see that, she hopes to have a better life for herself, coming from the backstreets and catching your eye, she's not good enough for you, Frankie?'

'You are wrong, Mother. She loves me and the money has nothing to do with it. Unlike you and your poodle Richard.'

Florence looked sternly at her son. 'You see, you are always judging me, but as soon as I have something to say, I am always wrong. You will thank me when the right woman comes along. Now, we will not hear another word about this Meg. Put her behind you.'

'I can't do that. I will marry her with or without your blessing. If it means that I have to go without my money until I am entitled to it, then so be it.'

'You are a fool, Frankie, just like your father would have been a fool if it had not been for my guidance. I wash my hands of you and you needn't suffer my company any longer. Richard and I will eat in our room this evening, and will be gone by the time you arise tomorrow.' Florence stood up and tidied her skirts. 'As for your inheritance, I will make sure that you have a long wait to receive it. Better that than to marry that backstreet scrubber and spend it all on her.'

'It was never to be spent on her. It was to develop my business and well you know it,' Frankie said as she made for the door, skirts rustling.

'Then your business dealings will have to wait because you are not getting your hands onto another penny until it is due legally.' Florence opened the door to the passageway and hesitated for a moment. 'I'll say my farewells now, Frankie. Please instruct your maid that we are to supper and breakfast in our room.'

'Mamma, please see sense! Don't leave like this.' Frankie watched as his mother climbed the stairs to her room and to Richard, her head held high. Hopefully, overnight, she would think better of her decision to leave him penniless and on his own. Frankie needed his inheritance. It was crucial that she came around to his way of thinking. Yet, it was clear she thought of Meg as some sort of trollop, who had seen her chance at fortune in luring Frankie in, and was dead set against the marriage. Maybe there was more to it. Perhaps she was worried about losing him as her son or didn't want to share him with another woman. Whatever the reason, she was determined not to like Meg and for him to wash his hands of the woman he loved.

* * *

Meg sat with her head in her hands, tears running down her face. 'She hates me, even though she doesn't know me. She thinks I'm after Frankie's money!'

'She doesn't know you very well then, does she?' Sarah replied. 'Even I know that it's his baking that keeps you interested in him and the fact that he's a sweet talker. He could be penniless if he made good

141

cakes and said the right things to you. I never want to be so besotted by anybody like you are with him.' She shook her head. 'Why don't you end it? You've always said he was way above our class. You'll always feel as though you don't deserve him, even though by the sounds of what you've told me, he's as poor as we are. It's just he doesn't show it.'

'But I love him, I can't help it. I should have married him straightaway and not told him to wait. It has given his mother the advantage to put a stop to our wedding plans and to withhold his inheritance.' But something inside of Meg had changed after this afternoon's events; she could feel it. She lifted her head and dried her tears. 'She will not stop us from marrying. Money should not make any difference to the love that we feel for one another. If it does, then he is as shallow as you say and I will leave him and everything he stands for.'

★ ★ ★

Dusk was falling as Frankie made his way into Sykes Yard. He needed to reassure Meg that, with or without his mother's blessing, he would marry her, although now he may not be able to assure her of the lifestyle that he had wanted for them both. In fact, he would probably have to sell Grosvenor House and move from affluent Headingley if he was to keep the two loves in his life — his patisserie and Meg.

Before totally giving in to despair, he would arrange to see his late father's solicitor in the morning and see if there was anything that could be done about an allowance without his mother's approval. Thankfully, the solicitor, Messrs Hartley and Son, were based in

Leeds on Commercial Street. Although he had never seen them without his mother's presence, it was time to do so.

He felt nervous as he knocked on Meg's door. This was the home that he had visited on many occasions but never with so much intent as now.

'Oh, it's you! Have you come to break my sister's heart again?' Sarah asked. He pushed past her without reply.

'Meg, I'm sorry. Please ignore my mother. She is nothing but a bigoted snob. Please don't think the same of me. I've left her and her poodle sulking in her bedroom. She is to return home tomorrow morning.' Frankie went to Meg, who was standing by the fireside and took her into his arms. 'Forgive her, forgive me for not telling you about my financial affairs. It should never have arisen and my mother did not need to bring it up in conversation. It makes no difference to my love for you.'

Frankie held Meg tightly and looked into her eyes. 'I know that you are not who my mother thinks you are. We are in love with one another, with or without money.'

'Oh Frankie, if you were a pauper on the street I'd still love you,' Meg said softly. 'I suppose your mother is only protecting you. It is what mothers do. Mine was just the same; she was always looking out for me and was relieved when you came along — a good honest man — and I know she would approve of you with or without money.'

'Well, I'm still intent on marrying you — if you will have me?' Frankie said and held her tightly. He told her of his plans to see the solicitor, adding, 'After all, I'm nearly at the age of twenty-five, I can't see what a few months' difference will make.'

'You need not just because of our marriage. It is not why I'm marrying you.'

'The sooner it is settled, the sooner my life is settled. I can plough on with my new bakery and give you the wedding you deserve. Without my money, I am not the best catch in Yorkshire, despite all my fineries and my business.' Frankie hung his head but Meg kissed him on the brow.

'You are the best catch any woman could possibly wish for in my eyes, Frankie Pearson. Now, when are we to be married? Let us set a date. Lately I've regretted making you wait. My mother would have understood and probably would have told me to get a move on before you change your mind about me. As for your mother, I'm sure she will come around. Besides, once we are married there is nothing she can do.' As Meg waited for an answer, Sarah shook her head in despair.

'Are you sure? I might yet end up in debtors' prison. I am not the man you deserve or the one you thought I was,' Frankie said, feeling anxious but relieved that Meg understood his predicament.

Meg held Frankie close and looked him deep in the eyes. 'You are the man I love and that is all that matters and you will never be penniless — you are too talented. Let's get married next spring, April, in Saint Mary's. We need not have a large wedding. I've no family besides Sarah and if you are not in favour with your mother then she will not be attending.'

'Spring it is then, with or without money. I'm not prepared to lose you if I am to lose everything else. I didn't think that you would want to be part of my family after meeting my mother and hearing my finances.'

'Oh, she wants you, don't you worry about that. You could be Jack the Ripper himself and she would still be daft enough to marry you,' Sarah said, stomping out of the room.

'Take no notice. She'll come around and anyway she's happy at the moment. She has been taken on at the music hall, the job of her dreams, so she tells me. Thornton's Music Hall and Fashionable Galleries, did you ever hear such nonsense?' Meg smiled. 'All will work out all right, I'm sure. Things are about to take a turn whether your mother wishes us well or not.'

'I hope so, I really do hope so, my love,' Frankie said as he held her tight. 'I want us to be happy together without any worries and at the moment I cannot see that at the moment . . . but I'm sure things will change eventually.'

★   ★   ★

It was Tuesday afternoon and Frankie was making his way across town. His mother and Richard had left at first light the previous day, saying only a curt farewell. Florence had not even deigned to visit his patisserie. Still, she would have taken delight in finding fault in everything that Meg and he had done.

He couldn't wonder if there was something more than his mother not wanting him to marry Meg. Why was she so against him having access to his inheritance? After all, it would only be a matter of months when he would be entitled to it officially. Surely, asking for a small amount in advance would not matter to anybody, especially when it was to be invested in yet another business. Hopefully, the whole affair would be resolved shortly when he spoke to the solicitor.

★   ★   ★

Frankie sat outside the office of Leo Hartley and listened to the grand wall clock tick away precious minutes. He couldn't help but think he should be back in his patisserie on the Headrow, planning for the next day and making sure the staff did as they were told. Hopefully, Meg would be taking care of all that. She could keep everything and everybody in line in his absence.

His palms were clammy with nerves. He disliked going behind his mother's back, but needs must if he was to survive. He stood to attention as Leo Hartley's office door swung open and the small bespectacled man emerged.

'Ah, Frankie, it is good to see you. I don't believe I have seen you since your father's death. That must be all of six years ago by now.' Leo Hartley held out his hand to shake; Frankie took it firmly and smiled.

'It will be seven come January, sir. I'm surprised and touched that you remember me,' Frankie said as he followed Hartley into the office and sat down in the chair that was offered to him as the solicitor went to take his own seat on the other side of the leather-covered desk.

'Time does fly, especially as you get older, but you'll not have that problem yet. You are still a young man.' Leo smiled and crossed his legs and looked across at Frankie, the son of his late best friend. 'Now, what can I do for you today? Transfer of deeds perhaps? I hear that you have been buying property in and around Leeds — a wise decision, might I say. Leeds is growing

146

daily and changing for the better.'

'Yes, indeed it is. That is why I have invested in new property. However, perhaps I have been a little foolish and hasty as I thought that in my latest buy in Headingley that I had a bargain. Which brings me to why I am here today.' Frankie caught his breath as the old man leaned forward. 'The property needs considerable repair and I was hoping that you would be able to grant me a small allowance from my father's money that he left to me.' Frankie registered the surprise that passed across Leo's face. 'I wouldn't be asking, but it has already cost me more than I expected and my business on the Headrow is only just starting to show a profit.'

Leo Hartley sat back in his chair. 'Does your mother know you are here?' he asked quietly.

'No, I'm afraid not. We are not seeing eye to eye at the moment,' Frankie sighed.

'I thought not, else you would not be here, telling me your sorry tale,' Leo said sharply. 'I'm afraid I have nothing more to do with your inheritance. Your mother took it out of my hands some months ago. She said that she was going to ensure that you had enough money when you needed it and not spend it on misguided whims. She didn't tell me that you were buying another property — she just warned me that you had extravagance tastes. That she would prefer for herself to hold the purse strings because of a situation arising just like this.' Leo sighed. 'You will have to ask your mother, who or what is in charge of your monies. We made a cheque out for all the amount, plus interest to her on the understanding that she would invest it well until the day you were entitled to it legally.'

'Wait, please tell me what you are saying is not right.

147

That my mother has all the money that I was entitled to! She can't have, she's never said anything to me.' Frankie felt himself turning white with fear.

'She was signed over every penny nine months ago. She told me that she was going to help set you up in business and then invest the rest. I understood that she had allowed you to buy your shop on the Headrow and, from what I hear, buy a bakery in Headingley. Property is always a wise investment in my eyes, although the direction of your business sense is a little lacking, catering for only the extremely rich.' Leo Hartley smiled. 'Surely you knew what had happened to the money? Your mother assured me that she would tell you that she was taking it in control as she was entitled to, as in clause 5 of your father's will?'

'She hardly gave me a penny, else I would not be here today. She has taken it without my knowledge.' Frankie held his head in his hands. No wonder his mother hadn't wanted him to have any more money or get wed — there would be no money available for her to spend. He knew now that there would be no money waiting anywhere for him. She would have found a way to make sure the money had remained with her, funding her decadent lifestyle.

Frankie saw the look of doubt on Leo Hartley's face as he stood up. 'I'm sorry, but your mother was adamant and I made sure all the paperwork was in order from us. It was still partly in her name. Your father had left it that way and, as I say, the clause allowed her to. After all, it was she and I who were in charge of your inheritance. I could see no reason not to entrust her fully with your money. After all, she is your mother.'

'Oh yes, she is my mother, and I am well aware of

that. Such a loving mother, always thinking of herself and nobody else. I know that you will have it all in order, else my father would not have been friends with you. Could I just see the paperwork and the clause that you speak of please?' Frankie reached across to the paperwork that was open on the solicitor's desk and read with horror the clause that did indeed give his mother sway over his inheritance.

Still ashen-faced, Frankie rose, top hat in hand. 'I'm sorry Mr Hartley, it is my mother who has questions to be answered from me. Thank you for your time. I won't be bothering you again.'

★ ★ ★

Meg looked up from her work and her hands froze. 'What on earth is wrong?' she said, as Frankie came into the bakery. He looked visibly shaken as he sat down on a stool, all the blood drained from his face.

'She's taken every penny. All my inheritance is in my mother's hands. Leo Hartley has listened to her tale of me being reckless with money and agreed to transfer it all to her in Paris, for safekeeping!' Frankie looked up at Meg. 'I'm ruined. She will not give me my money, even if she still has it.' Frankie sighed and held his hands out to be taken by Meg.

'Surely she will have invested it safely for you!' Meg said. 'She wouldn't steal money from her own son.' Meg held his face in her hands and kissed him gently as he shook with worry. She didn't know Florence Pearson well, but surely she could have her only son's well-being in mind when she had transferred his inheritance out of the hands of his solicitor.

'You have no idea what my mother would do to get

what she wants,' Frankie said bitterly. 'She respects nothing but her own needs. I will never see anything of my inheritance. What to do about my businesses, I don't know. I must stop my builders at the property at Headingley and put everything I have left into running this place. Either that, or sell my own home, but that would break my heart.' Frankie shook his head.

Meg ran her hand over his shoulders. 'Before you do anything, write to her or even visit her. It may not be as bad as you are thinking.'

'I only wish, my love. It looks like you will be marrying a pauper. That is, if you still want me?'

'I've always said, I love you, not your money. Now, the shop is busy. It makes you reasonable money, you are far from being a pauper. Stop seeing the dark side of things. Put the other shop on hold until you have seen or heard from your mother. Things will be all right.'

The two of them watched the customers coming and going into Frankie's shop. The bakery was always busy, but Frankie knew it could not carry two bakers. If he was going to struggle with money, there really was no need for a second baker at his patisserie. He loved Meg dearly — how could he sack the woman he loved so?

16

'Well. I didn't expect a lass, let alone one that was so small and as scraggy as you.' Larry Hopkirk looked at the reflection of Sarah as he peered into his dressing-room mirror while applying his stage make-up. 'I suppose you'll have to do. Burt Pickering is always tight with his money. He doesn't care that we artists have needs. It is true what they say: a Yorkshireman is a Scotsman with his pockets sewn up. Honestly, I don't know why I come up north. I'd rather be back in the smoke, on my own patch in Holborn.'

'I'm as good as any lad, and I can do anything a lad can do, if not better,' Sarah said sharply. 'And a Yorkshire man is nowt like a Scotsman, even I know that. I can't understand a word the jocks say when they come down to the cattle market.' This fella from down south knew nothing.

'Oh, you might be scrawny but you're not afraid of saying your mind.' Larry grinned. 'Now, pass me that green medicine bottle, it's my tonic before I go on stage. It's your job to make sure that it's always full, else woe betides you. As Vesta Tilly says, a little of what you fancy does you good.' Sarah passed him his bottle, wondering what was inside it and then watched, fascinated, as he leaned towards the mirror to add a line of kohl around his eyes. Then, he drew a stick of cream-coloured face paint down the bridge of his nose to highlight it.

'Does everyone put as much make-up on?' Sarah

asked. He was now swigging from the green bottle. Whatever was in there smelt very much like the breath of the town drunks.

'They do. It makes us stand out on the stage. Now, are my shoes cleaned? And have you got my clothes ready for when I come off stage? You are not here to ask questions, just to see to my needs. The less you talk to me, the better we will get on.' Larry stood up in his loudly checked suit and reached for his matching top hat.

'There, all done. Do you want me to see if they are ready for you to go on? I can hear the crowds clapping. You don't want them to get too rowdy.' Sarah reached for the door.

'Nay, we'll make them wait a bit longer, whip them up until they aren't bothered what they see as long as they are entertained. They've to wait for class like me.' Larry took another sip out of his bottle and patted his hat as he put it on his head. 'Lead on, Macduff. I'm ready for Leeds but is Leeds ready for me?'

Sarah looked at him and wondered why he called her Macduff and then led him through the labyrinth of passages to the wings where Burt Pickering was waiting with a stagehand. On stage, there was a backdrop painted with a row of houses and a false gaslight, which Larry Hopkirk was going to sing under, once the main curtain had been lifted.

'Larry, are you all right? Got everything you need?' Burt asked.

'Yes, apart from a complimentary bottle of whisky, but I'll make do and mend. It sounds like a full house?' The crowd was shouting his name.

'Aye, we will always do you proud here in Yorkshire,' Burt said and looked down at Sarah as she took in the atmosphere from behind the scenes and wished she was the one that was going on stage. 'Sarah seeing to your needs?'

'Yes, just as long as she doesn't rabbit on too much and gets on with her job.' Larry pulled his jacket straight and cleared his throat. 'Right, let's get on with it, then. The sooner I get my performance done, the quicker I can go for a drink.'

Sarah stood in the wings and watched as the stage-hand made sure the light was right for the outspoken cockney with his own style of comic verse and songs. The crowd clapped and cheered as the curtains drew back and Larry soaked up the applause before begin-ning his act, telling the jokes of the day and singing a song that he called his own but belonged to his one-time friend, Harry Randall, 'They All Take After Me'. Sarah smiled as she sang along, wishing that it was her on the stage, not singing but dancing as she joined in with the chorus:

Folks say I ought to think myself the luckiest of
    men-
I am the happy father of a family of 'ten'.
Not one of them will leave me while a penny I
    have got.
They are a nice fat-headed, ugly, lazy, and lowlife
    lot.

And they all take after me, they all take after me:
My peculiarity seems to run in the family.
They cadge, thieve, ev'ry chance they see.
There's Jack and Bill, they're on the 'mill',
And they take after me, And they take after me.

153

The girls all think they're handsome, tho' they're
 pug-nosed ev'ryone,
The paint and the powder they put on they have
 in by the ton;
To all the pubs and the pawnshops, too, they fre-
 quently visits pay;
They all love to stay out half the night and stay
 a-bed all day.

And they all take after me, they all take after me:
My peculiarity seems to run in the family.
They all drink whiskey in their tea,
They would all rather die than work,
And they all take after me, and they all take after
 me.

Now all the boys are champions at shifting pots
 of ale.
But never soil their hands with work, except when
 they're in gaol.
They never met a policeman but want to have his
 blood;
They delight in getting drunk and rolling in the
 mud.

And they all take after me, they all take after
 me . . .[1]

Burt Pickering stood next to her while Larry performed. He slapped Sarah on the back and bent
double laughing as he watched Hopkirk whip the

---

1   (They All Take After Me, Copyright 1893 Francis, Day and
Hunter. Words by T W Connor, Music by Harry Randall)

audience up into singing the last line of the chorus before he bade them farewell. 'Now, that's why this man is so famous. He knows how we all live and tells it as it is. Just listen, the crowd loves him, that's the second encore!'

Larry was called back on stage again and again. His song had reminded her of her next-door neighbours. There were plenty of them, and they always seemed to be in bother. *He could well have been singing about Harry's family,* she thought as she watched him wave and shout goodnight and thank everybody as he made his exit towards her.

'They'll be wanting my blood next, if I'm not careful. They've certainly had plenty of my sweat,' Larry growled. 'Towel, where's my towel?' He glared at Sarah, who hadn't realized she'd need to bring a towel out for him.

'Move yourself to his dressing room and get him one — quickly!' Burt Pickering yelled and Sarah ran like the wind back to his dressing room, nearly knocking over a juggler. She might have forgotten his towel but she was loving every minute. This was the life that she had dreamed of.

★　★　★

Meg waited outside the music hall. Although Sarah had said that Len would walk her home, she felt that she would rather see her home herself. Midnight was no time for a lass Sarah's age to be walking back with a lad not much older than herself, even though it gave her only a few hours in her own bed.

She hid in the shadows and watched the audience spill out of the wide main doors. Bright gaslight

155

shone down upon the cobbles and the steam from the crowd's breath disappeared into the cold midnight air. They talked and laughed as they made their way home, the night's entertainment a relief from the everyday humdrum of their lives.

Meg watched and waited as the crowds dispersed and the main doors were closed. Surely Sarah would be out shortly from the side entrance only the staff and performers used? She pulled her shawl around her. Suddenly, the door opened and the sound of Sarah laughing made her stand to attention. Meg smiled to herself; perhaps this was, indeed, the job for her sister.

Sarah came out with a man following her, holding the door open for her, followed by who she knew to be Len Pickering. Sarah soon stopped laughing when she saw her sister waiting for her and looked embarrassed.

'Meg, what are you doing here?' Sarah stared at her older sister.

'I thought that I would make sure that you arrived home safely. I was only sitting at home worrying about you.' Meg looked at the trio who had sounded so cheerful until she had arrived.

'There was no need. Len was walking me home and as it happens,' Mr Hopkirk is in accommodation not far away from us,' Sarah said. 'He says I can walk home with him each night.'

'That I have, my dear girl. Worry not, I'll see that your sister comes to no harm, she'll be fine with me.' There was a distinct smell of whisky on his breath. 'Young Len here is keeping us both company, so Sarah has double the escort.'

'That's very good of you, Mr . . .'

'Mr Larry Hopkirk, singer, comedian and panto-mime dame at your service, ma'am!' he called back over his shoulder. 'Now, if you don't mind I'm away to my wife, who I hope will have some supper waiting. I could eat a horse!' Larry bowed and tipped his top hat.

'Oh, you're Larry Hopkirk. I've heard of you, indeed you are famous,' Meg gasped.

'It is good of you to say so, my dear. I do believe I am, but I think of myself more as infamous,' Larry chuckled. 'Now, Len. Get yourself home, we will wend our way through these city streets without your help.' He patted Len on his shoulder and he was dismissed.

Sarah went quiet as the three of them walked down the dark streets.

'You must travel a lot, Mr Hopkirk. Do you not get fed up with wandering?' Meg asked.

'No, it's part of my life now, and I can bring my wife along with me most times. Annie enjoys seeing new cities and venues as much as I do,' Harry said, wending his way with a slight wobble along the streets.

'Was our Sarah helpful tonight? I hope she was. You know she has always wanted to work on the stage, she loves to dance,' Meg said, linking her arm through Sarah's.

'She will be my ideal helper once she gets used to my ways. If she loves the stage she should be encouraged. There's nothing quite like the smell of the greasepaint and the roar of a happy crowd to make the blood surge,' Larry said, splaying his arms open as if bowing to a crowd.

Meg said nothing as they approached Trafalgar Street where Larry Hopkirk said he had his lodgings. The man was obviously the worse for a drink and she was glad that she had taken the trouble to make sure that Sarah was home safely.

'I'll bid you farewell, my dear ladies. Until the morn, my Juliet!' Harry said as he opened the door to a voice that was shouting his name. 'The wife!' Larry grinned. 'I'll be in bother now, always am after celebrating my first night in a new venue.' Then he disappeared into the house, leaving Sarah and Meg on the doorstep.

'He was drunk, Sarah. Has he been like that all night? I'm glad I decided to meet you,' Meg sighed.

'He may be drunk, but I like him. I think he'll be good to work for. Len says he's one of the better ones. He's been firm with me but I've enjoyed working for him tonight and Len has taught me things that I never thought happened behind the stage. He was painting the backdrops and then he showed me how to mix the rouge that most acts use on their faces.' Sarah chatted non-stop until they reached Sykes Yard and home. She had found her niche in life, whether Meg liked it or not.

17

'Look, I'm sorry, but I'll have to put a stop to any further work on my shop and bakery.' Frankie stood in front of Jed Hurst, a man he regarded as a friend as well as an employee. He felt as if he was letting him down and losing face. 'I know I'm letting you down and that because you trusted me we have nothing in writing, but I'm sorry, I really need you to stop building.

'My bakery on the Headrow is not doing as well as I thought. I have to stop any extra layout,' Frankie said. He felt a flame of humiliation. Did he really want to share all the details?

'What about the brass you already owe me? It will soon be Christmas and my lads will need every penny. Can I expect to be paid by then? I bloody well hope so. I've my family to feed and these men to pay!' Jed glanced around at his men, who were starting to plaster the walls. Jed put his fingers to his mouth and whistled hard for them to stop. They all understood the signal, and turned to stare at the well-dressed man standing beside their employer.

'I'll see you right.' Frankie held his breath. 'I can manage to pay you if you can give me a week or two.' This was more than he'd ever asked of anyone, and to get a bad name as a late payer . . . that was the worst thing that could happen. His comment to Meg about debtors' prison could come true far more quickly than he feared.

'It better had only been a week or two. I thought you were rolling in it?' Jed said.

'It's all a simple misunderstanding.' Frankie didn't like the look on the workers' faces.

'Right, lads. Tools down. We're not wasting any more time here.' Jed turned back to Frankie. 'You'd better come up with the money before the end of the month, else you'll be hearing from me or my boys,' he said with raw menace in his voice. 'There's plenty of folk that wants the best, but can't pay for it. I thought you were better than that.'

Frankie felt deeply embarrassed. He never had any intention of not paying for the work that his friend had done. He always honoured his bills. 'I am, and I can pay. Just give me time.'

The men's tools clattered into their sacks and the plaster was left discarded. Everyone around him seemed to throw Frankie filthy looks. The men had guessed, even if Jed hadn't made it too obvious.

'Well, see that you do. Then we'll come back and finish the job. I hate being taken for a mug, especially by someone I thought was a good friend. You promised me this would all be fine!' Jed placed his cap on his head and picked up his bag of tools. 'I'll send you a bill for what you already owe. Prompt payment will be expected!'

Frankie watched as Jed and his workers walked out of the shell of a building. Some of the men spat on the floor, telling him exactly what they thought of him. He'd have to raise the money somehow, else his name would be mud all over Leeds. Jed could be handy with his fists, if he had problems with payments.

How have I come to this? he thought as he looked around at the half-plastered walls and the windows yet to be fitted. The bakery was in a worse state than when he had first bought it. Apart from a new roof, it was a long way from being finished.

★ ★ ★

Frankie stared at the letter in his trembling hand. It had taken his mother nearly a month to reply to his demands, and now he wished he had never heard from her at all.

He crumpled the letter up and felt his heart beating faster than it had ever done before. He didn't know what to do. He had cut everything back to the bone in the bakery and was living as meagrely as he knew how. Thank the Lord, Grosvenor House had been passed to him without any let or hindrance. It was his. If it came to the worst, he could sell it.

He opened out the letter, and read once more.

24 Rou de San
Paris

3rd November 1894

My Dear Frankie,
   Really! How could you write to your mamma in such a way?
   Yes, I did transfer your inheritance to a bank here in Paris, I thought that it was to be in both our interests. After all, my dear, you have had some of your inheritance already and you inherited the family home. I thought that it was time for me to intervene before you gaily spent it all frivolously on your wants.

I was willing to let you spend some of your father's fortune but I thought it only right that you invested half into something that would give you a good return for your money. Therefore, I have invested your money in purchasing three of the most fascinating paintings that you have ever seen. I'm sure they will triple in price in the years to come. Two of them are by a well-known painter called Henri de Toulouse Lautrec. He is a strange little man, although he has talent. I came across him at the Moulin Rouge. He did a series of posters for them. The other one is by my darling Richard. He really is going to be famous, a big name in the right circles. You'll see, my darling. You'll thank me eventually.

I do hope that you have changed your mind about Richard. He really is a darling. He treats your mamma with such care and love. I'm sorry we both left on such a sour note. Perhaps next time I come over (although it will not be for a while now) we can kiss and make up.

I do hope that you have changed your mind about marrying that common bit of a thing. You could do so much better.

I only have your best interests in mind.

All my love as ever,

Mamma

Frankie screwed up the letter again. His best interests!

It was her best interest that his mother had in mind. All the money was spent on three paintings, and he'd not even heard of the fella known as Toulouse-Lautrec. As for the one by Richard, that money had gone straight into her bank and well she knew it. His mother always had been jealous of the money that had been left him and now she was showing her true colours. No wonder she would not be seeing him in the near future. There was nothing there for her to come for.

In the meantime, what was he to do? He was struggling to pay the wages to his girls and hated himself for not being honest with his friend Jed. He must find the money to pay him somehow.

★   ★   ★

Frankie sat at Meg's kitchen table, his head in his hands. It was Sunday and he had decided to visit Meg. He needed to share his worries.

'She's spent every penny. Every blasted penny! It's all gone on her lover and a fella that I've never heard of before that she says is some well-known French artist. No matter how good he is, his paintings are not going to pay the bill I've run up with Jed. Besides, I'll never see a penny of that!'

Meg put her arms around his shoulders. 'You must be able to get it back from her somehow.'

'No, I'll never get it back. I'm ruined, Meg. She's ruined me! What a fool I've been, spending money before I actually had it.' Frankie looked at Meg. 'What am I to do? The debtors' prison beckons . . . '

'Stop it, Frankie. You are a long way off from that. You have no idea what it is to be really without money.' Meg sighed. 'You own Grosvenor House. You could see the bank, and get a loan against it. That ring on your finger must be worth a small fortune if you have to need to go to a pawn shop.'

'Mortgage my house, never! Nor will I ever sell it. It's my family home. I have thought about it but I love every brick in the place. So, never will I ever do that! As for the pawnshop, I couldn't! I couldn't show my face in somewhere like that. Everyone knows who I am. The scandal!' Still, Frankie looked down at the ruby dress ring that he had been left by his grandmother and knew it to be worth quite a bit.

'Well, that's what I would do. You'd rather have the scandal of not paying my bills or my staff? Besides, you don't have to show your face at the shop; I'd take them for you. I know how to barter with Ethan Leavesly. I've done it so many times over the years, he can't pull the wool over my eyes. We had to sell and pawn many things when my father died. That is why our house is so sparse. You get used to living without luxuries.' Meg sighed. 'If you came back into the money, you could always buy your things back — providing Ebenezer hasn't sold them.'

'I've never been so desperate. I should have known to learn how to walk before running headlong into trouble as I have.' Frankie started to pull his ring off his finger. 'It's twenty-two carat gold, set with the finest ruby. You'll try to get a good price for it? You'll not give it away?' He handed it over. 'I'll bring you some silver, as well. If I can raise enough to pay Jed what I owe him, that at least will be a relief.'

'I'll haggle for every penny. He'll give you two months' grace for you to retrieve your things although he'll charge you interest on the money he loans you. Will that be all right with you?' Meg looked at the precious ruby ring as it glistened in the flat of her palm.

Frankie clearly had no idea how a pawnshop operated. He looked for a moment as if he was about to argue then quietly said, 'Yes, I suppose it will have to be, but I can't see myself in a position of ever being able to buy them back. They are lost because of my stupidity and pride.'

'Stop blaming yourself,' Meg said firmly. 'Your mother is as much to blame — more, so. She has stolen your inheritance.' She kissed Frankie on the cheek. 'Don't worry, my love. Jed will get paid and I'll make sure the pawnbroker does not take advantage of us.'

★   ★   ★

Meg stood beneath the pawnbrokers' sign, the three brass balls hanging above her head. Along with the ring, she had a diamond necklace that had belonged to Frankie's mother, two silver candelabras and a set of silver fish knives.

She had worried about carrying such precious belongings along the streets on a Saturday afternoon, but now as she opened the door into the shop that she had traded with so many times, she felt quite faint at the thought of the money that she would try to barter for.

'Ah, Miss Fairfax. What can we do for you today? You always know I look forward to seeing your pretty face.' Ethan Leavesly spoke from a dark recess.

'I've come to do business for a friend. These aren't my things that I'm here to pawn, so I'll expect a fair price.' Meg looked at the grey-haired small man, dressed in a velvet smoking jacket and the hat to match, a gold-coloured tassel hanging down at the side. The shop was full of jewellery, gold and silver. The walls were alive with the ticking of clocks.

'My dear, I always give a fair price to you. A friend,

165

you say? They must be one of wealth.' He lifted up the silver to examine the mark, and weighed it on some scales as he glanced across at Meg. 'You've not been a-thieving, have you, Meg Fairfax? This is far higher quality than what you usually bring me. I don't want the peelers raiding my shop. I keep my nose clean in these hard times.' He peered at Meg as she delved into her pocket and put the ruby ring and diamond necklace down on the counter.

'No, no. They are genuinely for a friend. He's fallen on hard times.' Meg watched as Ethan took in the quality of the diamonds and the gold marks.

'They are indeed of good quality. Let me see what I can offer. Usual terms acceptable to your friend if my price is right?' Ethan's eyes narrowed to slits as he counted the money out.

'Two months to repay, if possible. You know that it's worth the wait,' Meg said sharply.

'Aye, Meg, I'll offer you a month and ten per cent interest on every pound that I'm counting out. Not everybody can afford stuff like this.' Ethan slid his notes and coins in front of Meg.

'Another five, and you make it two months' grace. Else, I'll take it back with me.' Meg counted the notes then reached for her shawl ready to retake the booty home within it.

'Three pounds more, and I'll agree two months' grace. Take it or leave it. You'll not get a better price in the whole of Leeds.' Ethan sat back, watching Meg's face.

Meg paused. 'You are a hard man, Ethan Leavesly. You know it's all worth more.'

'Aye, but I've to sell it on and who's to say it isn't stolen?' Ethan smirked.

166

'You are the thief, old man. I'll accept — although I am tempted to take it elsewhere, but you don't sell it in the next two months. My friend should be able to repay you by then.' Meg knew really that Frankie had no means to repay the pawnbroker — at least, not immediately — but at least this bought Frankie some time, with a way to pay his friend Jed and keep his family home.

'Nice doing business with you. If there is anything else your *friend* needs to pawn, tell him to come back to me. I pay the best prices, and well you know it.' Ebenezer smiled, showing his blackened teeth to Meg as she put the money in her bag and left the shop leaving the bell jingling behind her.

She hated dealing with Ethan Leavesly. It reminded her of when her mother was alive when they had to pawn things on a weekly basis. She had had no option then or now. But he was no different from any other pawnbrokers, and, by his own lights, he had given her a fair price. Still, she knew all too well that like all those in his business, he had no heart when it came to making money from the poor.

18

It was Sunday afternoon. Joe Dinsdale stood outside Ted Lund's bakery. Recently, Ted had sounded more and more desperate to sell his dilapidated bakery.

As of yet, he'd had no decent offers. Joe looked up at the roof that looked sound, and the windows that, once sanded and painted, would make the shop look ten times more respectable. He knew that inside was getting past its best, but when Meg Fairfax had been there she had made it clean and had kept it tidy and had many a customer. So, it couldn't be that bad and just needed some of his money spent on it to make it look better cared for.

He put his hands in his pocket and took a final look at the property he had almost decided to buy. Before he did, he had to ensure that he had the baker to go with it — and that would be the lass that Ted Lund had done wrong by. He'd visit Meg Fairfax first and make sure that she would come and work for him or even be his partner in his new venture. She'd made good money for Ted, and he'd never shown her one ounce of gratitude. If she could do the same for him, he would willingly make her part of the deal. It had to be worth a conversation, at least.

★ ★ ★

Meg's hands embraced a cup of tea, with Frankie sat across the other side of the table. Upstairs, Sarah was still in her bed. She had not returned from the music hall until well after half past twelve the previous night, accompanied by Larry.

'Did I get you enough?' Meg asked, as Frankie counted out the money that she had secured him at the pawnshop the previous day. Frankie had insisted on coming over as soon as possible — not because he didn't trust Meg, but because he didn't want the risk of someone talking and the money being stolen.

'He's given you more than I expected, but not the full price that the items are worth. But I suppose you never get the full price.'

Frankie picked up the wedge of money and looked at it. 'There's enough here to pay Jed and make things right with him. A bit leftover that will come in handy.' Frankie sat back, flooded with relief. 'Thank you, Meg, I don't think I'd have been able to do that without you. I should be able to keep going at the bakery now, the leftover money will pay for the ingredients I need for the coming months and with Christmas not far away, I should make more money over the counter.'

'Will you be able to reclaim your things from Ebenezer? He gave you an extra month to do so.'

'I don't know. I'll have to see. After all, like you say, they are only possessions. Much better that my conscience is clear,' Frankie sighed.

'If you like, I can bake you more down-to-earth items for the patisserie shop; they don't cost as much as your patisseries, and everyday customers would welcome them in the tea room. I thought that was why you were first attracted to me in the first place — my skills in everyday baking,' Meg said, trying to suggest a way that he could still make money but cut his costs.

'We will see. I'd prefer to see how things go. Then, if we need to, I'll bring your recipes into play.' Frankie noticed the hurt expression on Meg's face. 'I still have to build my reputation around my patisserie skills. Don't take offence.'

'I thought it might help . . . But, of course, you are right.' Meg smiled. Both stopped in their tracks and turned to look at who was knocking on the kitchen door. Neither Meg nor Sarah were expecting visitors and Frankie quickly put the money that he had been counting into his pocket before Meg went to open the door.

'Ah, Meg. I'm glad you are home,' Joe Dinsdale said. 'There's something I want to ask you. May I enter?'

'Yes, but I have a visitor already. You'll know Mr Pearson, I presume. He places an order with you occasionally.' Meg felt her cheeks blush, as Joe Dinsdale gave her a knowing look and she couldn't help but feel guilty at being caught with a single man in her house, not to mention the deals that she and Frankie had just undertaken. However, she knew Joe Dinsdale never visited anybody except for business.

'Oh, I'm sorry, I don't want to disturb you. Could you call into my shop tomorrow? That might be better?' Joe tipped his hat to Frankie. 'It's of a personal nature.'

'There's nothing wrong is there?' Meg asked, wondering just why Joe was on her doorstep and that it could only be bad news.

'No, no. Only something I've been thinking about, but it is best said in private. I'll be off and leave you two to your tea.' Joe stepped back and smiled. 'Hope to see you tomorrow. Say, just before five? It's my quietest time if you can make it then?' Joe noticed the puzzlement on Meg's face. 'It's nowt to worry about. In fact, it could be to the contrary, if you are happy with what I've to say.'

Meg watched Joe walk out of the yard and then closed the door behind him. 'Well, I don't know what that was about. I suppose if I don't go and see him, I'll never find out, so I'd better show my face.' Meg looked first at Frankie and then at the top of the stairs, where Sarah stood in her nightdress, yawning.

'If it's not him jabbering, it's somebody else knocking on the door to see you.' Sarah threw a dirty look at Frankie. 'Try to be quiet. I need my sleep,' she growled and turned to go back to bed.

'If you had a normal job, you'd not be sleeping at this time of the day,' Meg shouted back as she sat down to drink her tea but then regretted it. At least Sarah was working and bringing in money.

'Joe Dinsdale obviously didn't want to say what was on his mind in front of me,' Frankie said. 'You don't owe him anything, do you?'

Meg shook her head. 'I don't owe him a penny. I never ask him for tick, especially since that business with Ted Lund.'

'Well, he's obviously got something on his mind and it involves you. You had better meet him and see what it is,' Frankie said, before grinning. 'I don't have a rival, do I?'

'Don't be daft. He's old enough to be my father!'

'Aye, but he'll be worth a bob or two. Happen my mother was right, that you are just after my money!' To take the sting from his words, Frankie pulled Meg onto his knee and kissed her. Both laughed and pulled faces at one another as Sarah knocked her protest on

171

the floor and shouted down another complaint about the noise.

'Is that what you think, Frankie Pearson? Anyway, he'd not put up with that'en, so no, I'd better stick with the one I've got.'

Meg returned Frankie's kisses and found comfort in his arms. Whatever Joe Dinsdale wanted, it could wait until the next day. Frankie was in her arms. His money worries were settled for the coming weeks — thanks to her — and that was all that mattered right now.

★ ★ ★

After a long day at the patisserie, Meg quickly made her way to Joe Dinsdale's shop. She was tired and fraught. First thing, she had helped Frankie with the making of the eclairs and a new recipe of almond tarts. Then, while he went to see Jed Hurst, she had been up and down stairs to the tea rooms with no time for a break.

She had been surprised to see Frankie running to the cost of such expensive pastries after all the financial woes. She loved Frankie dearly, but when it came to money, he could spend it a lot faster than he earned it. She was beginning to realize Frankie had been so used to money all his life that without it, he was lost.

As she walked, she mulled things over. She didn't know how much longer she could work in the patisserie. It was trying — they loved one another, but their ideals were different. She gathered her thoughts as she approached Dinsdale's. She tidied her hair and skirts and then walked through the door to be met by a beaming George.

172

'Meg! I haven't seen you for a while. How are you keeping?' George smiled as she walked up to him and looked around for Joe Dinsdale.

'I'm managing, George. How are you? Still working for Mr Dinsdale, I see.' Meg saw the young lad blush as he looked at her; she knew he was sweet on her but too shy to say anything.

'Yes, he's a good boss and I like it here. I'm not frozen in winter, like some of my mates who work outside. There's a lot to be said for that,' George grinned. 'Mr Dinsdale is waiting for you in the back room. I've been asked to show you through. He's boiled the kettle and even opened a new packet of biscuits that came in from Crawford's this morning.' George hesitated. 'He's up to something, but I don't know what.' He went quiet as they heard Joe Dinsdale emerge from the small kitchen at the back of the shop.

'Ah, Meg, I thought I heard your voice. It's good of you to come, lass. Come and have a cup of tea with me. I've something I want to be asking of you.' Joe Dinsdale smiled as he ushered her into the small storeroom and kitchen beyond. 'Can I offer you a drink? The kettle's on the boil.' Joe nodded to the iron kettle that was sitting on the side of the small fireplace. Whatever Joe was about to ask her, it must have been important. He never offered tea to anyone.

'Thank you, that would be lovely.' Meg watched as he poured water in the teapot and placed it on the table, before opening a biscuit tin.

'Now, you must be wondering what this is all about. Tea and biscuits? There must be something I'm after, and you are right, there is.' Joe sat back in his chair and looked across at the young lass while she hesitated to sample the delicious looking biscuits. He motioned for her to help herself. 'I'll come straight to the point. I'm thinking of buying Ted Lund's bakery. But I needed to talk to you first because I want you to run it for me.'

Meg swallowed the piece of biscuit that she had just bitten into and looked across at Joe. She couldn't believe what she was hearing.

'I know that you made that place a success when Ted was in Ireland. Folk say they miss you like nobody's business. The old bugger has gone back to his old ways and now just wants to jigger off, back to the Emerald Isle. You know his heart hasn't been in his business for a long time. I think now is the time to make him an offer.' Joe shook his head. 'But I need someone to run the bakery and supply my shop, too. I know that you are just the lass to do that.'

Meg stared at him, wide-mouthed in surprise. 'Me! Even after Ted accused me of taking his money?'

'Aye, I know he did that and I know the truth of it. I also know you are as honest as the day is long. There's not a better baker in these parts. Now, I'd want you to work as hard as you did for Ted, but there would be better pay in the offing. You'd be your own boss, and — who knows? — after a few years, you'd happen to buy the bakery from off me. As long as you kept supplying me at this shop, I'd be open to offers. I know nowt about baking; it's the only thing we don't have in my shop.'

This was everything Meg had dreamed off. If she was careful, and if Joe paid her as well as he was promising, she would be able to save and make it a goal in life to buy the bakery herself.

'Of course,' Joe said quickly, 'I've to buy it first. Ted might decide that he doesn't want me to have it.' Joe narrowed his eyes. 'Are you interested?'

Meg gulped down a scalding mouthful of tea, giving herself time to gather her thoughts. Her heart was hammering in her chest and she didn't want her voice to tremble when she spoke. Carefully, she placed her tea cup back in its saucer. 'I'm more than interested,' she began. 'This is all I've ever dreamt of. I'd never let you down. You can bank on me.' Meg hesitated. 'There is only one problem. I work for Frankie Pearson at the moment and I wouldn't want to let him down either.'

'I know you work for him and seeing him at your home on Sunday morning, I'm guessing that he's more than just your employer.' Joe watched Meg struggle to consider whether Frankie would understand.

'He's my beau. In fact, he's asked me to marry him.' Meg smiled at Joe. 'He knows I loved every minute in Ted Lund's bakery. If he loves me, he'll not stand in my way. Besides, his place is a patisserie. We would not be in competition with one another. He'll understand. I've even offered to bake him some straightforward fayre but he's not interested, even though I'm sure it would sell in his shop.'

'Well, I hope he'll not begrudge me stealing you to work in my bakery — or should I say *our* bakery!' Meg saw a twinkle of excitement in his eye.

'Providing you can buy the place, and that your terms are acceptable to me, I think I'll be able to persuade him.' Meg stood up and offered Joe Dinsdale her hand to shake. With a few simple words, he'd made another dream of hers come true — and it meant that she would be working for her own kind. Frankie would understand, he would have to understand . . . wouldn't he?

Frankie looked at Meg and gave an indulgent sigh. 'How could I be angry? I know that bakery was your love long before I met you. You understand that I feel the same way about my patisserie. I know you think that I am irresponsible with the money I spend, that my customers are spoilt and rich — but it is what I love, too.' He shook his head. 'As long as you are happy, you have my blessing to go and work for Joe Dinsdale and I hope that the bakery soon becomes your own.'

'I love you, Frankie Pearson.' She went and hugged him tight. 'I just hope that Ted Lund sells Joe the bakery and I hope that Joe has the sense not to mention that I will be working for him, else Ted would never sell it to him.' Meg paused. She had to be sure. 'You really don't mind if I leave here to work for him? You aren't just saying that to keep me happy?'

'My love, you know my plight. I can hardly afford what staff I'm going to be left with. I'll simply work longer hours. As I say, you go with my blessing. Down the line, if you manage to buy Lund's bakery, then we can combine forces — if I am still trading. I do not doubt that you will make the bakery a success. In fact, I have more faith in you than I have in myself at this moment in time.' Frankie looked downcast.

'Frankie Pearson, you stop that! You have the best patisserie in Leeds and well you know it. Everyone gets money worries in their life. The only problem here is that you're not used to them. Between us, we will feed both the rich and the poor of Leeds and we will both be successful, so stop feeling sorry for yourself,' Meg said sharply.

'I hope that you are right. If only my mother had done right by me, I could have bought you Ted Lund's bakery myself.' Frankie kissed her and held Meg tight.

'We'll both have to knuckle down, but I'm not afraid of hard work and you aren't either.' That was one of the things she loved about Frankie most. 'It may be that in a few months we will own a chain of shops and bakeries, with our names above the door.' Meg had been given a chance, and she was going to grab it with both hands.

19

'You drive a hard bargain, Joe Dinsdale. You always have known when to strike a man when he's at his most vulnerable and wanting to make a new life for himself.' Ted looked harshly at the man he had known all his life, as Joe made his final offer for his dilapidated bakery.

'Now, don't be like that. It's a fair offer. You want to get rid of it and I'm offering you a decent price.' Joe held his hand out to be shaken.

'What do you want with a bakery, anyway? Your shop is full of tins and packets. You want nowt with taking on a bakery.' Ted hesitated and put his hands through his thinning hair. 'Tha's not a baker, neither is your missus, so you are going to have to take somebody on.'

'I might, if I can find the right person. I thought, if I had my own bakery, it could supply the shop. The amount of times George and I have to turn folk away when they ask for a loaf of bread is nobody's business.' Joe didn't want admit that he already had the baker in hand.

'I hope you send your customers my way when they're asking for bread. I'm the nearest to you.' Again, Joe didn't like to admit that none of his customers wanted to go near Ted's place.

'I do, but that's why I need your bakery. It's the closest. Folk want their goods, fresh.' Joe hoped that he was not losing the deal.

'Another fifty pounds and it can be yours. But you are buying yourself nowt but work, and you are not getting any younger.' Ted held out his hand to be shaken.

'Forty, and we've a deal. I'll get my solicitor to handle it straightaway.' Joe spat on his hand to seal the deal.

'I'll see mine tomorrow.' Ted spat on his hand, and they shook. The solicitors would do the necessary paperwork, but this was all the pair needed between them.

Ted looked around his old home with a hint of sadness. 'It's time to put the past behind me. Leeds is changing too much for my liking.'

'Who's bought your house, Ted? You've been here a long time. The street won't be the same without you.' Joe realized that Leeds was losing one of its well-known occupants.

'He's a fella called Tom Askew. One of the managers at Hunslet Mill.' Ted shook his head. 'He came around with his strumpet, that Daisy Truelove. He's setting her up in a house of her own, even though he's married with a family. She's a forward minx! She strutted around this house and found fault in nearly everything. Then they both told me to keep it quiet until they had bought it and moved in.'

Joe shook his head. 'You'd think she'd choose somewhere else to live with her fella. You don't wash your dirty linen in public. She always was a bit forward. I bet her mother has had plenty to say about it. She'll be ashamed of her, of that I'm sure.'

'It's these young women. They think they can do anything now that the government has given them more say in their lives, it was a sad day when they

179

could look after their own money and property when married.' Ted moaned. 'I'm glad I've not got one in my life.'

'Nay, Ted. It's nice to come home to a warm home and a cooked meal. I'd miss my old lass.' Joe stood up to leave.

'No, I'm best with my own company and that's the way I'll stay when I get to Ireland. Now, we'll get our deal done as soon as we can and then I'll be free of this place and the bakery and I can't say I'll regret leaving either behind.' Ted saw Joe out.

★ ★ ★

'Oh, Daisy, I can't believe you're doing that!' Meg sat across the table from her best friend and listened to her excited voice as Daisy told her about her move into her new home. 'What does your mother think? Surely she doesn't condone it all?'

'She's had to accept it. It'll make her life easier, anyway. She's only herself and my father to look after, then. Although things are not that rosy between my brother and his wife, even though they are only recently married. I can see our lad returning home yet.' Daisy sat back and grinned. 'You'd a close shave there with him. I knew it would never last, he's such an arrogant sod.'

'But you'll not even be living over the brush with your man. He'll still be with his wife and Ted Lund's house will need a lot of attention just like the bakery does.' Meg couldn't believe that her best friend could be so brazen with her life.

'I hear Joe Dinsdale's bought the bakery. What does he want with that? It's a pity your fella won't buy it for you, but I suppose he'll not want to lose your help in his bakery.' Meg wondered whether to tell her friend the news that she had not shared with a soul.

'Patisserie, Daisy. Don't forget, it is a patisserie,' Meg said with a grin. Then she hesitated, before plunging on. 'A bit is happening in my life as well. I can't let you be the centre of gossip.'

'What's Sarah done now?' Daisy said and folded her arms and laughed, waiting to hear.

'No, it's not our Sarah's doing. She's as happy as Larry working at the music hall. She's besotted by that Larry Hopkirk and his wife now. She's been invited into their home a time or two of late. No, it's about my news and we're not too far apart, me and you.' Meg watched Daisy's eyes widen.

'You are going to live with Frankie! If so, you should practise what you preach!' Daisy exclaimed.

'No, I'm not. But I'm the one that's going to be baking for Joe Dinsdale on the understanding that if I can ever afford it, I can buy the bakery from off him eventually as long as I keep supplying him with baking.' Meg looked at the delight upon Daisy's face.

'You sly devil! But what has Frankie to say about all this? Will he not miss you working for him? And won't you be his rival?'

'He's given me his blessing. He was looking at cutting back on his staff anyway. The patisserie is not as busy as he had hoped, although Christmas will soon be with us and then people will be wanting all sorts from him.' Meg hoped that Daisy would not detect her lying — she didn't want Daisy to know the truth that Frankie had no money because of buying the second bakery.

'He's doing all right though, isn't he? It always looks

181

so swish and he has a certain sort of folk that come and go. Anyway, everybody knows he's so wealthy, you can tell that by just the way he dresses — the dandy!' Daisy grinned.

'Yes, he's all right, but he's not as wealthy as he seems. Looks can be deceiving.' Meg distracted Daisy by offering her another piece of shortbread.

'Now, that is a surprise. Who'd have thought it!' Daisy said. 'But he's still a good catch, just like my Tom, even though he isn't totally mine.'

'No, Frankie will never be a hundred per cent mine. He's in love with his dream of the perfect patisserie. I will be glad to get back to serving my own kind, although I do love every inch of him,' Meg sighed.

'Men! There's always a fault with every single one of them, but we can't live without them. I know I shouldn't be moving into that house of Ted Lund's but I don't want to lose Tom and it beats skulking about behind folk's backs, meeting in a warehouse and down by the docks where nobody can see us,' Daisy said as she looked down at her feet. 'As long as his wife doesn't find out. I feel sorry for her, the poor cow. She looks after all his children while he plays about with me. I think I have the better deal. A paid roof over my head, a tentative lover — but I've still got my independence.'

Daisy might think that she had a good deal, but Meg questioned it. She'd have no respect from the married women of the district. They have no time for a floozy like Daisy, who might lift her skirt up for any of their men. Gossip would be rife and well she knew it would be when she moved into Ted Lund's old home.

'Are you not bothered what folk will say about you? I couldn't live like that. Frankie has asked me and

Sarah to live with him but it's not right until we are married,' she said.

'Meg Fairfax, you don't approve, do you? I never thought that you were that prudish! You know full well what we get up to but now we are doing it under a roof of our own, it's a different tale. I'm not walking the streets, you know. We are simply showing commitment to one another,' Daisy said sharply.

'But he's married, Daisy. He'll never be yours,' Meg said quietly.

'He says once his youngest is old enough to work, he's leaving them all behind. He doesn't love his wife. He's only eyes for me.' Daisy pushed her chair back. 'If I didn't know better, I'd say you were jealous.'

'Don't be daft! I don't want you to get hurt, that's all.' Meg looked at Daisy as her cheeks flushed in anger.

'Well, I'm off. It's up to you what you think. But if your fella is in trouble with money, I'd say I've got the better one. At least my Tom makes good money at the mill, unlike Frankie's posh bakery.'

'Daisy, I'm sorry, and Frankie is not in that much trouble. Please don't be telling folk that he is,' Meg said. She was beginning to regret ever confiding in her friend at all.

'I won't, but I thought that you'd be happier for me and Tom. He does love me, you know.' Daisy picked up her posy bag. 'I hope that it works out for you at Ted Lund's old bakery. At least I can look forward to a decent loaf of bread in the morning, one without sawdust in it. Now, I'll be on my way. I'm meeting Tom at one. We are choosing wallpaper for the front room. It will look a lot cosier by the time I've finished with it. Old Ted has never spent a penny on the place, just like he hasn't on your bakery. Mucky old devil! The sooner he's in Ireland, the better.'

'I don't think Joe Dinsdale will have told him that it is me that is going to be baking for him, otherwise he would have had something to say.' Meg walked with Daisy to the door and touched her arm. 'I wish you well, Daisy. As long as you are happy, I didn't mean to offend.'

'I know. You can't help who your heart loves, no matter what your head tells you. You make a success of that bakery and I'll wait for the day when my Tom is mine alone. I think I know which one will come first.' Daisy leaned forward and kissed Meg. 'Perhaps we are both as foolish as one another when it comes to our choice of men. And don't worry, your secrets are safe with me.'

Meg's hand lingered on Daisy's sleeve as she opened the door for her to go. 'Take care, my friend.'

'I will and don't forget, I'll want a fresh white loaf every other morning and I'll tell the lasses at the mill that you're back in business. You'll soon be able to buy Joe Dinsdale out. That fella of yours will have to look out. He's got a rival in you.'

20

'I can't believe that he's been making bread in these conditions.' Joe Dinsdale picked up the discarded bread tins and looked at the numerous mice droppings.

'He's certainly let it go to the dogs since I left.' Meg gazed around her and thought of how she had left the bakery. Tidy, clean and in good order. 'I'll soon get it back to how I left it, because I can't work in a scrow like this.' Meg picked up a bread tin. There was no end of work to be done before she would be happy to sell her bread from here.

'Aye, well. Whatever you need to get it decent, you let me know,' Joe said. 'We might as well get it right from the start.' He opened one of the oven doors, only to find a mouse nestled inside. Quickly, he shut the door again. 'These ovens are fit for nowt. The ovens themselves are rusty and they must take a lot of wood and coal to get them up to heat in the morning. Happen I should get gas ones for you or even worse, I'm beginning to think I should never have wasted my brass and your time. You'd have been a lot better baking with that fella of yours. He'll not be overrun with vermin and have ovens that have seen better years.'

'There's nothing wrong with the ovens — it's just Ted hasn't looked after them.' Meg ran her hand along the edges and smiled. 'They work well. In fact, I prefer to use these than the ones Frankie has. I'm not fond of using gas, even though coal and wood are mucky. Don't look so worried, there's nothing here that can't be sorted without a bit of elbow grease and hard work. You'll not know the place once I get down to it.' Meg looked around at the task in front of her.

'Let's start as we mean to go on. Put an order in with George once you are ready to start baking and I'll get the lad to bring it around for you. The rest, wood and coal and the such like . . . I'll order as the weeks go on.'

Joe leaned back and looked at his latest recruit. 'Now, let's talk about what brass! I've been thinking, seeing you'll be running this place and I know nowt about baking, that we go halves with the profits each week. Like I say, after a time, you could buy the bakery off me. Not that I'll be thinking of parting with it just yet.'

Meg knew he was talking about more money than she had ever dreamed of. She also knew all too well what she had been making for Ted Lund before he so ungenerously sacked her.

'I'm not going to argue with that. I'm just going to enjoy baking,' Meg smiled.

'Tha'll be baking for me, don't forget. I'll expect to see good profits and baking of a good standard. If I see both of them, then both of us will be happy.' Joe shook Meg's hand and looked around. 'Do you want to borrow George for a day, to help you get on top of it all? I can spare him.'

'No, don't worry, I can manage. I know this place and have always wanted it to be run my way. It's no chore to have it looking spotless. But could I request that you buy me some new mixing bowls? Most of them have chips. The large bread bath is all right and the loaf tins themselves will scrub clean. It's just the

186

bowls.'

Meg stood with her hands on the large wooden basin called a bread bath that she mixed the dough in and remembered the happy hours there previously.

'Aye, lass, I'll order you some. Do you want some floor clouts and dish clouts? Mops and brushes? I have all of those?' Joe watched as she went and picked up the brush that she had tried to use so many times on the floors of the bakery.

'I think so, and some soda crystals and carbolic soap, if I could. Some lime-wash and paint brushes. I want to freshen the place up, good and proper.' Meg couldn't wait to set loose on the old place.

'Aye, I can give you that and I'll ask Brian Alston to come and paint the outside windows and make a new sign for over the shop door. It will be grand to see *Joseph Dinsdale The Best Bakery in Leeds* over the door.'

Meg went quiet. Joe was going to put his name over the door with not a mention of her. She thought that she might have a little recognition seeing he was bragging it was to be the best bakery in Leeds.

'Now, I'll be away,' Joe continued, not noticing the expression on her face. 'I'll get George to come round with the things we have in stock. I'll order you the rest from the salesman when they call. I'll call in every so often to see how you are doing and leave me with a list of your wants as soon as you want to start baking. You don't have to hold back. I know whatever you make will sell. I've listened to folk singing your praises enough when you were here the last time. Ted Lund was an old fool, he didn't know when he had it good.' Joe looked at Meg. 'As long as you make money for the both of us, we will rub along just grand.'

187

'I'll not let you down, Mr Dinsdale. I owe you a lot for giving me this opportunity to prove myself.' Meg opened the door for him.

'We'll make a good do of it, lass. We are both the same — hard workers that know the value of money.' Joe left Meg leaning against the bakery door.

She would work hard, and she did value money. She'd make a go of this, for sure.

★ ★ ★

Frankie tipped his top hat to the various people he knew as he walked out of the bank. In his inside pocket was enough money to pay his staff the wages for the week, thanks to Meg's bartering with the pawnshop. Things would be all right now he had paid Jed, and the threat of being taken to the debtor's courts had been lifted from his head — or worse physical violence at the hands of Jed's workers. The shame of admitting that he had not the money to pay his friend would have been unbearable.

He walked back to his patisserie and thought about Meg. Since she had been given the opportunity to bake in her beloved bakery, she seemed a lot happier. Perhaps his mother was right. She was from the lower classes and perhaps not right for him. She might never be happy with him although he hoped that his mother was definitely wrong with her assumption. However, he loved Meg not for her status but for her true love of him. As long as she was happy, that's all that mattered to him.

He entered his shop and met an excited Norah. 'Mr Pearson, I'm so glad that you are back! She's been waiting for you for the last ten minutes. Marie

188

has served her coffee and a macaroon. We thought it was only the done thing,' Norah said without drawing breath.

'Who deserves such treatment?' Frankie frowned at the thought of giving anything away for free.

'Lady Benson, from Langroyd Hall. She asked to see you, said she needed to talk to you and only you.'

'Oh Lord! I would have been back earlier if I had known.' Frankie passed his cloak and top hat to Norah and quickly put his fingers through his hair before climbing the stairs.

Sat next to the window, he saw Lady Benson, dressed immaculately. The crowning glory upon her head of blonde curls was a jaunty pale blue hat, adorned with feathers and a mock hummingbird which matched her full-bodied dress of blue taffeta. A string of pearls hung around her neck and Frankie was taken aback by the beauty of her smile as she looked across at him.

Beatrice Benson rose from her chair and shook Frankie's hand. 'Mr Pearson, I'm so glad that you have arrived before my departure. I wanted so much to meet you and discuss your confectionery.'

'Lady Benson, it is I that am honoured. Please, sit down. I am at your service.' Frankie watched as she gently sat down, her perfume filling his senses.

Beatrice smiled. 'My friends keep telling me that they adore coming here. Indeed, when we hold our teas together, they invariably bring a box of your treats.'

Frankie dared to look straight into the sparkling blue eyes that assessed him with interest. 'Thank you. I'm glad that your friends enjoy my pastries. I've honed my skills in the best patisseries in Paris.'

'That is why I'm here.' Beatrice took a delicate sip

of her tea. 'Mr Pearson, I wondered if I could open a monthly account with you? My husband and I entertain various and numerous people throughout the year and with the party season nearly upon us, we will need a constant supply of treats for our guests.' Beatrice hesitated. 'We have two cooks, but neither of them can bake in such an extravagant style as yours. I need to impress some of the dignitaries that come to visit, hence my request.'

Frankie's chest puffed with pride. At last he was getting recognition for his work. 'It would be my honour. Of course, there is no question about you opening an account with us. I'm so impressed that your friends have told you of our small patisserie.'

'Well, that's settled then. My errand boy will tell you what I will need and when. Is that all right with you?' Beatrice drank the last sip of her tea.

'Yes, yes — of course! We are only small as of yet, so if you can give me a day or two's notice on each occasion, I would appreciate it.'

'I will. I like the way you say 'only small as of yet', Mr Pearson. A man of ambition.' Beatrice started to rise from her seat and Frankie quickly went to her aid, pulling the chair aside for her. 'And a gentleman. Perhaps you would like to join me and my husband at the hall this weekend? We have an informal gathering of friends for a pheasant shoot on the estate.' Beatrice looked at him in such a way it made Frankie forget all about his Meg for a second or two and then checked himself.

'Nothing would give me more pleasure.' Frankie thought of all the connections he could make.

'Do you shoot, Mr Pearson? I find it a terrible sport, shooting a poor harmless bird that has been bred just for that reason. They strut around the lawn and I try to shoo them away. The gamekeeper and I are not the closest of friends. He knows my views.' Beatrice walked towards the top of the stairs and waited for Frankie's reply.

'No, I don't. I'm of the same view as of you, although I do like to eat game,' Frankie said.

'Well then, you must come and keep us ladies company and let my husband and his cronies do the shooting. Shall I say Saturday at two-thirty? You could bring some of your pastries with you, my friends would like that. A new face, coming with temptations.' Beatrice's eyes glinted with mischief.

'That would be wonderful. I'll be with you at two-thirty. Thank you for your most thoughtful invitation.' Frankie led her back down to the main shop, where Marie and Norah watched in awe.

'Two-thirty Saturday. We will be waiting.' She picked up her skirts and walked out with her head held high onto the Headrow, leaving Frankie gazing after her.

Marie and Norah looked at one another and hid their smirks as Frankie turned and saw them both. 'What? She's asked me to tea, that's all. Now, get on with your work!'

★   ★   ★

Frankie sat back in the comfort of the hansom carriage and looked out of the window as the industrial streets of Leeds were left behind for the sprawling fields of the surrounding countryside. Langroyd Hall was out to the north of the city, set in its own grounds. It stood proud and impressive, a magnificent example of Georgian architecture. The main entrance was supported by carved pillars standing proud at the top of a flight of Portland stone steps with statues of guarding lions on either side of the doorway.

Beatrice and her husband are worth considerable money, Frankie thought as the carriage made its way to the bottom of the steps where a footman waited. He only hoped that first impressions were correct as he had reluctantly paid for the horse and cab to bring him in style and decided the box of petit fours and macaroons that sat on the seat across from him should be a gift for his host. He could hardly afford the extravagance but hopefully, it would be paid back with future orders if he made the right impression that afternoon. He also felt a little guilty that he had not told Meg of his visit to Beatrice Benson, but she had been so busy of late wrapped up in her new venture with Joe Dinsdale, she hadn't shown him much attention. Besides it was only a business meeting. She did not need to know of his visit to Langroyd Hall, he thought as the footman opened the carriage door and lowered the steps for him to walk down.

Parks the butler met Frankie at the top of the staircase. The footman had relieved him of the box. 'Ah, Mr Pearson, Lady Benson is expecting you. Hodges will see those are taken to the kitchen. Her ladyship will be delighted that you have brought her something special for her afternoon tea. Please follow me to the drawing room.'

'Thank you, I'm looking forward to the afternoon.' Frankie heard a gun blast and noticed smoke arising from a bank of trees at the side of the house. He didn't approve of the shooting of harmless birds for sport and he quelled his anger.

'That will be his lordship and his friends. They went out early and had their luncheon taken to them over at the shooting lodge. It will be like this for as long as it is pheasant shooting season. That is why her lady-ship is entertaining this afternoon.' Parks opened the solid doors for Frankie to follow him into the mar-ble-floored hall, with its paintings of Benson ancestry.

'Ma'am, your guest, Mr Pearson,' Parks announced as he opened the doors into the drawing room.

Frankie expected to find Beatrice and one or two close friends, but at least ten faces turned to gaze at him. He couldn't help but feel as though he had walked into a room of vipers.

'Mr Pearson. How delightful that you are able to join our little group today. My friends have been look-ing forward to making your acquaintance.' Beatrice smiled and stepped forward in a figure-hugging dress. Meg would never have dared to wear such an outfit.

'Come. Sit down by my side.' A young woman who Frankie had seen on occasion in his shop patted her seat.

'Now, Eunice, don't be greedy. Mr Pearson can sit here, and then we can all share him.' Beatrice beck-oned Frankie to sit next to her. Eunice's face showed her feelings as Frankie took his seat and looked around at the crowd of enthralled ladies. 'I've brought you all some pastries. The footman took them through to the kitchen on my arrival. I thought that you might like a sweet treat,' Frankie said nervously.

'Wonderful! We all hoped that you would. Now, Mr Pearson . . . or may we call you Frankie? Please tell us all about yourself.' Beatrice looked ready to hang on his every word.

Frankie tried his best to smile as the room erupted

with the sound of female voices. He was obviously the entertainment for the afternoon while their husbands were out shooting. How he wished he could escape as the pack competed for his attention. He wanted to be back in his bakery or visiting his Meg.

Anywhere but Langroyd Hall.

★ ★ ★

'So, you have been with my wife and her friends for the day?'

Lord Benson watched Frankie shake Beatrice's hand to say his farewells at the door. He slowly climbed the steps with his shotgun cocked, and his close group of shooting friends around him. 'Knew they were all up to something. I sensed the excitement and the fact that they couldn't get us all out of the house fast enough.'

'It's been an honour to be asked, sir.' Frankie assessed the portly lord, dressed in his shooting attire with a brace of pheasants in his hand.

'I bet it has! All those women! I bet you were spoilt for choice,' Lord Benson said gruffly.

'Lady Benson and her friends have been the perfect hosts, sir. You need not be embarrassed.' Frankie was thankful to see his carriage coming up the drive.

'I know her all too well, young man. You are not here without reason.'

'He is to supply us with pastries, that is all,' Lady Benson interrupted. 'Cook struggles with these new recipes and you do want us to keep up with society. They will be the perfect treat this coming party season.' Retrieving it from a footman, Beatrice passed Frankie's empty basket to him.

194

'That is all, sir, I assure you.' Frankie took the basket out of Beatrice's hand, eager to get away. The footman opened the carriage door and he climbed in, putting the basket on the seat across from him and giving instructions to the cabby man to return him home to Headingley. He waved and watched as Lord Benson took Beatrice's arm and heard him say, 'A bloody Frenchman, have you no shame?'

Frankie pondered as he sat back and gathered his thoughts. He looked across at the empty basket. What a waste of money. He doubted that he would be asked back if Lord Benson had his way, let alone supply the hall with his pastries.

Then, he noticed the note hiding beneath the chequered cloth lining the basket. He reached forward and pulled it out from its hiding place. Unfolding it, he read in the day's dimming light.

My dear Frankie,
   I hope you don't mind me being so candid. I have had such a wonderful afternoon with you by my side. You have kept my friends and me entranced all afternoon? Perhaps you would care to visit me again at your convenience.
   I look forward to your response.
   Bee

21

Meg stood back with a brush in her hand and a bucket of whitewash by her side. She was plastered from head to foot. Every bone in her body ached but she was happy with what she had achieved in such a short time. Now, the bakery smelt clean and was fit for a purpose. Walls were painted, floors scrubbed and the pans, baking dishes and trays stood lined up ready for use. All that was missing now was the ingredients and the coal for the ovens, both being delivered on Monday. Another day of stacking shelves, sorting cupboards, and making sure all was in place, and then she could open on Tuesday. Then the true work would begin.

She went out into the small backyard, now cleared of rubbish. She pumped water into a tin bucket to soak her painting brushes. She looked around her. Now, even the lean-to with outside lavvy was spotlessly clean. Likewise, the rooms above the bakery had never been opened and walked into for years and Meg had felt shivers going down her spine as she had walked up the previously blocked-off stairs and peered into the two rooms that told the story of Ted Lund's past family life.

The first room had been filled with old packaging and glass jars from the Leeds Glass Factory, boxes filled with long-gone delicacies that had disintegrated to dust. But it had been the second bedroom that had pulled on Meg's heartstrings. She had felt tears well up into her eyes as she had opened the door and had instantly realized that back in the day when Myra, Ted's daughter, had been alive, it had been her nursery. A place of safety for her to play in while her mother and father made a living downstairs in the bakery. In one corner was a cot still with its covers on. Scattered across the floor were various toys — a wooden top, building bricks and a clockwork clapping monkey. Things that had been played with by his precious daughter before her death. They had been left to gather dust and cobwebs just like the rest of the bakery. It was obvious to anyone that when Ted had lost his wife and daughter, he'd also lost his will to live — until, that is, his trip to Ireland earlier this year.

Hopefully, in his new life in Ireland, he will find peace and contentment, Meg thought as she watched the sun setting over the terraced house of York Street. It was time for her to be going home. In another hour, Sarah would be going to the music hall for her nightly stint with her latest fascination, Larry Hopkirk. Sarah was besotted by the music hall acts, but Meg still doubted if it was the right place for her.

It was Saturday night. Larry Hopkirk would be giving an encore, so Sarah would be back late — too late in Meg's mind.

Thank heavens tomorrow is Sunday, Meg thought as she walked back into the bakery. She could stay at home and see Frankie, who had promised to visit her. She'd not had time to think much about how his bakery had performed over the last few weeks but no doubt he would be telling her. She had not missed working for him, but she had missed his loving looks and warm embraces.

Sarah smiled to herself as she recalled the things that Larry Hopkirk had told her about Christmas in London. How all the shops were filled with everything you could ever imagine and want and how people thronged the streets with gifts for their loved ones. Then they would attend the theatre of an evening, to watch their favourite pantomime. He'd describe how he dressed up in a frock to play the leading lady and make people laugh until they nearly fell off their seats. By the sound of it, London was the place of her dreams! The place she wanted to live, not a dreary mill town in West Yorkshire.

'I'll not be coming home tonight,' she told Meg. 'Larry and Annie have asked me to stay the night with them. They say I'm the daughter that they never had. They make such a fuss of me.'

Sarah beamed and felt warm inside, hoping that she had found a love to replace her mother's. Meg, however, considered that perhaps something was not quite right for the young girl to be asked to stay with a couple she hardly knew.

'He's never said anything to me. It would have been polite manners if he had done so. Are you sure you're staying with them? You're not just telling me a tale?' Meg scrutinized her younger sister's face. 'I think I'll walk to work with you and have a word with Larry Hopkirk. See what he's playing at. Why would he want a young lass like you staying with him and his wife when you only live a few streets away?' Meg feared the worst of Sarah.

'That's it, show me up! Don't believe me. It's the truth, I tell you. Anyway, you'll be happy to hear that he'll be going back to London before Christmas. He's to play Old Mother Hubbard at The Grand Theatre in Islington!' Sarah snapped.

'More reason for me to go and see him. A man who dresses up like a woman! These theatre folk are a law to themselves.' Meg grabbed her shawl.

'Don't go to the music hall, please! You'll show me up.' Sarah pulled on her sister's arm. 'If you don't believe me, call in and see Mrs Hopkirk. She'll tell you that what I'm saying is the truth. She'll like your company as well. She says it's a lonely life travelling with her husband. She never sees anybody when Larry is on the road.'

'I can't go there! She hardly knows me from Adam.'

'I'll take you, we go past the door on the way to the hall. Please, our Meg. See her, not Larry. I'm not a baby anymore. They'll laugh at me at the hall if you go asking after me.'

Meg could see how concerned Sarah was at the prospect. 'All right, seeing you're making such a fuss, I'll just see her. Now, come on, else you'll be late and then you'll despair of me even more.' She pushed her younger sister out into the darkening streets. She was uneasy about Sarah's growing theatre friendships, but perhaps if she met Annie Hopkirk herself, her mind might be put at rest.

★ ★ ★

'Sarah, I thought that you'd have gone with Larry. He set out over ten minutes ago.' Annie Hopkirk stood on the doorstep of her rented property accommodation, and looked at her two visitors.

'I would have been, if it wasn't for my sister here.

199

She insisted on checking up on me, Mrs Hopkirk! She doesn't believe that you've invited me to stay tonight, so I've had to bring her with me.' Sarah looked up at the kindly woman whose face was made up with powder and lipstick.

'Sarah!' Meg snapped. 'I was worried, that's all. I didn't want you wandering the streets at night.' She sighed and looked at Mrs Hopkirk, who was watching Sarah closely. 'I'm sorry, I just wanted to check that she wasn't being a nuisance.'

'Nuisance? Not at all. Sarah is welcome to stay, always. She has been such a help to Larry and me. I don't suppose she has told you that she comes for an hour every day while you are busy with your bakery? She helps me with my various jobs and gets my shopping.' Meg looked at Annie in surprise. 'Anyway, dear — don't stand out there. Come in and see where she will be sleeping. Then you can make up your own mind about our arrangement. I know we showpeople have a reputation and I want to assure you that we are no different from you.' Annie turned and took her walking stick to help her walk. 'You'd better get a move on, Sarah. You know what Larry's like if he doesn't have all in place for his performance. I'll see you later.'

Meg followed behind Annie and noticed how lame she was, relying on her walking stick for support.

'She's an angel, is your sister. I don't know what I'd do without her. I've not been well of late, so her smiling face was a blessing. Larry says she's the best stagehand he's ever had.' Annie slumped down in her chair while Meg looked around. 'This is the place that the manager at the music hall has put us up in. It's all right — nothing like home, though. I miss my china.'

200

'It looks grand.' Meg noticed various doors leading off to further rooms. It looked warmer and more homely than her own place. There was a full plate of biscuits on the table, along with a chocolate box and a bowl of fruit. There was more food on the side table than Meg had had in her house all week.

'Sarah likes looking in Larry's box of make-up over there, she plays about with it.' Annie pointed to a box on the sideboard and smiled. 'You know she wants to go on the stage, herself. Larry keeps encouraging her. He believes in folk following their dreams.'

'I know she's always sung and danced but we never thought it would come to anything,' Meg replied. 'It was just Sarah being Sarah. Perhaps we should have paid more attention to her although she has always been loved by our mother and me.'

Mrs Randall hadn't been nasty in any way, but Meg still felt as if she had just been told that her parenting skills were abysmal and that she should be grateful that her younger sister was in good hands.

'She's looked after here, you don't have to worry,' the older woman continued. 'She's like the daughter I never had. Larry and I have a son, but he never calls on us. He's like a lot of folks, doesn't understand the world of music hall, even though he was brought up with it.'

'It's just that I worry about her. Since our mother died I've tried to keep her on a straight track and sometimes it has proven difficult.' Meg couldn't help but sigh.

'Aye, she's wilful,' Annie agreed. 'That's why Larry likes her! Don't be too hard on her. She works her socks off at the music hall, and she's thought a lot of. I only hope that she finds another Larry when we return to London. He's in pantomime down there and he's in the middle of buying an old theatre at Clapham Junction. He's talking about renaming it The Grand Hall of Varieties. He says acts from all over the world will be performing there. You should have seen Sarah's face when he was telling her about it,' Annie smiled.

'He's buying a theatre?' Meg hadn't imagined that the actor and his wife had a penny to their names.

'Oh, yes! He's waiting to hear if his plans for a new theatre in Waltham Green have been accepted. He never stops working, does Larry. He's a good man. He's provided me well with a lovely six-bedroom home in the middle of London. I perhaps should stay there while he tours but I don't like to be away from him too long.'

'Oh, I see.' Meg felt foolish. She had thought the worst of the man that she had only briefly met, and there he was with his wife showing every kindness to her sister. 'I'm happy now that I know Sarah is definitely staying with you this evening. Sometimes her imagination gets the better of her.'

'Yes, we agreed the other day that she could stay. I think she likes to visit us and, if you don't mind me saying, I don't think she is keen on your beau.' Annie appeared to hesitate. 'Does he come to visit you on a Sunday? She seemed to not want to be at home come Sunday morning, even though if she's anything like Larry, she'll still be in her bed when the bells at eleven ring to attend church.'

'She thinks he poisoned our mother. When, really, he eased her pain with a bottle of laudanum. She also thinks I will abandon her, which I would never do,' Meg confessed.

202

'That's her imagination for you. That's why she gets on so well with Larry. Now, don't you worry, she's safe with us. You enjoy a Sunday on your own with your young man. I'm sure he's a respectable soul and that Sarah is perhaps a little worried that he's going to come between you both.' Annie smiled. 'It is hard when you lose your mother. She is your best friend, even if you don't know it at the time. You don't realize it but she's gone forever and no one can ever replace her.'

'I know it isn't just Sarah that misses her. I do every day,' Meg said softly, holding back her own tears. 'As long as I know that Sarah is all right, that's all that matters.'

★ ★ ★

'No Sarah this morning?' Frankie grabbed Meg by her waist, pulling her onto his knee.

'No, she's found a new part-time home with Larry and Annie Hopkirk. They seem to have taken to her. I think she helps Annie Hopkirk around the house, as she isn't good on her legs.' Meg kissed Frankie as he held her tight.

'That doesn't sound like Sarah, doing something for nothing. She still doesn't give me time of day. I thought by now that she would have come around to me.' Frankie ran his finger around the top of Meg's bodice.

'Frankie Pearson, you can stop that just because Sarah isn't here,' Meg grinned. 'Anyway, with Sarah and the Hopkirks, I think that it maybe only cupboard love; I could see that from the amount of food that was displayed next to Annie. There has to be something in it for our Sarah for her to show the devotion that she is.'

'It seems everybody is out for what they can get nowadays. Even I am taken for an idiot by some,' Frankie sighed.

'Never! Everybody respects you.' Meg realized he was being serious. 'Has something gone wrong?' She turned upon his knee.

'I've made enough to keep me afloat. No, it is the case of a slight misunderstanding on Lady Benson's part and I like a fool didn't realize that there was more to it than an order of fancies. She expects a little bit more for her money.' Frankie reached into his pocket and took out the note but before he showed Meg, he saw the shock on her face.

'Were you her latest fancy? Did you go to the hall, like all the rest?' Meg tried to hide a smirk at the look of surprise on Frankie's face.

'All the rest? What do you mean? She was infatuated with me!' Frankie puffed out his chest.

'You and her gardener . . . the butcher on George Street, the watchmaker on Canal Street. She's working her way through all the tradesmen in Leeds. She's well known. She comes into your business, reckons to place an order with you. Then invites you back to the hall. There you have to take her a gift, and then her friends play games on who can win your attention the most. She's well known for it.' Meg couldn't wipe the smirk from her face.

'But she gave me this.' Frankie passed her the note that he had wondered whether to confess to.

'Yes, and if you'd gone up to her bedroom, the husband would have been hiding — watching what you got up to. Dirty old devil. But you'd get a good

204

order from her each week if you performed well.'
Meg blushed. She had never spoken of the suchlike
to Frankie before.

'How do you know all this? She's a lady, surely. She
doesn't do things like that with just anyone?' Frankie
asked with indignity.

'Daisy told me. Your Lady Benson is the talk of
Leeds. She and her friends place bets on who will
come back and bed her.' Meg looked at the disgust
on Frankie's face.

'I thought that she was a true lady and that I could
rely on a decent order from her. I thought she was
going to be my saviour as far as the patisserie was
involved. Well, I won't be playing her games; I'm not
replying to her note. I only hope that she still buys
pastries from my shop.' Frankie took the note back
from Meg and screwed it up before throwing it onto
the fire.

'Good, because you are mine. How can I compete
with a well-to-do lady?' Meg kissed him on his cheek.

'Believe me, she is no lady after what you have told
me. Besides, you are twice the beauty that she is. I
don't know how any man could love a woman like
that,' Frankie said.

'They love her money. You must have been tempted?'
Meg asked quietly.

'No. I will always be true to you, whether I am a
pauper or a prince.'

'You will never be a pauper, Frankie. No matter
what happens to us in life, you will always be my
prince. Even a king — the king of my heart.'

22

'You have enough stuff here to stock up twenty bakeries,' George said, as he carried in yet another bag of flour from the flat cart.

'Believe me, it will all soon be used. I'll need a good order every week but not as much as this next time — it's only because every shelf and all the flour bins have been emptied. Ted Lund didn't exactly keep a clean house,' Meg laughed as she took tins of syrup and treacle from the cart and saw how red George's face was glowing after carrying ten bags of flour into the back of the bakery and the same of sugar.

'I'm glad to hear that; you should have seen Joe's face when he totted up how much this had cost him.' George leaned against the counter and drew breath before tackling the crate of baking apples that Meg had added to her list along with cherries, spices and dried fruit. He watched as each item was given a place in the bakery.

'I've ordered some things for Christmas. It's time to make figgy pudding and Christmas cakes. I'll feed them both with a drop of brandy until nearer Christmas and then they will be so moist, people will love them,' Meg said.

'He's not sent any brandy.' George went for another haul.

'No, I'll get that from The Horse and Trumpet later this afternoon, when I make my way to see how Frankie is doing.' Meg looked around her with pride.

The bakery was starting to look like she had always dreamt it could be. Clean, well stocked, the ovens ready to be lit, the bench scrubbed ... Now, all she had to do was to be up early in the morning and start as she meant to go on.

'You are still walking out with him, then? I heard that things are not that good with him. The salesman from Hebden's was telling Mr Dinsdale that he has cut his orders down.' George stopped to draw breath. 'I bet he's missing you working for him.'

'Well, that salesman shouldn't be discussing other folks' business,' Meg said sharply. 'Frankie's not doing so bad. His patisserie is more for the upper classes. Once he gets a good reputation with them, he'll be all right.' Meg went on to tell George that Frankie had visited Langroyd Hall and had secured an order with Lady Benson. Anything to stop the gossip.

'He'll not get the reputation that he wants if he goes there too often,' George grinned. 'He might get a backside full of lead shot if her husband finds him there too often, depending upon his mood, from what I hear.'

Meg looked at George sharply. 'I thought you were too young to know about things like that.'

'I'm sixteen next month! Besides, everybody knows about Lady Bea Bedding Benson. All the fellas keep clear of her. Those that want to, that is. She can be persuasive, and I'd keep my eye on that fella of yours. I've heard that what she wants, she gets.' George mischievously winked. 'Right, that's me unloaded and you stocked. What time do you want me to collect the baking in the morning?'

'Hmm ... Seven, or is that too early? The bread should be out, and I'll have a few basics made by then.' Meg struggled to concentrate after George's little joke. Lady Benson obviously had her sights set on Frankie and it was a fact that Frankie liked to get and spend his money easily. If she was putting temptation his way, might he succumb?

'Right you are. See you then. I can't say I'll be right chatty at that time of the morning, but I'll be here in body if not in spirit.' George put his cap back on as he departed, whistling to himself.

Trying to put her worries to the back of her mind, Meg started to find homes for everything that George had left. She filled the spice drawers and located a dry place above the ovens for the salt and sugar, and then she went and looked at her now spick and span shop. The shelves were covered with doilies, ready for the morning bakes. There was a set of three large glass biscuit barrels that she would fill with a batch of rock buns and coconut tarts. They would keep fresh for at least four or five days before she needed another batch. She would be late home that evening, but Sarah had already been told that there was some cold veal pie in the larder for her supper.

Everything was just as it should be, nothing out of place. Meg looked about her and felt a thrill of pride. It was happening! Her dreams were finally coming true.

★ ★ ★

Meg turned the corner onto the Headrow and immediately noticed the coach that belonged to Lady Benson, with the familiar crest upon the doorway, outside Frankie's bakery. The coachman stroked his horses as they chomped at their bits. They looked uneasy as if they had been standing there for a while. Her heart started to beat wildly, and she felt colour coming to her cheeks as she pretended to look into one of the shop windows two doors down. She wanted to see the jezebel who was intent on taking her beau away from her.

She didn't have long to wait. There was a distinctive voice, followed by a swish of skirts. The lady's coachman opened the carriage door and another servant carried her pastries carefully, waiting until she was comfortably seated in her place in the carriage. Meg watched as Frankie followed Beatrice out of the shop, giving her his hand as she stepped into her waiting vehicle.

'It has been a privilege, Mr Pearson. Such a delight. My ladies were so entranced by you and, of course, the temptations that you brought.' Lady Beatrice gathered her skirt around her. Meg felt the blood rising to her face. The cheek of the hussy! She set off at a pace towards the carriage and Frankie. She wasn't going to have an upper-class prostitute pinch her beau.

'You can keep your hands off him! He's mine!' Meg heard herself cry.

Frankie's eyes grew wide. 'Meg, dearest! Please . . . Lady Benson has come to pick up this week's delivery because she happened to be in town. Everything is all right. See, the pastries are across on the other side of the carriage from her.'

'I thought, I thought . . .' Meg stuttered.

'You thought what? That I was here to ravish and abuse your beau? Really, you should not listen to idle gossip. I have not the slightest interest in bedding your man. I simply enjoy the company of men, much more than that of women.' Lady Beatrice instructed her

209

driver to close the carriage door. 'Frankie has made it perfectly clear to me that any business we will do is strictly that — only business. He's a gentleman, and you are very lucky to have him.' Lady Benson waved for her coachman to mount and to drive off but before he did, she looked at Frankie.

'Don't worry, my order still stands. I can understand your beloved being jealous. It is the attractive ones of society that attract all the gossip and scandal. The working classes have nothing better to do than make up lies.' She snapped down her blind and left Frankie and Meg standing in the street as the carriage pulled away.

There was a moment's silence, then Frankie turned to Meg. 'You could have lost me her order. Why do you listen to the locals' gossip, especially Daisy's gossip and scandal?'

'It isn't just her. Lady Benson is known not to be any sort of a lady. Even George said the same this morning. And when I saw her, I thought the worse.' Meg looked downcast. 'I'm sorry, Frankie. I couldn't help myself.'

'Well, thankfully she'd already said she wouldn't withdraw her offer of an order, even after I made a fool of myself and told her that I was faithful to you and that I had no interest in her.' Frankie breathed in. 'She found it amusing that I thought she would be flirting with me. She obviously knows that her reputation is not what a lady's should be.' Frankie breathed out heavily. 'You could have ruined everything.'

'I think you'll find that there is no smoke without fire.'

'Shush, stop it. Do you want the whole world to know my business?' Frankie glanced around at the passing strangers who were watching them quarrel.

'I think you'll find that in the business world of Leeds, gossip quickly spreads, and what they don't know they make up!' Meg said sharply. But almost as soon as the words had left her mouth, she wished she could have snatched them back.

'What do you mean by that? Has somebody said something about me?' Frankie pulled Meg to one side.

'No, nobody has said anything. I shouldn't have said that. It's just that you can be such a hypocrite. You always say that you want people of all classes to shop in your bakery but when something goes wrong you always sneer at the more lowly.' Meg pushed him off and started to walk away, her eyes filling with tears.

Frankie followed her. 'I don't. It is just that I can't understand the pleasure that everyone gets from discussing other peoples' worries. Especially when people rejoice when somebody who has made something of their life falls upon hard times.'

'You are privileged, Frankie. I don't think you will ever truly know what it is to be without money. You worried over nothing when you couldn't pay your builder. The likes of us can't afford to eat some days, let alone buy your fancy patisseries,' Meg told him. 'Perhaps you should keep with the likes of Lady Benson, she's more your class. Your mother is right, I'm not good enough for you.' She let out a sob and started to run down the Headrow to get away from saying or hearing any more hurtful things.

'Meg, Meg, come back! Don't be so daft. Please, this is all over nothing!' Frankie called after her but Meg kept running.

* * *

211

Meg tried her best to concentrate. She got on with making the rock buns, mixing flour and butter, sugar and currants together, rubbing everything into fine breadcrumbs before adding eggs and milk. Baking always gave her a sense of calm and the knowledge that by the end of her putting her measured portions together, there would be something scrumptious gave her a deep satisfaction. She placed the mixture into rough clumps on the large baking tray before sprinkling them with a glistening of sugar and placing them into the oven.

She tried to control her sobs. There had been tears flowing down her cheeks as she had worked on the buns and now her heart felt as if it was about to burst.

What had she done? What had she been thinking, showing her jealousy to her beloved Frankie? She sobbed and wiped her eyes before reaching for the flour and lard to make pastry for the coconut tarts. She thought about the harsh words that they had said to one another and the look on Frankie's face when he had told her to stop listening to Daisy and her gossiping. It wasn't gossip! Everyone knew about Lady Beatrice Benson — everybody, it seemed, but her Frankie. He trusted the word of the upper classes more than that of Meg and her friends. But what a silly thing to have thrown their love away for! She started to mix her pastry, only pausing when she heard the door's bell jingle and her name being called from the shop.

'Meg, are you there? Please, I've come to apologize,' Frankie called.

Meg felt her heart flutter as she saw him standing looking around the newly spruced bakery that she had spent so much time in of late. He too looked upset;

212

perhaps he was regretting the argument earlier in the day and the hastily chosen words. But she couldn't help but think that it was his mother's voice coming out of Frankie's mouth. She had brought him up and sometimes it showed in his words. No matter what he said, Daisy and George were probably right. Lady Benson was definitely one who liked to play games, but she should have kept her cool else she could have cost him her Ladyship's custom if she had said anymore.

Meg wiped her hands and brushed a tear away before she went through to the shop. She could hardly look at Frankie standing in front of her. She dropped her head.

'I'm sorry, I didn't mean you any harm, I thought that she had tempted you away from me,' Meg sobbed. 'I'm sorry for my cruel words. You do care about folk like me.'

'Come here.' Frankie held his arms out to her and she went to him instantly, sinking into the warmth and comfort of his embrace. 'You do not need to apologize, I'm as much to blame. I blame my mother. She's brought me up a snob and sometimes I hear the worst of her coming out in me. Please forgive me.' Frankie bowed his head and held Meg tightly as he kissed the top of her head.

After a few moments, he gently let her go, wiped away her tears and put his hand in his pocket. 'Here, look, I've been meaning to give you this for a while. I found it when I was looking for things to pawn. Please stop crying, you break my heart when you sound so upset.' He pulled out a small velvet case and laid it on the palm of his hand. 'It must be a family heirloom,' he explained, 'though I can't remember either my mother or grandmother wearing it. But it is quite beautiful and perhaps it will prove my love to you.'

Meg's eyes widened as she opened the small box and she was struck dumb.

'You don't have to wear it, if you prefer not to,' Frankie said hastily.

Meg felt her cheeks flush with emotion as she gazed at the ring. It shone in the shop's candlelight, its sapphire sparkling blue as she held it in her hand. 'It's beautiful! But I couldn't take this. It must belong to someone . . . your mother?'

'You take it. Try it on. If it does belong to my mother it doesn't matter. She owes me enough. Please try it on and wear it as proof of our intention to be married. An engagement ring which I should rightfully have given you some months ago. I'd never be untrue to you, surely you know that?' Frankie took her hand and slid the ring onto her wedding finger. 'Look, it is a perfect fit. It was meant for you.' He held her hand as she admired the ring, and then he kissed her tenderly. 'I love you, Meg.'

'And I you, Frankie. I can't believe that I have your ring on my finger. I'm engaged to be married!' Frankie squeezed her so tight she thought that every breath in her body would be expelled.

'We need to definitely set a date for our wedding; I know April was mentioned but neither of us did anything about it. I'm not going to let you slip away from me.' Frankie held her at arm's length and looked at her. 'Maybe we had to have our tiff today to make us realize how much we mean to one another.'

'I think you're right. We will both sit down on Sunday and set an actual date. I don't want to lose you, either. I know I have kept delaying but that was only because the time was not right. Now I know that we both need one another,' Meg finished softly.

'Yes, we do, we both have our strengths and weaknesses but together we will always be strong.' Frankie held her tight again, then paused and sniffed the air. 'Have you something in the ovens?'

Meg rushed from his arms. 'Oh Lord! My rock buns!' Meg ran into the bakery where she flung open the oven door. 'Saved! Just in time. It's a good job you noticed the aroma.' Meg balanced the hot tray on a cooling rack and inspected the golden buns. A few more moments in the oven, and they'd have been ruined.

Frankie stood by the table and grinned. 'See, you do need me, if only to save your baking.'

'I need you for a lot more than that, Frankie Pearson. That's why I wasn't willing to share you with Lady bloody Benson!' Meg exclaimed.

'And I need you to keep me grounded. I take things for granted. You can keep my feet on the ground.' Frankie looked around the spotless bakery. 'You've been busy, Mrs Pearson-to-be. You are going to be a rival for your husband. It's perhaps a good move on my part that I've put that ring on your finger.' He smiled as she turned to him.

'We'll be a good partnership. Give me time and my name will also be spoken in the parts of society you admire. We are equals and don't you forget it.' Meg smiled and kissed him.

'Just don't change your ways or your baking. I love you for both. I'm so glad that you accepted my ring, I would never want to lose you.'

Frankie held her close once more. It was true. He was nothing without Meg by his side.

23

Meg wiped the sweat from her brow. Outside, bitter winds blew down the street — but in her bakery, it was roasting. She'd been here since five o'clock, busy making bread for her customers and making sure she had everything in place for her first day. She always had taken pride in her work, but now she wanted everything to be perfect.

She might not have enjoyed working for Frankie in his patisserie but it had taught her a lot, she realized as she rearranged a jar of homemade biscuits to tempt her customers and tweaked various cakes to show them off to their best advantage. On the top of the old stove, a big pan full of plum puddings simmered away, ready to be sold in the bakery at Christmas, along with Christmas cake, gingerbread men and brandy snaps.

She loved Christmas! The smell of spices and the look on people's faces as they gazed through the shop windows. However, it wasn't quite that time yet. This morning, the shelves were filled with freshly baked bread, fruit tea cakes, scones and the coconut tarts and rock buns that had been salvaged last night.

Meg hummed to herself and smiled as she looked around her new kingdom before turning the sign on the bakery door and peering out into the darkness of the early December morning. Lamps and candles were beginning to be lit as the residents of York Street came to life, ready to start another day of toil. Hope-

216

fully, they would soon be coming through her door for their daily bread, now they knew that it would be a decent loaf and not filled with sawdust. She waved at the dairy man and he, in turn, wished her a good morning in his broad Yorkshire accent. He snapped his horse's reins and his cart of milk cans moved off along the street as the local women came out of their homes, carrying empty jugs to be filled with his fresh milk.

'I'll be across in a minute, Meg,' Mrs Blackwell called over as she paid for her milk. 'By 'eck, it's good to know that you're back and I can get a decent loaf instead of that rubbish Ted Lund was feeding us afore he packed up altogether.'

'Will it be your usual?' Meg called back cheerily. 'I'll wrap one up and put it on the side ready for you.'

'Aye, but I'll have a look at what else you've got. Our Jimmy has started work today, so I'll have a bit more brass to spend, thank the Lord.' She gave a wave and scurried back inside, closing her door on the cold winds.

Up the street came George with his horse and cart, slow but steady out of the darkness.

'I could do with another hour in bed,' George said, not looking like his usual tidy self and wiping the sleep out of his eyes.

'I've been up at least two hours,' Meg laughed. 'It's a good job you're not a baker.'

'There must be an easier way to make a living! Either that or you are mad,' George growled as he tethered his horse and took the wooden tray filled with fresh bread for Joe Dinsdale's shop that Meg passed him.

'Then I must be mad because I wouldn't change it for the world,' Meg said as she passed him a batch of tea cakes and scones and told him to take care with them as George, half asleep, nearly dropped them.

The young lad climbed back onto the cart. 'Well, that's all well and good but I'll be mad in the head if I have to keep this up every day for old Dinsdale.'

'Tell him he needs an errand boy and then you can get your beauty sleep,' Meg joked.

'Aye, but then I wouldn't get to see you,' George said and then blushed.

Meg knew the lad was sweet on her. 'Well, we had better leave it like it is then. There's an extra scone in there for you. Don't let Joe Dinsdale see you eating it.'

'Thanks, Meg, I'll eat it now. It'll do as my breakfast. I didn't waken my mam to make my breakfast at this unearthly hour.' George flicked his reins over his horse's back. 'See you in the morning. It'll be worth it if I get something to eat every day. You are a good 'n.'

Meg watched George trundle down the street and hoped that her baking would sell well for Joe Dinsdale. He was her saviour and she'd always make sure he got exactly what he needed for his shop.

The doors along the street began to open, the men of the house the first to leave for work. Soon the cobbled street would echo to the noise of clogged feet as the mill lasses followed suit. She went to check that her puddings hadn't boiled dry and that the ginger biscuits had baked.

It was grand to be back in charge. She was happy on her home turf and she was even happier that she had Frankie's ring on her finger. She smiled and twisted it on her finger as she thought of him. She balanced the hot tray of ginger biscuits as they came out of the oven and heard the shop door bell tinkle, heralding her first customer. With the air filled with the aroma

218

of fresh bread and Christmas pudding, she smoothed down her pinny, left the tray of biscuits to cool, and went with a smile on her face to serve her first customer.

'Now then, missus. Have I caught you lurking in the back of the shop? You've not got Frankie there, have you? Not having a bit of how's your father?' Daisy grinned and winked at her friend.

'Only you would think that way, Daisy Truelove. I was getting some biscuits out of the oven, as it happens.' Meg smiled but couldn't help but think about what Frankie had said about her friend's tendency to gossip.

Daisy looked over at the perfectly displayed shop shelves. 'So, how does it feel to be back in your own bakery? I bet you're enjoying every minute. Just look at what you've got on your shelves. It's a good job Ted has gone to Ireland. He'd have had a fit if this had all been paid for by him.'

'So, Ted's actually gone, has he? I'm glad, I didn't want him to be looking in at me from outside or talking about me behind my back.'

'Aye, he's gone. We got his house keys on Saturday,' Daisy said as she looked over the loaves. 'The amount of carbolic soap and scrubbing brushes that I'm going to go through to get that house clean is nobody's business. The dirty old devil.' Daisy looked at the coconut tarts. 'Lord, you have too much to tempt me. I can see I'm going to be spending all my hard-earned brass with you.' She delved into her purse to pay for what she had in front of her and placed it into Meg's hand.

'What's this, you sneaky monkey. You've not said anything about this!' Daisy took Meg's left hand and turned it over to reveal Meg's engagement ring. 'Look at that! Now that is a sapphire if ever I saw one.'

Meg felt herself blush. 'He gave me it the other day. It's a family heirloom. He said he found it in a drawer, but I do love it.'

'I thought you said he was struggling? He can't be struggling if he's got something like this lying in a drawer. I'll never get anything like that off my Tom. Best I'll get is help with the rent. He's never any money by the time he's seen to his wife and family's needs.' Daisy looked wistfully at the ring as the next customer came into the shop.

'I'm sorry, Daisy, but as long as Tom loves you, that's what matters most.' Meg wrapped the loaf of bread for her friend and passed it over.

'Aye, well, it's my fault for loving the wrong man. If Frankie's got things like that just lying about the house, you're right, he's not really short of a bob or two,' Daisy smiled. 'I'm glad that you are up and running. My mam will call in later, she said she couldn't wait to see what you're up to.' Daisy took her bread and acknowledged one of her new neighbours as she left the bakery.

'Aye, she's a brazen thing, that'en. Living with another woman's husband. I don't know how she has the nerve,' the newcomer said, before looking around her. 'It's grand to see this bakery back to what it used to be like. You'll soon be making money, now it's something like. Two cobs and I'll have four of them coconut tarts. I bet they'll be good with a drop of custard for pudding tonight.' She made way for two mill lasses who were calling in on their way to work.

Looking out of the window after serving them, Meg wondered if she was going to be this busy all morning. If so, she was going to be run off her feet! She was happy to be back in the bakery that she had fallen in love with. She would make it into a good business, and as soon as she had the money, she could buy it from Joe Dinsdale. Then she would be a woman with her own business and not need to be supported by Frankie once they were married. She was determined to be her own woman, even if it was not the convention of the day.

★   ★   ★

Sarah sat up in her bed. The house was quiet, and she was on her own again. Meg had left early and Sarah had returned late from the theatre so neither had seen one another.

She thought about her mother as she looked across the room at the other, empty bed. It had once been where her mother lay, but was now Meg's bed. She missed her mother's company. She hadn't realized until she had died how much she had loved her mother. Mama had always been there for her, tender and kind, understanding but firm. She regretted not showing her love more openly. Christmas was not going to feel like Christmas this year without her mother. Of late, Annie Hopkirk had been the closest thing to a mother that she had.

Meg certainly wasn't, with her fancy man and ideas above her station. This new bakery wasn't helping. All she thought and talked about was baking and Frankie, with that ring on her finger that sparkled in the moonlight as she lay sleeping.

The church clock struck eleven. It would soon be one, but unlike the old days when Meg used to come back from Ted Lund's bakery once he closed, she stayed now, baking and getting ready for another day. Meg had no time for a younger sister in her life. A tear welled up; Sarah sniffed hard and brushed it aside. She'd nobody to share her worries with — except the warm and friendly Annie and Larry Randall.

It was a busy time at the theatre. The folk of Leeds were rushing to see Larry's last few appearances before he disappeared back down to London for the pantomime season. He and Annie would be gone soon, and then what? A new performer to work for that she didn't like or who wouldn't like her. She would be totally alone.

Sarah wiped another tear away. The Hopkirk's temporary home had been a sanctuary to her of late. It was somewhere she could unload her troubles, be fed and have a good night's sleep, warm and cared for when Meg was too busy to bother about her. When the Hopkirks left she would have no one, especially if the worst happened and Meg went ahead and married Frankie Pearson.

If only her mother was still alive, or better still, Annie was her mother. She would have everything that she craved. She lay back in bed and looked at the damp bedroom walls. The Hopkirks didn't live like this. Even the temporary accommodation that they were in now was dry and warm, but Annie had told her of the six-bedroom house that they lived in at Islington, how she had a maid and a butler, and could walk and shop the streets of London, and even see the Queen when she passed by in her carriage.

London sounded much finer than the dark and dreary streets of Leeds, a world away from the noisy cotton and woollen mills and the iron furnaces that roared down by the forge. Sarah smiled, remembering

222

Annie laugh when Sarah had asked if the streets were paved with gold. But she also recalled her reply: she'd said the streets were, if a person grabbed an opportunity.

Perhaps, Sarah thought, she should take advantage of her own opportunities. She breathed in and stopped crying as a wonderful idea started to blossom in her mind.

She'd get up, get dressed and go and see Larry and Annie. Meg wouldn't know — she'd not be back until late afternoon but anyroad, she didn't care what Sarah did nowadays. Once there she would work her charm on the couple and see if she could persuade them to come round to her way of thinking.

A new life in London as Larry's assistant in the theatre would make her life complete. A new life in London, the biggest city in the world, and a good home if Annie and Larry would let her stay with them. She wouldn't need to live with Frankie Pearson, because as sure as eggs were eggs, Meg was going to marry him — and that would be a disaster for Sarah.

★ ★ ★

'Does your sister know that you're here?' Annie Hopkirks asked as she let Sarah into their house. 'You don't usually visit at this time of the day. Is there anything wrong?'

'No, nothing is wrong, it's just I'm all on my own, like I am most days now. I never hardly see my sister. She's too busy for me and then I'm either at work or asleep. Meg isn't bothered about me, anyway.' Sarah looked sorry for herself. 'She'll soon be getting married and then she definitely won't want me, especially if she has her own children to worry about.'

'Oh dear. I didn't think things were so bad between you and your sister,' Annie said as Larry looked at her. It sounded like she had no real home life at all.

Larry folded the edition of *Variety News* he had been reading and looked at the young lass who had been such a help to him. 'What are you going to do and where are you going to go when we leave at the weekend? You can't just wander the streets.'

'I don't know and I don't want you two to go. I don't know who I'll be looking after once you've gone. I overheard Mr Pickering saying that he might not need me anymore. I even tried to show him that I could dance and join one of the troupes but he just laughed at me.' Sarah hung her head and began to cry. 'I don't know what to do!' she wailed. Then she looked across at the couple, hoping that she'd pulled a heartstring or two.

'I shouldn't ask this and please don't feel obliged. But I wondered if you could find me a job in your new theatre? You know I'd work hard and I'm eager to learn. I'm really going to miss both of you and Meg has no time for me.'

There was silence for a short time, broken only by Sarah's sobs. The Hopkirks looked at each other, and then at the young girl. 'I don't know, Sarah,' Larry said eventually. 'Both Annie and myself would need to talk to your sister. I'm sure she loves you and only tries to do the best for you, even though it doesn't seem to be that way.'

Annie put her arm around the lass they had both taken to. 'Now, stop your sobbing, we will work something out,' she reassured Sarah. 'I'll talk to your Meg. She obviously doesn't know how you feel, but I'm sure she's only doing her best. She'll be busy trying to make ends meet, especially with the run-up to Christmas, when everybody expects something special on the table.'

'I know but she'll soon be married and then I'll be on my own. She hasn't told me but I noticed that she's wearing an engagement ring now. She knows I hate Frankie Pearson. I never want to live with him and she knows it,' Sarah wailed.

'Shush now, we'll sort something out. As Annie says, we'll talk to Meg before we do anything.' Larry shook his head. 'Now, Annie. Did you say we had some nice ham for dinner? I think we'll have a bite to eat and then we'll all feel better.'

'Yes, let's have something to eat,' Annie agreed. 'That'll make us all feel better and I've some fancy biscuits that a fan of yours gave you. You'll like those, Sarah. They have chocolate on them. Now, stop your blubbing and we will sort something out.' Annie headed towards the small kitchen.

'Thank you, thank you,' Sarah called as she went. 'I'm sorry to ask but I really have nobody else to talk to but you two.'

Annie put a plate of delicious-looking ham with some pickled onions on the table and set a place for her.

'Then we will do something,' Larry said and looked at Annie.

Lasses like Sarah were two a penny down in London. There was always somebody trying to take advantage of Annie's good nature and his money once they found out that they both had soft hearts. However, he knew Sarah had really touched Annie's heart and he knew she would worry about her once they left her behind.

Larry smiled to himself as he watched Sarah tuck into a good slice of ham. He'd been around enough actors all his life to know when all was not what it seemed, but he smiled as Annie kissed Sarah on the head. Perhaps they could make a place for Sarah in their own home? A parlour maid? Or, on second thoughts, a scullery maid. She was far too outspoken to be a parlour maid. He'd have to think about it. After all, Annie had always wanted a daughter.

24

Meg looked out of the shop window. Snow was beginning to fall and the streets were desolate. It was just after one o'clock and now she realised why Ted Lund had always closed so early — there was never that much afternoon custom, especially on a winter's day. Perhaps she should, too — particularly on days like this.

She watched the roofs and streets gradually disappear beneath the snow. The street's working horses put their heads down against the wind as the winter chill started to take hold. This was the season that ordinary working folk hated as they struggled to keep their family warm and fed, and make Christmas Day special for their loved ones, no matter how basic the presents and the food.

Meg smiled as she remembered the wooden doll that her father had carved for her and that her mother had lovingly dressed in offcuts of old clothes for Christmas. Sarah still had it by the side of her bed after Meg had passed it down to her. The crude doll was the one tie to their parents that they both shared and was still loved by both of them.

She sighed and leaned upon the counter, looking at the plum puddings wrapped neatly in muslin ready to be steamed by whoever bought them. For every other pudding and small Christmas cake that she sold, she put a sixpence to one side in a small glass jar. This was for her and Sarah's Christmas money, to help buy coal and food for the one day that they both enjoyed together. It gave her hope that she would one day be able to buy the bakery from Joe Dinsdale as she watched the little jar grow and her pay got better each week after Joe had taken his cut. Hopefully this year, they would have a good time and she hoped above all else Sarah would bury her dislike of Frankie just for that one day.

She looked at the ring on her finger and smiled. She loved Frankie so much. It didn't matter if he was wealthy or not — it was the man she loved, not his money. He hadn't been able to reclaim the things that he had pawned; the only thing he had really missed was his father's ring and that had now disappeared out of the pawnshop window. The rest he hadn't missed, and now he was starting to make money with his posh clients and Lady Beatrice's regular order. His patisserie window brimmed with special cakes for the festive period, which he had advertised in both English and French to impress his new clientele. *Eclairs au Café*, *Tourte a la Frangipane* and *Tartlettes la Parisienne* were just a few of his delicacies. His Christmas Cake was called *Gâteau de Noël. Posh names, but just ordinary baking,* Meg thought as she tidied her row of rock buns, coconut tarts and gingerbread.

The shop door opened quickly with a tinkle of the bell. To Meg's surprise, Annie Hopkirk entered, covered from head to foot with snow, her fox fur looking to be alive as the animal's glass eyes shone at Meg from beneath the covering of snow upon the other woman's shoulders.

'Mrs Hopkirk, what brings you out on a day like today? Is our Sarah all right? She's not pestering you too much, I hope? I'll tell her to stay at home if she

228

is.' Sarah had never been away from the couple of late.

Mrs Hopkirk looked at Meg, her cheeks blushing as she felt the warmth of the shop. 'No, my dear. She's no pest. Me and Larry welcome her company,' she assured Meg. 'She says that you are so busy here in your job that you haven't time for her. I think she gets lonely. It is best she is with us, rather than wandering the streets. A young girl like her could end up in terrible trouble.' Meg looked at her with a questioning gaze. 'You know what I mean. There are plenty of men out there who would take advantage of her.'

Meg felt as though she was being judged. What had Sarah been saying to make Annie think that she had no time for her younger sister? 'I do care for her! I'm always there for her. She knows where to come if she needs me, and I do all I can for her. Our Sarah is never satisfied with her lot in life, no matter what you do for her. However, I do appreciate your concern.' Meg looked at the worry that came over Annie's face.

'Larry and I have been talking,' Annie said and paused. 'We haven't got a daughter of our own, and to be quite honest, I've taken a liking to your sister. I know she's a mind of her own, but she's not a bad girl. She asked if she could come back to London with us, for us to find her a job on the stage or working on it. Of course, we have promised her nothing as of yet — we needed to talk to you first.'

'Take her to London, she asked you to take her to London with you? She's never said anything to me about that — is she that unhappy with her lot?' Meg shook her head in despair and shock at the words Annie was saying. 'She's my little sister — if she went to London I'd never see her again. She can't do that, she belongs here with me. I do my best for her, I really do.'

'I think she knows you do,' Annie said, seeing how upset the conversation was making Meg. 'But she feels that she is a burden to you, I think, since your mother died. And if you don't mind me saying, she has a strong dislike of your intended. She says he killed your mother, although I don't for one minute believe that.

'We would look after her. She'd be free to come home at any time and we would pay for her train fare to accompany us to London.' Annie paused. 'Larry says he can't promise her a job within his company but we would find her employment and accommodation and make sure she is well looked after. Perhaps this is an opportunity for both of you to do what you want with your own lives.'

'We were both doing perfectly all right, thank you,' Meg replied. 'Sarah has no right to be tittle-tattling about how hard done by she is. With every day I work, her life gets better!' Meg exploded. 'If she thinks I'm going to let her disappear down to London with a couple I hardly know, she can think again.'

'I'm sorry. We only thought that we were doing you both a favour. As I say, we think a great deal of her. Larry laughs at her antics. She'll never make a dancer, but he hasn't the heart to tell her. Why don't you talk to your sister about it all? We are to travel back to London on Saturday for the pantomime season. Larry always has a starring role. He enjoys Christmas.' Annie turned to leave. 'We really do have her best interests at heart. She would be safe and well cared for. Please at least consider our offer.'

230

Meg watched as Annie Hopkirk pulled her wrap around her neck and stepped back out into the winter's weather. She felt her temper rising again as she wondered what Sarah had said to make Annie Hopkirk think that she would be better under their care. She had done everything possible to give her younger sister a good life, yet here Sarah was telling tales of how badly done by she was.

She looked once more out of the window. The snow was coming down harder now, and there would only be a few more shoppers before nightfall. She'd close the shop and confront her ungrateful sister to see exactly what was going on. She turned the sign to Closed and took her apron off.

$$\star \quad \star \quad \star$$

'Meg, you're back early!' Sarah exclaimed as she looked up from where she sat, warming her toes in front of the open fire.

'Yes, I'm back! You look cosy, and I see you've had some dinner. Not gone hungry or cold then?' Meg looked at her sister's empty plate, with the evidence of the pie that she had left out. 'Things have got a lot better since I started working for Joe Dinsdale, haven't they?' She shook her shawl free from the snow and stared at her sister, trying not to lose her temper.

'I suppose so, but we still haven't got much — not like some people.' Sarah stilled in her chair, as she saw the expression on Meg's face. 'I'd say Annie or Larry Hopkirk have been to see you. Can I go, our Meg? Please, can I go to London with them? You don't want me here! You could marry your fella then and you'd not have me to worry about.'

'What have you been saying to the Hopkirks? Annie was telling me that Frankie had killed our mother and that I never had any time for you and that I don't want you under my feet. Now, you know that just isn't true! I'd do anything for you, and so would Frankie. He might not show it, but he's quite fond of you. He knows that when we marry, you will come with me to Grosvenor House.' Meg sighed, knowing that Frankie's feelings were rather more complex, but this wasn't the time for that. 'Sometimes, Sarah, you can be so selfish! We would all like another life but we have to deal with what we've been given or make the very best of what we have got.'

'You've been given an engagement ring, but you've never said anything to me,' Sarah cried. 'I refuse to live with Frankie. In fact, I hate him, so there! I'll run away and make my own way down to London if I can't go with the Hopkirks.'

'Oh, Sarah! The ring doesn't change anything. That's why I didn't say anything. I'd still be marrying Frankie in the future, ring or no ring. But not until next year at least. We've talked about April but there is no date set yet. He's building his patisserie and I want to prove that I can run my own bakery. We'll not be moving in with Frankie for some time yet, so you mustn't worry about that.' Meg sat down and looked at her young sister, whose face was set in anger.

'So? Until then I'll still be living in this place, sharing my room with you, with damp coming down the walls and rats running about in the yard!' Sarah snapped.

'We'll not always be here. Besides, you could be sharing your bedroom with a lot worse. Think of those next door, sometimes five to a room and a baby screeching all night. Look at what you've got, not what you haven't.' She gestured around her at their once welcoming home.

Sarah folded her arms. 'Well, we might not have this place for much longer. A man from the council came round while you were at work. He insisted I let him and some other nobs in. They were muttering about a new development. They called at all the houses on this row. Daisy's brother was with them, in fact — he said that Leeds would be the better without housing like ours. So, you might have to marry Frankie to keep a roof over your head and I definitely will be running away if you don't let me go with Annie and Larry.'

'You're making that up, you spiteful devil! I know nothing about any of this. You are lying just to get your way,' Meg said, but felt her legs go weak and her head spin. What would they do without their home? It was an instant worry — for them both to be without their home would be a disaster.

'I am not! Ask Betsy. She nearly chased them out of the yard with her brush in hand. I think it was Daisy's brother who was with them. They said they'd be putting notices of possession through our doors, so you'll happen believe me when that arrives.' Sarah grinned savagely. For her, the men from the council's planning department could not have come at a better time.

'What are we going to do? They can't take our home from us? Surely they can't do that.'

'They called them slums!' Sarah said, taking delight in making her sister worry even more. The more she played on it, the more Meg was likely to let her go with the Hopkirks. 'You'd be better off without me, if we are to be homeless.'

'Look here, young Sarah, this is a bit too convenient for my liking, the council coming around at the same time as you are wanting to trail off down to London with a couple we hardly know to a city we definitely don't know,' Meg said firmly. 'Don't you think for one minute that the council repossessing our house will make my decision easier on you going to London! I'm still against it. We'll have to find somewhere else to live, if that's what they are about. So, you can look smug but I'll not be letting you go with the Hopkirks.' She stood facing Sarah, her hands on her hips.

'Well, like our mam used to always say, you can't always have your way. I'm going with them and just you try and stop me. I'll seek my fortune on the stage! Larry will see me right and you can stay here with your fancy French man — you up to your elbows in bread dough. I want something better in my life.' Sarah shoved her feet into her boots, not bothering to button them as she grabbed for her shawl. 'I'm off to where I am believed and wanted.'

Sarah slammed the kitchen door behind her, and walked out into the darkening evening.

* * *

'I thought that you'd be round,' Betsy said to Meg, as she shouted at her family to be quiet. 'Bloody bastards and right before Christmas. Did Sarah tell you that our landlord has sold all the row to the council on the understanding that we are out by the end of the month? End of the month! I ask you, does he not have any heart? Where are we all to go? What am I going to do with all my tribe?'

Betsy was too fraught and angry to cry as she stood in the doorway. 'I don't know what to do. My mother will take some of us, but my lodgers will have to go and Jim swears he'll not live with my mother. Lord knows what we are going to do.'

Meg looked at the chaos that Betsy called home and felt sorry for the family. At least there was only her and Sarah to be homeless, which was bad enough — but to find somewhere for a family like Betsy's? That would be a nightmare. Meg felt a panic come over her; Sarah had never said that the council expected them to be out of their home by the end of December. Where were they going to go? Frankie would take them both in, but she had more pride than to live with her beau before getting married. She had heard all the scandal that Daisy was getting and she had no intentions of being talked about in the same way. Besides, she had started to make a life for herself and once married to Frankie she aimed to build her business, and that of Frankie's, larger and stronger.

'I'm sorry, Betsy. If I hear of anywhere to rent, I'll let you know. It's going to be an upheaval for all of us.' Meg watched Betsy pick up her baby and start to sob.

'I suppose you'll be all right. You'll be going to live with your fella. It's a good job he has his own house. Sarah will not like it though.' Betsy wiped her nose on her sleeve.

'I don't know what we'll be doing. I'm not ready yet to live with Frankie and Sarah's got it in her head that she's going to London with the folk from the theatre. But I don't want her to go — she's too young and I hardly know them.'

'Well, I'm letting our Harry go to Hull,' Betsy told her. 'He has a job on the docks and lodgings, so he's one less to worry about. Sometimes you have to let them go. They want to make their own way in the world and they can always come back home if they're not happy. I'd let her go, if I were you. She's not daft, isn't your Sarah. She can look after herself. Two of a kind are her and my Harry, but we should be grateful that they know how to survive in this world.'

Meg sighed. 'But they are both so young and London is so far away, I can't bear to think of her on her own in a large city.'

'But she's not on her own if these folk are willing to take her in. I'd be glad to see the back of her, if she was mine! One less to worry about.' Betsy looked around her at two of her children squabbling. 'I'll have to go, Meg. These two are pulling the hair out of one another and besides, you're getting sodden standing on the step. It looks like we're going to be in for some real snow.' Betsy smiled at Meg. 'Whatever you do, it'll be the right decision. You always try to do the best for that sister of yours, no matter what she thinks, and let's just hope that we can all find new lodgings. I'll have to go, else they'll be disturbing my lodger and he's in a bad enough mood finding out that he's going to be out on his arse.' Betsy closed the door and left Meg to wander back home.

25

Meg had tossed and turned all night. Exhausted, she dragged herself out of bed on the dark winter's morning.

From the smooth counterpane, Sarah's bed clearly hadn't been slept in. She'd not returned home from her evening's work at the music hall. Of late, she had often stayed with the Hopkirks, preferring the warmth and comfort of their home. She was growing up and Meg was starting to lose her, that much was clear. Perhaps Betsy was right — she should let Sarah go to London with her blessing. After all, there was nothing here for her once the Hopkirks had gone. Much as she didn't want to admit it to Sarah, Frankie had made it clear he would not really want Sarah to live with them.

Meg dressed quickly, noticing the frost's leaf patterns on the windowpane and the snow piled up. It would be a cold walk to the bakery this morning.

She left her home without a warm drink inside her or breakfast. She'd see to both, once she had the ovens going at the bakery. Trudging through the dark streets, with a fluttering of snow falling on an already heavily laden way, she thought about her predicament. Sykes Yard had been her home all her life and although it was dilapidated, she'd be heartbroken to think of it being demolished.

However, if she was to let Sarah have her way and go to London, she had thought of somewhere for herself to live that didn't include Frankie, no matter how much she loved him, just until they were married. Indeed, there was even enough room for Sarah if she decided to stay and she would be warm and dry and well fed.

Turning the key in the bakery's lock, she felt a sense of relief. *The answer has been here under my nose all along*, she thought. Needs must. She lit the dry kindling under the bakery ovens and filled the kettle to put on the fire for her first drink of the morning, turning the brass control knob to full on the paraffin lamp and taking it up the stairs. She gazed around the two vacant rooms above the bakery. She'd thought about them as she had dropped off into her restless sleep and they had played on her mind all night. It made perfect sense to live above the bakery. It would be better for her and Sarah. The rooms were always warm with the heat from the bakery and there would be no early morning walk for her. She smiled, imagining the rooms transformed into a bedroom and living room. They'd be perfect! She couldn't wait to tell Sarah once she returned home that afternoon. That was one problem solved, once she had asked Joe Dinsdale's permission and she could not see him saying no to her idea.

She would go and see the Hopkirks on her way back home and see exactly what they were proposing. Maybe they would be willing to send for Sarah in another year's time, when she would be a little older and hopefully wiser. Then Meg would gladly give her consent. By then, she would be getting married to Frankie and Sarah could follow her dream. Sometimes things happened for a reason.

* * *

'Lord, it's a cold one this morning!' George said, smelling the air. 'I'm frozen and my feet are soaked. I love the sight of the snow, but not on the streets as soon as the horses and the trams get going. It goes to slush and is splattered with horse muck. You are nice and warm in here though — and it smells good this morning, all nice and spiced. What's in the oven?'

'Christmas pies, or mince pies as they are now called. It's ironic that people have started calling them mince pies, when there's no longer any meat. Just suet and fruits.' Meg smiled and passed George her tray of loaves. 'I'm sending Mr Dinsdale two dozen to sell in his shop and I'll send some more Christmas cakes towards the end of the week as well as another batch of gingerbread men.'

George looked at the mince pies, with their dusting of icing sugar.

'Put these on your cart and then come back in for one extra and a drink of tea. They'll warm your bones before you head back to the shop.'

'Are you sure, Meg? Have you the time? But I have got an excuse that the snow was heavy and made me slower, so that would be grand.'

'Yes, come on. I'm ready for another drink and all the baking is in the oven. The bread is out under the counter and it will be another half hour before any customers come in, especially with the day being so wild. Come through to the back and warm up.'

Meg poured the boiling water into the old enamel teapot that she had inherited with the shop and stirred it before filling two mugs for George and herself. She pushed a warm mince pie on a plate underneath George's nose. He took a bite out of it and grinned. 'My that's grand. Better than any breakfast I've ever had.' George caught the crumbs that fell from his mouth.

'Good, I'm glad you like them. I only hope the shop's customers do.' Meg quickly checked the sponges that were baking in the ovens.

'Oh, they do and will. Old Dinsdale was saying it was the best thing he had ever thought of. He's talking about opening another shop because of your good work,' George said.

'Yes, I've noticed his order is getting bigger each day but he's not taking any trade from me — both places are doing well,' Meg smiled. 'I'm coming to see him after I close this afternoon. I need to ask him something.'

George blushed. 'I'd like to ask you something, Meg — but I know I shouldn't, what with you being already promised to someone.' The lad hesitated. 'There's a dance at Sackville Street Hall on Saturday night. Would you come with me? It would be such an honour to have you on my arm.'

'Oh, George! That is sweet, but you know I can't. I'm betrothed to Frankie. I'm sorry, but I'm sure that there will be lots of girls who'd love to be on your arm. You are such a handsome young man.' Meg watched the disappointment and embarrassment pass over George's face.

'I should have known better than to ask you. I've made a fool of myself.' George got up from his chair. 'I'm sorry.'

'No need to be sorry, George. You will always be a good friend.' Meg went and kissed him lightly on the cheek. 'There, that seals our friendship with no harm done. Now, I'd better get on and you had better get back to Joe Dinsdale. He'll be waiting.'

Meg's visit to Joe Dinsdale's shop was short and sweet. He was busy taking orders for geese and turkeys, ready for Christmas Day. The fowl were already hanging by their necks outside his shop doorway and folk were debating who was going to pluck them before roasting. He hardly listened to what she had said to him, she thought as she walked along the streets towards where the Hopkirks lived — but at least he had agreed to her living there. That part of her plan had worked out all right. So, now Meg was left with the delicate task of telling Sarah the news of her new home and hoping that both she and Annie and Larry Hopkirk would agree to inviting Sarah down to London the following year. That way Sarah knew it wasn't an outright no and it would give her time to save up for her leaving and make sure she would be looked after by the Hopkirks. Meg's feet were wet, her boots leaking. The sooner she talked to them, the better. She stood shivering on the doorstep, waiting for their door to be answered.

An unfamiliar man dressed in a thick jacket with a cap on his head and a checked muffler answered the door. 'Yes?'

'Oh, sorry! I must be knocking on the wrong door. I thought Annie and Larry Hopkirk were staying here.' Meg started to walk away.

'They did until this morning, when they decided to go back to London. They couldn't risk getting stuck by the snows with him performing on stage all Christmas down there. They caught the train first thing. I'm just checking that everything is all right for the next visitors to the music hall.' The workman shook his head.

241

'My boss is playing hell with them. He's got nobody for the top of the bill all this week. These southerners are not used to a bit of snow. Bloody soft, they are.'

'Did you see them go? Were they on their own? A young lass wasn't with them, was she?' Meg could feel herself starting to panic. Sarah surely wouldn't leave without saying goodbye.

'Can't tell you, love. I've only just arrived. But I do know they've taken the two towels that were here. No matter how well off they are, they always pinch the towels.' The workman grunted and then closed the door to keep the cold winter from entering the house.

Meg's heart was beating so fast she thought she was going to collapse as she ran down the slush-covered streets, her feet skidding on the ice.

Sarah, please be home!

She turned the corner into Sykes Yard. All the chimneys along the row had smoke coming out . . . except theirs. The fire had never been lit. She ran up the steps to the house and flung open the door to an empty cold kitchen.

'Sarah! Sarah! Are you here? Please say you are here!' Meg shouted. She ran upstairs and looked at the bed, the top sheet missing. Besides that, the drawer that kept the few clothes that Sarah had lay open.

Empty.

'No, no, what have you done you, stupid girl? Why, for once in your life, didn't you listen?'

Meg sat on the edge of the bed and sobbed, wrapping her arms around herself and rocking. 'Why have you gone and left me? I did everything a sister could, if you only had realized.'

There was nobody there to reply.

242

She sobbed until the daylight started to fade and then she made her way down the stairs and started to light the fire, the cold seeping into her bones as she looked into the dancing flames.

Only then did she spy the note balanced on the fireplace, recognising Sarah's erratic handwriting. She reached for it and read.

DEAR MEG
  I KNOW THAT YOU ARE GOING TO BE REALLY UPSET WITH ME WHEN YOU ARE READING THIS, BUT I HAD TO GO. YOU ARE FOLLOWING YOUR DREAMS. LET ME FOLLOW MINE.
  MY NEW ADDRESS IS NUMBER 2 LONSDALE SQUARE, ISLINGTON, LONDON. LARRY AND ANNIE HOPKIRK ARE LETTING ME LIVE WITH THEM AND THEY HAVE GOT ME A JOB. PLEASE DON'T WORRY, ALTHOUGH I KNOW YOU WILL. I'LL WRITE WHEN I CAN.
  YOUR LOVING SISTER, SARAH

Meg watched as her falling tears smudged the writing.

The two sisters may not have seen eye to eye, but Sarah was her only living relative. She had gone down to London without a penny to her name and with only Larry and Annie Hopkirk as friends — if indeed they were friends. She'd heard of people down there who took advantage of young people like Sarah.

'Please let her be all right,' Meg whispered as the night drew in around her, alone and missing her headstrong sister. 'Please.'

The following morning, Meg was in no mood to open her bakery. All she could think about was her young sister as the bread got an extra-hard pummelling. The ingredients she usually took so much care with were abused. She needed to close the bakery early and talk to the manager at the theatre — and then to Frankie. There was so much she needed to tell him, to share her worries with someone she knew would care.

The weather was as dark as Meg's mood and she was thankful that it deterred people shopping with her just for once. George came as usual for his delivery, but she didn't offer him a drink to warm him. Daisy came in and yacked on about her Tom, but Meg couldn't take in a word.

'What's wrong with you, then? You look as if you've found a penny but lost a pound,' Daisy said as she gave up on any decent hope of conversation with her mate before going to work. Even her bread seemed heavier than usual, which matched Meg's mood.

'It's Sarah and your brother!' Meg said and looked at the dismay on Daisy's face.

'What! He might like his women, but they are usually women, not young girls — and he's calmed down since he got married.'

'No, he's not done anything like that. It's worse than that — your darling brother is on the planning board that aims to knock my home down. To make it worse, our Sarah has run away to London with Larry and Annie Hopkirk. She left on the train with them yesterday and didn't tell me. I found a note last night.'

'Well, I don't know what to say about either! My brother is an idiot since he got married. All he does is suck up to his father-in-law. New houses are all he thinks about, new houses and new shops; he's no feeling for anybody or anything.' Daisy sighed. 'Will you be all right? Have you somewhere to go?'

Meg nodded. 'I'm going to live above here until I get married. There was room for Sarah and me, if she had only waited and given me a chance. Instead, she's fled. Your brother gave her the opportunity she was waiting for.'

'Has she left you an address? You must be going mad with worry.'

'She has, and I know the Hopkirks have her best interests at heart — but you never know, do you? I hadn't heard of them until Sarah was put in charge of Larry's needs. She's left without a penny to her name and only the few clothes she had and that is not many. She's too young to go to London. I wouldn't dare go even at my age. She can be so gullible sometimes.' Meg felt tears well up in her eyes.

'Oh, love.' Daisy went behind the counter and hugged Meg. 'She'll be all right. She's a tongue in her head and she's not daft. She kept everybody on their toes when she worked at the mill.' Daisy smiled. 'If you've an address, that's something. You can write to her and send her things.'

'If it's the right address! I don't even know if the house exists. As soon as I've closed my doors, I'm going to the music hall to check that she's not lying. They surely should have the Hopkirk's address that I can check against.' Meg tried to smile as she heard the mill horn summoning all their workers. 'You'd better go, you'll be late if you don't run.'

'It doesn't matter. They can sack me if they want. I can't leave you in this state.' Daisy continued hugging

245

Meg.

'No, go. You need the money, like the rest of us. I'm all right, go. Once one o'clock comes around, I'll close like old Lund used to do. It's a wet day and I've business of my own to sort. Blood comes before brass.' Meg watched as her friend made for the door.

'I'll give that brother of mine a piece of my mind, if nothing else,' Daisy promised. 'Bloody bastard! Let me know how you go on with Sarah. Keep smiling, chuck. Things can only get better for you.'

Daisy ran off down the cobbled street with her clogs sparking beneath her feet.

★ ★ ★

One o'clock couldn't come soon enough for Meg. She tried to smile as her regulars came in for their bread and placed orders with her for Christmas pudding, cake and mince pies and asked if she had anything planned for Christmas.

In honesty, she didn't feel like celebrating Christmas now. Both she and Frankie had been so busy of late, it had never been mentioned between them. Christmas would not be Christmas this year without her mother and now Sarah. What if things didn't work out between her and the Hopkirks? She would be wandering the streets of London, alone and penniless.

Meg turned the key in the bakery's lock after damping down the ovens and getting everything ready for the next morning. The sooner she went to talk to Burt Pickering, the better. She rushed down the busy streets, full of early Christmas shoppers. She had no time to dally; besides, now she had no one except

246

Frankie to buy anything for.

Meg walked down the White Bull Yard that led to the music hall's entrance. She'd been there with Sarah many a time, but today it was imperative she saw Burt. Her heart raced as she saw his son up a ladder, plastering a new poster over the one of Larry Hopkirk. So, they knew Larry had gone? But had Sarah also told them of her departure?

'Here you are! Sarah's sister, aren't you? Where is she? We expected her in last night but she never showed her face.' Len looked down from the top of his ladder. 'She's all right, is she?'

'I don't know! She's gone and she won't be coming back. That's what I'm about to tell your father.' Meg looked at the puzzlement on young Len's face.

'What do you mean, she'll not be coming back? She loves working here. You can't drag her away from watching folk on stage.' Len started to climb down the ladder and followed Meg through the warren of backstage passages to his father's office.

'She's not gone and done it, has she? She's not convinced Larry to take her to London?' Len asked, as Meg knocked on his father's door. 'The stupid cow! I told her not to be so daft.' Len shook his head and walked away as his father opened the door.

'Well?' Burt said, after Meg introduced herself. 'What's your daft sister's excuse for not turning up last night? She can't be that busy helping Annie Hopkirk — they've packed up and left for London.'

'No excuse, she's gone to London with them. Run away from the lot of us, driven by a brighter life upon the stage.' Meg nearly started crying again.

'Well, she'll not have much of a life on the stage. She's got two left feet and she sings like a strangled cat,' Burt growled. 'Bloody hell, Larry Hopkirk should have more sense than to drag a young lass from her home, although I know his wife had a soft spot for your sister. I suppose they were taking pity on her. She could tell a good sob story.' He shook his head.

'Well, she's gone. She's given me an address but I don't know if it's true or not; knowing our Sarah, she could have made it up.' Meg hesitated. 'Do you have an address for the Hopkirks? She left without a penny to her name.'

Burt walked over to his bookings ledger and leafed through. 'Number 2, Lonsdale Road, Islington. That's where he lives, for his sins. By heck, I wish I'd known what she was going to do, I'd have stopped her. You must be worrying. I would be if it was my lass or even Len.'

Meg's face filled with relief. 'Well, at least she hasn't lied about that,' Meg said, with a flush of relief. 'I can send her some money.' She tried to smile.

'Aye and a peace of your mind, I hope,' Burt said. 'As long as she's safe, she'll be all right with Larry Hopkirk. He's not a bad man. I've known him for a few years now. Likes a drink while he's performing, but there's not a bad bone in his body and he's wealthy. She could do worse.'

26

Frankie's patisserie was heaving with well-to-do people shopping for that extra bit of something special to be shown off and displayed on their Christmas dinner table. The tea room was thriving too, with ladies taking a break from their Christmas shopping.

Meg stood at the back of the shop and listened to the conversations of Frankie's customers and smiled. They spoke completely different to her customers. Frankie's customers required more cosseting, asking for gateaux to be delivered and puddings to have more brandy added. They were extravagant with their money and their ways.

'I'm sorry, Miss Fairfax,' Norah said. 'I saw you standing there, but the customers are so demanding, at the moment. They need everything just so and the orders that we are receiving for Christmas . . . I don't know how Mr Pearson is going to cope on his own. I take it you are here to see him?' She looked into the back of the bakery to see if Frankie was busy.

'Yes, please,' Meg said.

'Go on through. He's up to his elbows making our latest meringue recipe. It's not just any meringue — it's meringue in the shape of swans and filled with cream. There's nothing like making your life hard,' Norah sighed and made way for Meg to walk past her.

'Well, it wouldn't be Mr Pearson if it wasn't a bit challenging and fancy. I bet they're popular. I can see them on many a posh table this Christmas,' Meg smiled. Frankie loved designing his cakes and Christmas must be extra special for him. She approached slowly, as he piped a delicate swan's neck onto his baking trays.

'Meg! Sorry, I didn't hear you. I'd have come out to you if I'd have known you were in the shop.' Frankie stood back to look at his work, before putting the piping bag down. 'Are you all right? You look worried.'

'Oh, Frankie! I've had such a bad few days, I don't know where to begin.' Meg folded into his arms for comfort. 'The council are evicting all our row. We have to find new homes by the end of the month.'

'Well, that sorts that then. You both move in with me and we marry this spring. So there's no need to worry about that,' Frankie said, very matter-of-fact.

'No, that's already sorted. I'm going to move in over the bakery until we are ready for marriage. It's our Sarah that's the problem. She's run off to London with Larry Hopkirk and his wife. I've just been to the music hall to check that she's given me the right address.'

'Now, just wait a minute! You'd rather live above the bakery before living with me yet we have no more Sarah to worry about?'

'Just until we get married. It makes sense. I'm over my place of work and we can both concentrate on building our businesses. Besides, before I get married I want to be able to buy my bakery and then it can be part of our chain. I want to contribute to our financial stability. But that's not my main worry. It's Sarah running away from home. I'll never see her again!' Meg cried.

'Write to her. Tell her to come home, and offer her rail fare to do so,' Frankie said. 'She'll quickly realize that London is just another city — a huge city, granted — but no different from Leeds. If she replies and says she is happy down there, then be content. After all, plenty of young girls move miles away from home to find work or be in service. She must have trusted the Hopkirk family for her to have gone with them.'

'She's so far away, Frankie. She's never been anywhere on her own.'

'I'm on my own — that's why I want you to marry me. Plus with Sarah gone, it makes the move into my home easier.'

'You've never got on with Sarah. You're probably glad she's gone to London,' Meg accused.

'Not at all,' Frankie said quickly, 'because I know that you will worry about her until you know that she is safe and looked after. I was just thinking . . . Now is the time to wed and start our life together. Otherwise, what is the use of both of us working and making every penny that we can, only to leave it all behind when we are both dead in our shrouds? If we are lucky and when eventually we do have children, unlike my darling mother, I want to be able to set them up in business as they grow older, and revel in their success.'

'All the more reason to wait just a little longer to wed — perhaps April is a little too early?' Meg replied. 'You're only just starting to show a profit and I don't want to throw my bakery away just yet. I've only just got it. You're still not right about Sarah. She is perhaps older in her ways than I give her credit for — but oh, I worry so.' Meg looked up at Frankie and smiled. 'I'll write tonight and make sure all is as it should be. I'll offer her forgiveness and the rail fare back home if

251

she wants it. I've been saving sixpences up for Christmas treats but I'd rather spend them on her return home if I have to.'

'You will at least come and stay Christmas Eve with me?' Frankie kissed the nape of Meg's neck. 'I've arranged for a few neighbours and friends to come around to have a sing-song and perhaps even dance, if I can move the furniture in the drawing room. I'd love to be able to show you off to everyone.'

Meg paused. 'Stay the night? Do you think I should? What would people think? We may be engaged to be married, but I don't know if I should.' Despite her protests, Meg felt a thrill of excitement at the thought of sharing Christmas Eve and the day after with the man she loved.

'You'll have your own room. Anyway, what business is it to anybody but us? I promise I will be honourable.' Frankie held her tight. 'Don't you worry about Sarah. She can look after herself, that one. Perhaps it is a blessing that she has gone her own way. She hated me.'

'I know, but I'm more of a mother to her than a sister and she is a force to be reckoned with.' Meg looked up at her betrothed. 'I will stay Christmas Eve. It's a time to be with the people you love.' Meg kissed him before leaving his embrace.

'Mr Pearson? Mr Pearson!' Norah stood in the bakery's doorway. 'Sorry to disturb you, but there are a number of ladies who won't go until they have seen you.'

'I'll be right with you, Norah. Let me guess . . . is it Lady Beatrice's friends?' Frankie looked at Meg and smiled.

'Yes, it is. They all insist on seeing you.'

'Excuse me, my dear, my adoring public awaits.' Gently, Frankie extricated himself from Meg's arms. 'I knew that they would be calling this week. I received an invite to Lady Beatrice's annual ball at the hall, but I've no intention of going. After all, it is on Christmas Eve — and I hope to have my true and only love on my arm that night.' Frankie looked at Meg and smiled. 'Let me go and appease them.'

Meg looked at the swans he'd made with so much love and care. Filled with fresh cream, they would look absolutely beautiful on a Christmas dining table. She then went and listened to the eager chatter of the young women baying for Frankie's attention.

'I've brought my diary for the dance on Christmas Eve! I'd hoped that I could book you for a dance. Please promise me at least one!' Meg heard a voice she did not recognize.

'Yes! We have all brought our dancing cards in the hope that we can secure you!' another voice rang out.

'Ladies, please! I will dance with each and every one of you. There's no need to add me to your dancing cards. You will get my utmost attention. Now, if you don't mind . . . I have business to attend to.'

'You are very popular, Mr Pearson,' Norah said with a wry smile as the ladies departed.

'A little too popular for my liking. They are all respectably married women. The last thing I want is their husbands after my hide.' Frankie laughed and returned to Meg.

'You are nothing but a cad, sir,' Meg smiled. 'You've told me that you have no intention of attending the Christmas Eve Ball.'

'I'm no cad! I said that I would dance with them . . . which I might, at some later date. But not this Christmas Eve. I have better things to do.' He kissed Meg gently on the cheek. 'Now, I must finish piping these swans before my meringue spoils. They are proving popular.' Frankie picked up the piping bag and looked at Meg. 'I wish you would choose to live with me, but I'll see you at the weekend or before if you need me. When do you think you'll be moving out of Sykes Yard?'

'As soon as I can get someone with a cart to help me. I'm going to ask around the market. Mick at the veg stall will help, I'm sure, if I offer him a bit of money.'

'I'm here if you need me. Don't you be stealing all my business with that bakery of yours,' Frankie grinned.

'I wouldn't dare! Besides, my customers wouldn't thank me for your posh stuff. A meringue swan will not fill their bellies.' Meg kissed him quickly on the cheek. She was going to return home and write to Sarah, before sending anything down for Christmas. Frankie was right. If the Hopkirks had taken her down to London with them, her dreams would make her happy.

Now, it was time for Meg to live her own life.

★ ★ ★

Meg made her way home across the market to ask Mick if he could help move her on the coming Sunday. She might as well move as soon as she could. Get settled and warm before Christmas. Once Sarah wrote back, she would feel more content. Frankie loved her, she'd a new home and her business was thriving. What more could she wish for?

★ ★ ★

It was the Sunday before Christmas — moving day from Sykes Yard.

Both Meg and Sarah had been born here, in the house they had always known as home. As she placed the bedding onto Mick's flat cart, she felt a wrench, deep in her gut.

'Tha's not got a lot, lass! Two beds, table and chair, dresser and drawers.' Mick loaded the dolly tub and posser onto the back of his cart as Meg looked long and hard at her old home.

'I've taken a lot of the pots and things already, each day as I've walked to work. It was easier for me to do that. Besides, half my life is already in that bakery so I don't need much.'

Meg hoped that she was doing the right thing but there was no other option but to move from the square and the neighbours she had always known.

'We'll miss you, Meg,' Rosie, the oldest of Betsy's lasses, came out to say goodbye.

'I'll miss you too.' Meg walked over to Betsy for a final farewell. 'Will you be all right? Have you some-where to go?'

'Aye, we've worked it all out. Harry and his older brother have gone to Hull. I and the lill'ens are going to live with my mother, although I don't know where we'll all sleep. My old man and the lodgers will stay in the doss house down by the canal until we can find somewhere we can all live. It'll give me a bit of peace, if nothing else.' Betsy did her clear best to smile. 'We are not going until they come and throw us out though. They must bloody well wait.'

'I hope all goes well for you. You'll come and see

255

me from time to time at the bakery? There will always be a loaf of bread waiting for you.' Meg smiled. Poor Betsy.

'You are a good'en. Have you heard from Sarah?' Betsy said as she hugged Meg tight.

'Yes, she replied to my letter from last weekend. She's living with the Hopkirks in a big posh house in Islington. She's fallen on her feet good and proper, so I've nothing to worry about with her. Perhaps these things have to happen.' Meg looked for one final time at the street she would miss with all her heart.

'Aye, happen they have. But it's a bugger!' Betsy called, as Meg climbed up beside Mick and set off down the road to her new home above the bakery.

27

Meg looked around at her new home. It was sparse, but better than Sykes Yard. The rooms were not damp and there was enough space for her and Sarah — if Meg's sister ever decided to return home.

Not that Sarah had given any hint of returning home, in the letter that she had received. It had been brief, but Meg put that down to her sister's hatred of writing.

Sarah would be all right. Larry and Annie Hopkirk had shown nothing but care for her when they were in Leeds, so why should it be any different when she was living with them and working on the stage, as she had written she was doing in her letter? However, that didn't stop her from worrying; she knew so little about the Hopkirks and Sarah was young and alone in the capital city of England. All she could do was pray that she would be safe and well.

Tomorrow, Meg would parcel up the sixpences — along with a Christmas cake and card — to send in the post to her sister. That would help make Christmas special.

Slowly, she undressed and lay down in her bed. It felt strange not to be in her usual room with her sister. She suddenly felt terribly alone. She knew she had Frankie and that she loved him dearly, but he was not blood. Sarah was the only person she had left and already she was missing her.

She closed her eyes and said a prayer for her young

257

sister to be kept safe and gave thanks for having Frankie in her life. It had been a full day, and the next few days were the run-up to Christmas — the busiest time of the year. She started to think of all she had to make in the morning, like the gingerbread men and houses to place in the window for the children. She was lucky, Sarah was lucky. She dozed off, reminding herself that everything would be all right.

★ ★ ★

'You have a parcel, Sarah. It came in with the master and mistress's post. Don't let it happen again. You give your address as the basement of number 2 Lonsdale Square, like the rest of the staff. Mr and Mrs Hopkirk don't want to handle your mail, and I certainly don't,' Parsons the butler said to Sarah as he passed her the package.

'What you got there, Yorkshire pudding? Are you going to share it with us all? Go on, let us see!' Ethel, the Hopkirk's cook, walked over to inspect the latest scullery maid's business.

'Stop calling me Yorkshire pudding!' Sarah answered back. 'I might be from Yorkshire, but I'm no pudding. And no, I'm not going to show you what came for me. It's private.'

'You'll get the back of my hand if you give me any more cheek. Now, show us.' The cook tried to snatch the parcel out of her hands.

'I've told you — no!' Sarah clutched the package tightly to her and started to leave the basement that acted as the kitchen for the three-storey house that was home to Larry and Annie Hopkirk.

'You'll not leave this kitchen without my say so!'

258

Ethel glared.

'Leave her be, Mrs Nelson!' said Dorothy, the parlour maid. 'She wants to look at her present. She's been up since five this morning! Surely, she deserves five minutes to herself to open her parcel.'

Sarah ran up the back stairs, out of the sight of the main household. Up to her bedroom in the loft. She looked with love at the parcel in her hand and held back the tears. How she longed to be back home in Leeds with her sister! The sister that she thought had hated her. Now, she knew it was only love and care that Meg had shown her.

She peeled back the brown paper to reveal the Christmas cake carefully packed in a tin with a card showing a fat, red robin. Inside the envelope, there were four silver sixpences taped to the card. She'd never seen so much money in her hand before as she tore them away from the card and hid them under the pillow on her bed. If Cook found them, they'd soon disappear! There might be enough money here to take her back on the Leeds train. She could just smell the aroma of Christmas cake. Memories came flooding back.

Larry and Annie Hopkirk had promised her a life on the stage, or at least a job helping out. But all she had been given was the scullery maid's job.

If only she had listened to Meg. She was no better off in London than in Leeds. In fact, she was worse off — her hours were long and any interest that Annie and Larry Hopkirk had shown in her had soon disappeared.

But pride had stopped her from telling Meg that.

Instead, she had written and said how happy she was — looked after well, with a promising job in the theatre. Meg must never know that she was a lowly scullery maid, alone and frightened in England's biggest city.

Sarah would tell her anything but that.

She put the cake in the bedside drawer and hid it under the few clothes that she had. She swept tears away from her eyes. There'd be no Christmas for her this year — she'd be too busy cleaning. Why hadn't she realized the good life she'd once had? Now, it was all gone and she'd have to make the best of her foolish mistake.

★ ★ ★

Meg smiled at the children with their noses pressed hard against her bakery window. It was Christmas Eve, and the shop was filled with the smell of Christmas spices. The window was full of cakes, pies, gingerbread men and houses covered with sweets.

On the shop's counter, she had a straw basket full of sugar mice, coloured white and pink with string tails, priced at a farthing each, just right for that special gift at Christmas — no matter how poor the family.

This is a heart-warming time of year, she thought as she served customer after customer, all wishing her the joys of the season. All that had been missing was the snow, she thought as she turned the sign on the bakery door sign to — *Closed!* Two days while people enjoyed the only holiday of the year.

Another hour, and Frankie would arrive in his carriage for their own Christmas to begin. She was tired as she climbed the stairs but her heart beat fast, thinking of the evening in front of her — dancing, meeting Frankie's friends . . . and staying the evening under his roof. She felt nervous as she plaited her hair and put on one of her best dresses, the one that Frankie had bought her when they had first met, packing a bag of overnight clothes. She looked at herself in the mirror, finding herself plain and not well enough dressed for a Christmas Eve party at Frankie's home.

She glanced across at the bedroom mantelpiece and picked up the card that had arrived that morning from Sarah:

Happy Christmas, Meg. Thank you for everything. Your loving sister Sarah and then on the back of the card she had scribbled. *Sorry, I'll write later, I'm busy helping with the pantomime.*

At least Sarah was happy. A life on the stage was what her sister had always wanted. Maybe Larry Hopkirk had been meant to appear in her sister's life.

Meg quickly drew back the curtains and peered down on the street to see Frankie climbing out of a carriage and horses. True to his word, he had arrived to take her to his home. She felt her heart flutter as she quickly picked up her belongings and the gift for Frankie that she had taken so long to choose.

She clattered down the stairs to join him, checking the bakery door was locked and all the fires well and truly out. Frankie kissed her, before opening the carriage door and helping her climb into the warmth.

'You look as if you have come prepared, my darling. You are only staying one night . . . or perhaps two if I can persuade you?' Frankie kissed her again as the carriage started on its way.

'Two nights? Oh no, I can't do that.'

'Oh no, might the neighbours gossip about us both, do you think?' Frankie said mockingly. 'You'll be meeting most of them tonight and if you are staying one night, I'm sure that they will not raise an eyebrow.'

Meg looked down at her feet.

'Don't worry, I'm only teasing. Now, I have a surprise for you when you get to my house.' Frankie squeezed her hand. 'Something that I hope you'll really like.' He smiled warmly at her.

'You've not been wasting your money, have you? We are both supposed to be saving up for our businesses.'

'I've had a good few weeks. Lady Beatrice and her friends have seen to that. I'm sure I can spend my money upon the woman I love. I've told Jed the builder to recommence his work on the Headingley bakery in the New Year. In fact, he will be one of my guests tonight.'

'You are sure? You'll not end up penniless again?' Meg asked cautiously.

'Listen to you. You'd think you were my wife already. No, don't worry. Even my mother must have been feeling guilty about thieving my money from under my nose. She sent me a cheque in the post for fifty pounds. That terrible fella that she lives with? His paintings have sold so well that she wanted me to benefit. The cheek of the woman! She never mentioned the other artist — that La Treche man. He must not be that good.' Frankie grinned at Meg as she looked out at the busy streets of Leeds.

Before she knew it, they'd arrived at Grosvenor House.

Taking her hand, Frankie helped her alight. Immediately, she spotted the Christmas tree standing proud in the bay window with glittering glass baubles that caught the gaslight.

'Oh! A Christmas tree!' she cried. 'We never had one. And look at the holly wreath upon the door.'

'There's mistletoe hanging, too.' Frankie drew her over beneath the garland as a maid took her bags. Holding Meg close, he kissed her and smiled. 'That's just the start to a wonderful Christmas I hope.

'Now, run upstairs. Your room is the second on the left. I'll make sure everything is in place for this evening's entertainment. Ada and the young girl I have hired for the night have cleared the drawing room for dancing and have laid out a buffet that I prepared this morning. You won't believe it, but I've been training Norah in the bakery. She's not a bad hand, so I left her to make various things this morning. But enough of work — we are in for a glorious night. Graham Windle, my dear friend, is bringing his fiddle! We will enjoy our Christmas Eve in style with good friends and good food. Now, go, find your gift. The guests will be arriving soon and I want to show you off to them all.' Frankie watched as she quickly ran up the stairs to see what was so important.

Opening the door to the room she had been told she was to stay in, Meg caught her breath. Draped across the bed was the most beautiful deep red evening dress, dripping with beads. Beside it was a feathered headband and on the floor was a pair of red leather shoes, just waiting for her to slip her feet into. She took the dress and held it against her body, admiring her reflection in the full-length mirror of the wardrobe.

'Do you like it?' Frankie whispered as he entered the room. 'I thought that it would make you feel special.'

'Oh, Frankie! It's beautiful! How can I ever thank you? It must have cost a fortune.' Meg ran and kissed him.

'It's worth every penny, just to see the smile on your face. Now, do you want Ada to come and help you dress? She will do so, willingly.'

'Oh, no. I can dress myself. I don't need anybody's help — thank you.' Meg wouldn't want anyone to see the bloomers she had on underneath her skirts.

'I'll wait for you downstairs. I think I can hear the first guest has arrived — Robert Pitcher, a wealthy wool merchant and a good catch.'

'A bit like yourself,' Meg teased.

'Not at all. I am neither a good catch nor wealthy . . . nor do I consider myself single.' He paused, and took a breath. 'You have captured my heart and I can hardly bear to wait for our wedding day.'

★ ★ ★

Robert Pitcher drank his brandy and regarded Meg. 'My God, Frankie! You never told me what a beauty your wife-to-be is.'

'She is, and clever. I am truly blessed.' Frankie looked across at Meg who was making herself known to all his friends and neighbours and enjoying the music of his dear friend, Graham, as he played jigs and reels which had all the room dancing. 'Excuse me, gentlemen. I think the next dance is for me to have with my wife to be.'

Frankie gently took Meg's arm. 'Well, what do you think? Could you live your life like this? Everybody is in awe of your looks. None of the other women can hold a candle to your beauty,' he whispered as he waltzed Meg around the room.

'Nonsense! There are some beautiful women here.

264

Graham Windle's wife is stunning in that cream dress and then there's the lady in turquoise. But yes, I think I could get used to living this life — although we couldn't afford to live like this every day.'

'No, we couldn't now. But once we've made our fortunes?' Frankie held her tight and whispered into her ear. 'Stay with me tonight, please. I love you so much.'

'Oh, Frankie! I don't know . . . we shouldn't.'

'It's Christmas Eve. We should be together. I'll come to your room when everyone has gone home, and Ada has retired to her bed. No one will ever know except us two. I'll be back in my bed by the break of day.'

'Maybe. But I'd like our love to be pure for just a little while longer.' Meg said, remembering her mother's strong advice.

'Very well, I'll behave. We don't want to spoil your most special day by having to get married in a hurry. Our wedding day has to be special.' Frankie kissed her cheek.

'Then, yes, I'll be waiting for you, once the doors are locked and everyone else is in their beds.'

The music swelled around them, and Meg knew that there was nothing left to be said.

★　★　★

Meg stretched against the sheets and gave a lazy yawn. She was warm, content and happy. Frankie had been the perfect gentleman. He had shown her love, care and respect. She hugged her pillow and smiled to herself. She had everything she needed — and more.

Ada, the maid, knocked on her bedroom door and entered carrying a breakfast tray. Instantly, Meg pulled the sheets up around her.

'Mr Pearson thought that you would appreciate breakfast in bed this morning,' Ada said, as she pulled back the heavy velvet curtain against the early morning light. It was snowing outside.

'The perfect Christmas, miss,' Ada said as she placed the breakfast tray beside her bed.

'Happy Christmas, Ada. Is Mr Pearson up and about?'

'Yes, miss. He's gone for a walk in the park. He said that he will see you in the drawing room when you are up and dressed. Christmas dinner is at one. We've a fine goose this year and a plum duff pudding that Mr Pearson made himself.' Ada smiled and closed the door after her, leaving Meg looking at the largest breakfast that she had ever seen. She curled up beneath the crisp, white sheets and wondered how she would ever eat it all.

★ ★ ★

'You slept well, I trust, my love,' Frankie said. He sat next to the Christmas tree, which now was adorned with candles that glowed all over.

'I did. Very well.' Meg blushed, remembering his tender embraces before she fell asleep.

'You may like to stay another night?' Frankie smiled as she looked at him and then bent down to the base of the Christmas tree to pass him the present that she had so carefully hidden from him until that time. He looked at the small box that had been so lovingly wrapped and tied with red ribbon and wondered what was within it.

'We'll see.' Meg watched Frankie unwrap her gift.

266

'It's only small, but I do know that you will love it — indeed have loved it.' Meg smiled as the wrapping paper fell away to reveal...

'You've bought my father's ring back from the pawnshop! I thought I had lost it forever when I no longer saw it in the window. I have missed it so much. You really should not have spent that amount of money.'

'Why not? You are my husband-to-be and I have no one else to celebrate Christmas with. Sarah's happy, you are happy — and so am I. A more perfect Christmas, I could not imagine.'

'I second that. I love you.' Frankie kissed her. 'We have our whole lives to look forward to.'

Meg felt warm and complete. It was a wonderful Christmas, one of dreams, she thought.

'Let us hope that it's a life full of joy. We have seen enough sadness. Happy Christmas, my love.'

Meg's Christmas Recipes

Rich Christmas Pudding

100g (4oz) self-raising flour
Pinch salt
½ tsp grated nutmeg
½ tsp mixed spice
75g (3oz) shredded suet
100g (4oz) raisins
100g (4oz) sultanas
100g (4oz) currants
100g (4oz) soft brown sugar
50g (2oz) mixed peel
½ grated lemon rind
2 medium eggs
2 tbsp brandy or milk

Grease a 1.2 litre (2 pint) pudding basin, place a small round of greaseproof paper in the bottom to prevent sticking.

Mix together the dry ingredients.

Add eggs and brandy or milk, and mix well.

Place mixture in a prepared basin, cover with grease-proof paper and foil or a pudding cloth.

Steam for eight hours. Allow to cool completely then store in a cool dry place.

When required, steam for two hours before eating.

Christmas Cake

350g (12oz) plain flour
1 tsp mixed spice
100g (4oz) ground almonds
4 medium eggs
150ml (¼ pint) milk or half milk/half brandy
225g (8oz) butter
225g (8oz) caster sugar
225g (8oz) currants
225g (8oz) sultanas
225g (8oz) raisins
100g (4oz) glace cherries halved
100g (4oz) cut mixed peel

Heat oven to 150C / 300F / Gas Mark 2. Grease and line a 23cm (9 inch) round or 20.5cm (8 inch) square tin.

Sieve together flour, spice and ground almonds.

Beat eggs with milk.

Cream butter and sugar, stir in flour mixture and egg mixture a little at a time.

Lastly add fruit, mix thoroughly. Place mixture in the prepared tin and protect with brown paper around the outside tied tightly with string.

Bake for about three and a half to four hours.

Remove from the oven tin and allow to cool on a wire tray.

If desired, feed with a small amount of sherry or whisky, by pricking the top of the cake and dribbling a small amount in each hole.

Gingerbread People

300g (10oz) self-raising flour
100g (4oz) caster sugar
50g (2oz) margarine
3 tbsp golden syrup
4 tbsp milk
Currants and glace cherries
Glace icing

Heat oven to 160C / 325 F / Gas Mark 3. Grease a baking tray.

Place flour, salt and ginger in a bowl.

Warm sugar, fat and syrup together and add to the dry ingredients. Mix well.

Add milk and mix until firm consistency. Knead lightly with hands.

Roll out and cut out shapes or shape bodies, arms, legs and heads, and place on a baking tray.

Mark the eyes with currants and put some down the body, use a piece of cherry for the mouth and bake for about 10-15 minutes.

Allow to cool slightly then carefully lift onto a wire rack. Decorate with coloured glace icing.

Brandy Snaps

50g (2oz) margarine
50g (2oz) caster sugar
2 tbsp golden syrup
50g (2oz) self-raising flour
½ tsp ground ginger
1 tsp brandy
A few drops lemon essence
Whipped cream if needed

Heat the oven to 180C / 350F / Gas Mark 4. Grease a baking tray and the handles of one or two wooden spoons.

Melt the margarine, sugar and syrup in a saucepan. Remove from the heat and stir in the remaining ingredients.

Put small spoonfuls of the mixture at least 7.5cm apart (3 inches) on a baking tray and bake for 7-10 minutes. Cool slightly.

Roll around the handle of a wooden spoon and leave to set. Place on a wire rack.

If the biscuits become too stiff to roll, reheat for a moment to soften.

Refill the baking tray until all the mixture is used.

Use a piping bag to fill each snap with whipped cream before serving.